A Fragile Marriage

A Fragile Marriage

Juliet Dymoke

PIATKUS

For Mary and Bill

First published in Great Britain in 1995 by
Judy Piatkus (Publishers) Ltd of
5 Windmill Street, London W1

**The moral right of the author
has been asserted**

*A catalogue record for this book is available
from the British Library*

ISBN 0 7499 0292 2

Phototypeset in 11/12pt Compugraphic Times by
Action Typesetting Limited, Gloucester
Printed and bound in Great Britain by
Biddles Ltd, Guildford & Kings Lynn

Chapter One

A family row was always a source of great distress to Sophie and this one was particularly nasty. Her younger sister Alethea, however, usually contrived to make the most of them, 'stirring the pot' as their old nurse used to say. But this was one that touched Alethea too closely and she was on the verge of a tantrum.

'It's not fair,' she burst out in a goaded voice, 'it just isn't fair. Why should that spiteful old witch leave all her money to Sophie and nothing to me or Frank?'

With unusual sharpness Dr Sterling said, 'Really, Alethea, your language is sometimes too much by half, especially for a girl not yet eighteen.'

His wife, full bosomed and in practical matters the power in the house, broke in before her youngest, a boy of fifteen in the uniform of a midshipman, could put his oar in. 'You must admit, my dear, that your aunt could be extremely tiresome. I never went to see her without getting the rough edge of her tongue.'

'You seldom went,' Dr Sterling pointed out. 'Not one of you, except Sophie, put yourselves out to visit her. Battersea is not so far from Clapham as to make it impossible.'

'Well, I hated going,' Alethea protested. 'The house was so dark and gloomy and full of those horrid Indian relics – you know it was, Papa, and she always gave me a company book to look at, which I'd seen a dozen times before, as if I was a silly child.' Frank opened his mouth on a broad grin and his sister snapped, 'Don't you dare! Anyway, you only went at Christmas, hoping for something to put in your

1

pocket. And she was horrid, Papa, she never had anything nice to say.'

'That's because you had no idea how to conduct a conversation with her,' her father said with some truth. 'Her tongue may have been somewhat caustic but she was a great age, you know.'

'Well, I thought she was the most grumpy person I've ever met, and mean too. Five shillings at Christmas was all we ever got, even Sophie. She might have made it a guinea.'

Sophie, who had been silent so far, looked down at her hands folded in the lap of her simple grey dress, the skirts spread by the three obligatory petticoats. 'Well, I suppose if one is as rich as Great-Aunt Adela, one is entitled to be disagreeable at times, especially when people are only interested in what one will do with it.'

Alethea gave her a swift and not very amiable glance. 'Oh, we all know you sucked up to her as if butter wouldn't melt in your mouth.'

'Where do you find such expressions?' their father asked. 'From the delivery boy or the scullery maid, I shouldn't wonder. Sucked up indeed!'

Mrs Sterling smiled indulgently. 'Just a tomboy, my love. But it is time, dearest Thea, that you started to behave in a more ladylike way. If you are going to find a rich husband, you will need to mend your manners.'

'How can I catch a rich husband if I don't have a proper dowry? Sophie will, because money goes to money. She doesn't have to be beautiful.'

'Cat!' her brother said. He was lying lazily back in his chair, white-clad legs crossed. He had been home for two weeks' leave but could hardly bear to be parted from the prized uniform. 'It's you who are the spiteful one − perhaps you get it from Great-Aunt Adela herself! Not but what I couldn't do with some more tin in my pocket.'

'Be quiet, sir,' Dr Sterling said sharply, 'As for you, Alethea, I am surprised at you. Such talk is very unbecoming and unkind to your sister, for none of this is her fault. As for dowries, when the time comes, though we are far from being wealthy, you will have an adequate settlement. But I don't like to hear you showing such ill-nature.'

2

'I don't mean to, Papa.' Alethea turned her soft blue eyes on him, fully aware of the effect this generally had; this morning, however, it totally failed to move the doctor. 'It's all so unfair,' she repeated. 'Sophie can do anything she likes now.'

'You are quite wrong there. Nothing will be any different, though your sister may have a little more pocket money. I really am distressed that you younger ones should be so ungenerous. Neither of you made the slightest effort to be pleasant to your great-aunt and last Christmas you, Alethea, never stopped yawning, which is bad mannered in the extreme, and as for you, Frank, you couldn't or wouldn't trouble to hide the fact that you were bored.'

'Well, so I was,' he admitted. 'No one there except aged relations, all hoping for a slice of the cake. Won't they all have their noses put out of joint now!'

'That is enough,' the doctor broke in. 'I can see I have been far too lenient with you young people, allowed you too much freedom, and this ill-nature is the result.'

'Oh, Papa!' there was a chorus of protest from the two younger ones while Sophie hating the whole conversation, refused to join in, staring out of the window instead. It was a pleasant room opening on to a garden, wintry now, the trees bare, the only green a few laurel bushes hiding the house from the road. Smyrna Villa was double-fronted, a spacious house, this room running from front to back, folding doors dividing it into two for warmth, opening for entertainment. Breakfast was always taken in here at a small table, the dining room on the other side of the hall being used as a waiting room for carriage patients, while a small single storey building to one side served for the poorer folk, an outer door admitting them up a few steps to a plain room, lined with kitchen-type chairs. A short staircase at the rear of the hall led to the doctor's consulting room. Not a pretentious house, but large enough to be comfortable and in a tree-lined road leading to Clapham Common.

'If there is one thing that disgusts me,' Dr Sterling said, 'it is when anyone is abused for doing what they wish with their property. I have seen far too much of that sort of behaviour when I have attended a deathbed. Sophie is quite right there.

3

And she has always liked Aunt Adela, which you two have not. I'm not saying it isn't a pity that she didn't leave you a modest sum, but considering your behaviour it is probably better that she did not.'

'Modest!' Alethea burst out again. 'She was rich enough to have provided for all three of us, but oh no, Sophie is to get it all. What about *me?* And Frank?'

'Aye,' her brother agreed, 'it is always hard to keep up with the rich fellows. A little extra – '

' – would certainly be frivolously dribbled away,' his father finished. 'I am ashamed of you both. And perfectly capable of taking care of your future, Frank, while as for you, Thea, you have been blessed with looks that will no doubt procure you a number of offers, young men being what they are. Sophie has other qualities, not so easily found out but appreciated later. A fortune won't come amiss with you, eh, my dear?'

Mrs Sterling, who doted on Alethea but found little in common with her more intelligent elder daughter, shrugged her shoulders. 'Well, I know you always put Sophie above the other two, but – '

Her husband was becoming considerably annoyed. 'I hope I have not been guilty of favouritism. It is merely that Sophie and I have many interests in common.'

Sophie smiled, but said, 'I do wish you would not all talk about me as if I wasn't here. Papa, may we not drop the subject?'

'Willingly,' he agreed, 'Rose, pour me some more coffee, if you please.'

The coffee was poured in silence. Used to being considered by her mother in many ways her younger sister's inferior, Sophie was content merely to have his approval. Alethea could play the piano dashingly, compared to her modest efforts, arrange flowers attractively whereas hers always fell on one side, embroider exquisitely though when it came to general sewing Sophie knew herself to be superior, Alethea having no patience for it. At intellectual pursuits, however, Sophie was on her own. Alethea seldom opened a book and if she did it was to put it aside with a yawn after five minutes. She had no patience either with the few household tasks allotted to her. Dr Sterling believed in women knowing how to run a home efficiently, and would often say, 'Sophie, do be a dear and do this for me' — which Sophie generally did, without seeing either virtue or talent in herself.

Mrs Sterling, however, was less inclined to leave the subject of the legacy, unable to resist remarking that she wondered what Lord Randolph had to say about the matter.

'It makes no difference what he says,' was her husband's short reply. 'We were both equally related to Adela Crabtree.'

'She was well named,' Frank muttered under his breath, 'a real old crab.' At which his father turned towards him with one speaking glance so that he clapped both hands over his mouth, before removing them to say, 'I'm silent, sir. Not another word.'

'I should think not.' Dr Sterling surveyed his family. 'Considering only Sophie cared to accompany me to the funeral — yes, I'm aware you hadn't returned then, Frank, and you, my dear, had an unfortunate headache — I believe it shows how little anyone else cared for her. As for my cousin, we had no chance to speak privately at the time.'

'He has seldom made any effort to speak to us at all,' Mrs Sterling drew herself up and puffed out her bosom. 'No doubt he thinks a physician's family beneath his notice.'

'Our ways went differently. Being the youngest of seven, as you well know, I had to earn my living and I've never regretted my choice. I'm glad my parents, God rest them, did not live to see the decimation of their family.'

Sophie was the only one who had been really interested in the distant Northumbrian relatives. Her grandmother Mary had been a sister of the then Lord Randolph and had married Hugh Sterling, a gentleman from Alnwick. He had gone into the wine business and lived there happily with his wife and brood of children, but none of his five girls had married and of his two sons one died in a shipwreck on his way to Australia, so that only the young David Sterling survived to go to medical school in Edinburgh. In 1825, after his training, he had come to London to gain experience in a large London hospital and had never returned north. Meeting Rose Mayfield, the daughter of a chemist, he had thought her a fine young woman who would be the kind of wife a doctor needed. She had indeed fulfilled this hope in that while he had no head for figures or management himself, she was a model of efficiency and he was grateful for this. That she had become somewhat overbearing and self-willed was only a small misfortune. His children were a delight to him, and he was happy to occupy himself in caring for his patients, both the well-to-do in the area around the Common and the poorer and needy folk in the mean little streets behind which dwindled away to open country. He was long out of touch with his august cousin, Lord John Randolph, and had never been one to foster a relationship for mere gain. His lordship had an estate in Oxfordshire, as well as a London home, but their adult paths had not crossed until the recent funeral. The only link had been their shared aunt, Adela Crabtree, and she had spent most of her adult life with her husband in India. She returned as a grieving widow to shut herself up in a house in Kensington, filling it with mementos of her life abroad. Mrs Sterling had long given up urging her husband to keep in touch with their titled relations and contented herself now by saying, 'Well, with Sophie being Great-Aunt Adela's heir, perhaps now his lordship will take notice of us.'

At that moment a bell rang and Dr Sterling got up thankfully. 'Ah, that will be my first patient. May I suggest you all try to exercise a little charity. Your reception of the news has hardly been to your credit.' Refusing to foment the affair further by singling Sophie out from this rebuke, he nevertheless gave her a quick smile, adding, 'And one other thing. I don't want this matter spoken of outside the family. Is that clearly understood?'

When the door had closed behind him Alethea burst out again. 'Well, I still think it's beastly that I don't get a penny, nor Frank.'

Sohie had had enough. 'If I could share it with you, I would, but it's not in my hands. Do let's stop talking about it.'

Ignoring this, her mother said, 'When you marry you will no doubt be able to do something for your brother and sister, which I'm sure would be acceptable to your husband, who would of course have the managing of your fortune.'

'And that's all wrong,' Alethea was petulant, 'Why should a husband have all one's property, such as it is? That's not fair either. If I were a member of Parliament I'd bring in a law about that.'

Frank gave a shout of laughter. 'If women, especially ones with your silly notions, ever got into Parliament I'd live abroad, I can tell you!'

'And good riddance,' was his sister's reply. 'Women can go to college now and have a University education, so there!'

Their mother told them to stop talking nonsense, adding, 'I'm sure I don't know why ladies should want to do such a thing. Anyway, marriage is what I expect for you two girls.'

Sophie gave a wry smile. 'Considering I don't even have a beau, Mama, I think the possibility of a husband is a long way off. Thea is far more likely to marry first.'

No one disagreed with this and she went away upstairs to her room ostensibly to write to her friend, Verity Willsher. Instead, however, she sat down in front of her mirror and looked at herself. Quite accustomed to the idea that she was no beauty, nevertheless this morning she studied her reflection in a newly critical fashion. The last thing she wanted was for a man to marry her for her money, but it now seemed possible and she hated the thought. Something advantageous to both parties would be 'arranged' for her, no doubt, though she was sure Papa would not allow Mama to push her into something she did not want. So far she had had no offers. Social life consisted in dining with neighbours and family friends, going to a ball now and again, to the nearest Assembly Rooms, or to Mr Willsher's entertainments. He and his wife lived in a much larger house facing Wandsworth Common, and having a family of sons and daughters, enjoyed seeing the young people dance. Dennis Willsher was dangling after Alethea, but that minx, encouraged by her mother, was setting her sights far higher than a callow youth whose father was an attorney. Sophie danced with young men on these occasions but was on the floor far less than Alethea, who floated about the room, casting limpid blue-eyed glances at her partners, her lovely face bright, her fair hair dressed in the latest style. Mrs Sterling prophesied a great marriage for her if only she could be launched into London society. Alethea demanded to know how this should come about when they were restricted to Clapham with its businessmen and lawyers and the like, while Mrs Sterling was of the opinion that, having two marriageable daughters, her husband should bestir himself to contact his rich relations and find someone to sponsor them. A London season would surely see Alethea at least snaring a titled gentleman. Sophie had cared for none of this and thought it a great deal of pretentious nonsense, though she never said so.

Looking into the mirror now, she saw a rather long face, with a straight nose, a well-shaped mouth admittedly, but no striking looks. Only her eyes, large, grey and set well apart, could claim anything like beauty. Her light brown hair was parted in the centre and drawn neatly to each side in a knot of curls − no blonde locks for her. But the effect was far more pleasing than it seemed to her.

This morning's altercation had upset her. She loved her family, though she was not blind to their foibles, and she was truly fond of her sister, joining in the spoiling of that engaging child, though that had not been, perhaps, the most judicious thing. What was she going to do with all this money? At least she couldn't touch it until she married. The regular income would no doubt be more than her present allowance but it seemed unlikely that it would disturb the even tenor of her days. It would be fun of course to be able to buy little presents for the family, but as she had no idea how much she would have to spend she saw no further than that.

Was she dull that she found her contentment at home, mainly in the company of her father in his spare time, often going with him when he drove out to see his patients, helping her mother in the running of the household? Alethea was only just released from the schoolroom where a daily governess had taught her and Daisy Patterson who lived next door, and was restless, finding no similar contentment in the daily round. Alethea craved excitement and had persuaded her father to buy her a pony to share the stables with the carriage horse. She had learned to ride with the ease with which she seemed to master anything she set her mind to, telling Sophie it was the most exhilarating exercise and that she should take it up. But to Sophie the horse seemed a large and rather overwhelming animal with a mind of its own, and she had no desire to set herself on the back of such a creature when a carriage or her own two feet could convey her anywhere she might want to go. There always seemed to be plenty to do, visits to make, regular walks to the subscription library, mending to be done. Whenever the doctor found a poor family in need he told his wife and girls to see that they received food and any cast-off clothing. This generally devolved on Sophie but she didn't mind. With their maid, Minnie, she would walk any distance, her compassion drawn to hungry and sick children, combined with pity for wretched women trying to manage on what was barely a subsistence wage, or coping with a drunken husband. Mrs Sterling protested once that such visiting was not suitable for her girls, to which the doctor replied that the relief of the sick and poor was to his mind a Christian duty.

'They will catch some horrid disease, you mark my words,' his wife told him, to which he replied, 'You let me worry about that.'

So the days passed in multifarious occupations and Sophie was never bored. She had friends among the local families and her closest, Verity, had recently become engaged to a gentleman from the Foreign Office. Verity seemed to be so happy that Sophie wondered if she herself would ever be so fortunate. This enormous amount of money must surely complicate matters, and was likely to rule out a man of modest standing such as Daisy's brother – not that she had any real interest in him. She heartily wished it had been divided between the three of them, but her great-aunt had spoken plainly about the other two. She thought back to a conversation they had one autumn afternoon in Mrs Crabtree's dark drawing room.

'Alethea will be heading for trouble if I'm not mistaken,' Aunt Adela had declared. 'She's flighty and too pretty for her own good.'

'I know,' Sophie had sighed, 'which I am not.'

9

'Nonsense.' Adela Crabtree had been a small birdlike woman, her face brown and withered from long years in the heat of India. Always intelligent, acute, and never one to suffer fools gladly, she was now over ninety, no longer able to go out in the world, contenting herself with caustic strictures on everyone from the young Queen Victoria, the Government and the judicial system down to the most modest public figure whom she read about in *The Times*. She had a penetrating stare which discomfitted most people and on this occasion had bent it on her great-niece. 'You have talents, child, never think you have not. Even if you are not very good at arranging flowers' − this was a standing joke between them − 'or tying a bow so that it falls in place, still you paint very nicely and you can play the piano.'

'Indifferently.'

'Quite well enough, my dear. Only I am not thinking of these things so much as character. You are untried yet, but you will see. I think life may ask much of you because you set high standards for yourself, yet I am sure you will respond in ways you don't guess at.'

Sophie had laughed and shaken her head, but her aunt went on, 'Oh, I am right. Alethea is bright and full of nonsensical chatter, but shallow, I fear. As for Frank, I believe in young men making their own way. An inheritance too young can be ruinous − I've seen it many times. He will do well enough if he applies himself without having money poured into his pockets.'

Recalling this conversation, now Sophie feared the sharp remarks were all too true. Loving her brother and sister as she did, did not prevent her from being aware of their failings. On these visits she and her great-aunt had not only spoken of the family but covered a wide area of topics and she had loved these twilight talks. To be accused of sucking up to the old lady was wildly unjust. Only Papa understood and before dinner, when she knew he would be in his study, she went down to knock on the door. No one, not even Mrs Sterling, entered that sanctum without knocking.

He smiled up at her. 'Well, my love, what is it? You look bothered. Is it the money?'

'Yes, Papa.' She sat down in the patient's chair opposite

him. 'It is such a very great deal. I would rather it had been perhaps five hundred pounds.'

'More manageable, I agree, but there it is. Her entire wealth cannot but be overwhelming, and may cause a great deal of ill feeling. Still, she was very fond of you and you gave her so much pleasure with your visits.' Doctor Sterling was a short man, balding now, with a neat moustache, his blue eyes kindly, and he was much loved in the district, especially by his poorer patients who had cause to know of his quiet generosity as well as his medical skill. 'Do you remember how pleased she was with your painting of Brixton Mill? She wouldn't have had it framed and hung in her sitting room just to please you, would she?'

Sophie chuckled. 'No, Papa, that would not have been in character, but I hope I did please her. I'm only glad I didn't know what she was going to do. It would have made me so uncomfortable.'

'You must try not to worry about it, though I must admit it may be more a millstone than a pleasure. You don't receive anything of course until you marry – or reach the age of twenty-five. I forgot to tell you that. But Mr Patten has been my man of business long enough to know us all and to administer it for you with Aunt Adela's lawyer. They will see it is properly invested, not put into some fly-by-night venture. The interest will go into capital investment and also provide you with a quarterly allowance, which may be near a £100.'

'Oh, Papa! I could buy presents for everyone.'

He laughed and said, 'I think I will open a bank account for you. Don't be tempted to spend too lavishly on your sister or your brother, and certainly not on your Mama or myself. Let it stay there earning interest until you need it.'

'Yes, Papa, you are quite right, of course, but it will be so – so useful in an emergency.'

His eyes twinkled. 'Such as a particular evening gown, or more likely one for Alethea! But I won't have her bother you for such things – send her to me if she does! I don't mean you shouldn't be generous, but that you should be sensible. Well, I've no doubt on that score – you're a careful girl. My father taught me to be careful with money and I think

11

you have inherited that very necessary trait.'

She smiled across at him. 'Grandpapa was a border Scot, wasn't he?'

'And that's nae a bad thing.' He lapsed into the accent of his childhood and gave her an impish smile. 'Come along, there's the gong for dinner.'

Of course the legacy came up for discussion again at dinner until Dr Sterling said firmly that he thought it had been aired enough, bringing the talk to the subject of a great new exhibition to be held in London some time in the next year or two, when a site could be agreed on.

'Exhibitions can be very boring,' Alethea remarked. 'That one you took us to last year was the dullest thing I ever saw.'

'I must admit it was not very well done, and the latest gadgets for labour saving in the kitchen might not interest young ladies, but this proposed one will be very large and encompass every trade and craft there is. Every country is being invited to send exhibits, and as Prince Albert is very much involved in it, it will probably go further than the drawing board. And of course as he is eager for it so too will the Queen's interest be engaged.'

'What an example she is to everyone, and still so young,' Mrs Sterling agreed. 'Such a happy family life and a desire to do some good in the country. I swear more than half the babies born now are christened Victoria or Albert.'

With the conversation safely led away from her inheritance, Sophie was relieved. It was a burden she had no wish for, but it was going to be difficult to escape. At bedtime she and Alethea went up together as they usually did, but tonight Alethea followed her into her room and bounced on to the bed, her annoyance somewhat turned aside by the thought of an elder sister actually having funds in her hand.

'Have you thought, Sophie, what you are going to do now you are an heiress? I'm very grateful for the allowance Papa has given me since I was released from the schoolroom, but it doesn't go very far, does it? At least I can't make it stretch to all the things I want. I saw several lace collars in Patterson's the other day and couldn't afford any of them. I do think Mr Patterson might give us a discount.'

12

Sophie laughed. 'He's a tradesman and can't bring down his prices for all his friends.'

'Yes, well, when you get your first allowance will you buy me one? I've such a fancy for some blue silk for an evening gown too, with matching velvet bows. I can draw exactly what I want and Miss Sedley might be able to copy it, though she's not usually very imaginative. Or perhaps we can look for a better dressmaker, even if they are a little more expensive.'

'How you do run on.' Sophie sat down at her dressing table and began to loosen her hair. 'It's all a while off yet. Papa says the lawyers will take a long time to sort out the estate.'

'But you will think about it? Mama will be sure to say I have enough dresses, but it will be so boring to wear the yellow again, or the pink satin.'

'Or the white with the blue sash,' Sophie teased her. 'Mama is quite right. I seem to manage on half the clothes you think are necessary, and Papa has always given us what we need.'

'Oh, need, yes. But to have a little extra for a change — luxury! And you can't want to wear that old blue of yours again to Mr Willsher's next party. You know he always has such a splendid ball for New Year.'

'Well, I may have to. I won't have any of the money before that. In any case, if I wanted one I have sufficient left of my own quarter for a modest length of silk. But I like my blue. And Papa's not mean, Alethea, you know he isn't.'

'Oh, of course not, but he's always saying we have to learn to manage, and it becomes such a business explaining why I want something, and he looks at me in a teasing way as if I was a child wanting a lollipop.'

'Which you are.'

Alethea slid off the bed. 'I can see you're going to be horrid about it. I hope you don't end up like Great-Aunt Adela, all mean and cross.'

Sophie sighed. 'You never tried to understand her.'

'Because she treated me as if I was six years old! If Mr Dennis Willsher offers for me, that will prove I'm grown up. I shall be eighteen at Christmas.'

'And I suppose that makes me an old maid at twenty-one. Would you accept him?'

'Good gracious me, no. He's pleasant enough and good-looking, but Mama hopes for better for me − and you,' she added hastily. 'Papa is bound to be in touch with Lord Randolph now, and who knows where that will lead.'

'Who indeed?' Sophie countered absently. 'Do go to bed, Thea. I'm tired.'

But once in bed it was hard to sleep. Such a turn of fortune was totally unlooked for, nor was it comfortable to be singled out above her sister and brother. Frank was easy-going enough and too absorbed in his new career to worry about it beyond looking hopefully for the coveted compass on his birthday, but Alethea was a different matter. It must not be allowed to cause a rift between them, or the least unpleasantness with Mama.

Fond of her mother as she was, however, Sophie had to admit that she was, in plain words, a snob. She herself was always happier with her father who, being of an aristocratic family, had no need to be. Sitting up in bed, hugging her knees and staring into the dark, she tried to assimilate the fact that she was an heiress. Tomorrow she would do all the usual things − dust the ornaments in the drawing room, a task not entrusted to the housemaid, take their dog Dash for a walk, drive out with Papa − everything would seem the same, but it was not. Such news could not be hidden, and as an heiress she would be in demand. While wanting a home and children, she had always hoped she would meet a man whom she could love and who in return would love her for herself. Now, how would she know if they only wanted her for her fortune? 'Oh Papa,' she whispered, 'help me to choose wisely, when − if − it happens.'

Suddenly angry, she wished with all her heart that her great-aunt had not done this to her. She didn't want so large a fortune. They had had such a happy relationship and of course her aunt meant it to be the most generous compliment, but she didn't want it, couldn't even give it away to the poor or the missions, for no one would let her, least of all Mama who would probably have an apoplectic

14

fit at such a thought! No, there would be talk of stocks and investments and interest rates and it would all be too tiresome for words.

The next fortnight slipped by as if nothing had happened. Frank returned to his ship and though Alethea brought up the subject now and again she got no response from Sophie, still less from their father, and at last Sophie said plainly she was sick and tired of discussing it. At which her sister pouted, and forgetting their father's injunction, flounced off to talk it all over with her friend Daisy. Hearing what had happened, Daisy's mother, who had a son of twenty-three learning to be a lawyer in the Middle Temple, called to give her congratulations to her dear friend, Mrs Sterling.

'Dear Sophie', however, would not be drawn while Mrs Sterling explained that though it was a great surprise to them all, it was no more than might have been expected, having the connections they had. There was no doubt as to her meaning and Sophie escaped in disgusted embarrassment, on the pretext of ordering some refreshment. None of them, she thought bitterly, were heeding Papa's order not to speak of it outside the family. Certainly Mrs Sterling did not appear to think the order applied to her and had already whispered the news 'in confidence' to several ladies at the whist table.

After having tea sent up, Sophie went to the study where her father, who attended the local hospital twice a week, was at work on a paper of suggested improvements.

'Well,' he glanced up, smiling, 'what is it, dearest? You look ruffled.'

'I am, Papa. I hate it, this money. It makes everyone — I don't know — different.' Gazing out of the window into the front garden, she could see her sister and Daisy walking up and down in the shrubbery, arm in arm, fair head close to dark, and it was easy enough to guess at the source of their confidences. She added, 'Thea goes on and on about it, and Mama — underneath a lot of smiles, of course — is being quite unbearably condescending to Mrs Patterson. I do wish — '

'You wish Aunt Adela had not singled you out?'

'Yes, oh yes.'

15

He took her hand. 'Don't worry, my love. I won't let it ruin your life, nor will I allow a fortune-hunter to sweep you away, whatever your Mama thinks. We'll keep our feet firmly on the ground won't we?'

Leaning against him, she whispered, 'Oh, dear Papa, what would I do without you?'

At that moment there was the sound of a bell and he sighed. 'A patient, I suppose. I do wish they would keep to my surgery days. They all know that if it's urgent, I'll call.'

Sophie peeped out of the window. 'Papa! It's a carriage with a coat of arms on the door.'

'I wonder who that can be? Yes, William?' as their footman knocked and came in.

'Lord Randolph, sir. I've shown him into the dining room as he asked particularly for you, and Mrs Sterling has company in the drawing room.'

'Quite right.' Dr Sterling rose and exchanged a surprised glance with his daughter, before crossing the hall to enter the dining room, and she heard only, 'Well, John, it has been a long time — ' before the door closed.

Chapter Two

A week later another family exchange was taking place, but this time at a very different house, a tall and elegant mansion in Mount Street, which led to the Mount Gate into Hyde Park. There Lord Randolph of Redesdale was sitting by the fire in his library, while his elder son George stood leaning against the carved mantelshelf that was one of Robert Adam's finest. After six years abroad he had been home for precisely three hours, during which time he had bathed, removed the dirt of travel and changed his clothes.

'Well, sir, I observe that far from being at death's door, you are obviously in better health, for which I rejoice.'

His father gave him a sour look. 'I am sorry to disappoint you, but as you see, no doubt owing to the perversity of my nature, I am very much alive. Do you think that I don't know that if you hadn't had such adverse reports of me from that interfering old fool Warburton, combined with the doctor's pessimism, you would not have come back.' George made a deprecatory gesture, but it was recognized as no more than a formality and the old man went on, 'Certainly I myself would not have summoned you so precipitately.'

'I'm aware of that.' George moved away, oppressed by the heat of the fire and the stuffiness of the room. 'But our quarrel was a long time ago. Shall we not try to bury the hatchet?'

Lord Randolph stared into the red glow and then with his stick pushed a log into place so that fresh sparks flew upwards. 'You caused an unpleasant scandal, dragged our name through the courts. Nothing else would serve but your − prolonged − absence.'

George raised one eyebrow. 'Six years might seem excessive. You've never asked me to come back. No doubt you would have liked to disinherit me and put Maurice in my place.'

'Your brother doesn't come into this. Anyway he is at sea, at the end of a two-year voyage to the South Sea Islands. And when he is here he appears to be as frivolous and extravagant as ever, chasing women and getting up to God knows what else. How he goes on aboard ship I can't imagine. The pair of you −'

'Oh, pray don't put us into one drawer, sir. We are not in the least alike. I have my faults, but they are different.'

'Very probably. Your letters to me consisted of barely two or three lines, dictated no doubt by a hidden streak of duty of which I have been hitherto unaware.'

'As to that, I have had but one letter from you, letting me know my uncle Henry was dead − and that was dictated to Warburton.'

Lord Randolph brushed this aside. 'I believe Gibraltar was your latest stay.'

'I had a post in the Governor's household. He was a more than halfway decent man, and anything was more tolerable than being at our Embassy in St Petersburg to which you banished me.'

'I found you a better position than you deserved.'

'Too damned cold, Russia.' George walked across to a small table. 'A brandy, sir?' Pouring two glasses, he handed one to the old man. 'It seems I returned for nothing if we are going to quarrel again. I see no point in digging up old recriminations. And you might give me credit for being a little older and wiser.'

His father stirred uneasily. Never wearing anything but black, his frock-coat and the stock about his neck only emphasised the pallor of his thin, hawk-like face. 'Perhaps. But you seem to have tried many things, wasted your time, no doubt, in the capitals of Europe. I never knew where the next letter would come from, so apparently you have found nothing to make your life satisfactory.'

'You see no virtue in being a dilettante?'

'Don't fence with me, George. You take my meaning perfectly well. But you are right in that there is no point in looking back. Among the participants in the affair, Captain Horton is long gone to America and Mrs Horton is dead.' He saw his son's mouth twitch. 'You didn't know?'

'No. No one saw fit to tell me that.' The long dead scandal was doubtless forgotten in London, but Emily Horton had left a scar deep in the heart of the twenty-one-year-old he had then been. 'How — '

'There was a notice in *The Times* a year or so ago, if I remember rightly — a sudden illness, I think — so there is no need as you say to bring all that up again. There have been plenty of other scandals since then and society will have forgotten yours.' There was an edge to his voice as he saw the instant closing in of his son's face, but all George said, in a voice devoid of expression, was, 'Do you go into society these days?'

'Not much. I miss Melbourne, of course, my oldest friend. He's been gone nearly two years now, but Sir Robert Peel dines with me now and again. As PM he rubbed people up the wrong way at times but in private he's an excellent dinner companion. Wellington too, we share old men's reminiscences. I go to my club for a game of whist now and again, and sometimes to Court — Her Majesty is always very gracious to an old man. The Prince is highly educated and interesting to talk to, but I go less and less these days.' He stopped, one hand gripped on the arm of his chair, for to talk about his affairs was the last thing he wanted. Never a man to show the least sentiment, he nevertheless knew a moment of inner panic in case he should lose this first-born again. He went on, 'Well, now that you are here we must consider the future. You are my heir and I've had one brush with death. There is a great deal to be considered. Plummers — '

George set down his glass, trying to thrust the late Emily Horton to the back of his mind. 'As a matter of fact, I do have some plans. If you — ' He hastily changed this tack from 'if you had died' to 'if you approve, I would like to set up a stud there. I've brought home a stallion and

19

two mares. They're Arabs, and it could be a profitable prospect.'

Lord Randolph gazed at him in astonishment.

'Arabs? I've not seen the breed.'

'I suppose not. I believe I am the first man to bring them to this country – pure white, beautiful creatures.'

'So you've lost no time in appropriating Plummers!'

His son shrugged. 'It wasn't planned. I had the chance to buy these horses and it seemed too good to miss. I was in Morocco at the time, and when I returned to Gibraltar to find Warburton's letter awaiting me, I shipped them and myself home as well. You know horses have always been my great interest – well, I want it to be more than a hobby now.'

'You can't tell me you had been intending to set them up on the Rock?'

'Good God, no. I was going to send them home anyway, and write to you suggesting I should take over Plummers. You never go there, do you?'

'No, I do not – a damned draughty place too large for comfort, and none of the windows fit.' But he paused, remembering far-off happier days when, full of hope, he had taken his young bride to Oxfordshire, and the idyllic years they had spent there. With her death he had turned from the place with revulsion and left the working of it to his steward. But he remembered the two little boys who had played there, climbing the old cedar and taking a boat out on the shallow mere. He glanced at the strong, well-built figure of his son. 'You have changed, George.'

'Hardly surprising, sir. It's been a long time.'

'Yes, it was time you returned,' the old man said pensively. 'You can look to Plummers. At least in this house I have some comfort – for as long as I am here.'

George ignored this proviso and turned to what was pressing on his mind. 'Warburton hinted that all was not well financially, that I should have a task on my hands.' He watched his father shift again, the wrinkled hands twisting on the ebony stick from which he was now inseparable, and in a voice that was less harsh, asked, 'What is it, father? What has gone wrong?'

'Investments,' his lordship muttered. 'Cursed Stock Exchange. Warburton's fault, he listened to my broker's bad advice and passed it on to me, damned old fool.'

George felt a certain sympathy for the cautious and much tried Warburton. 'It must have seemed good at the time. What was it?'

'Oh, another South Sea bubble or some such thing. Better invest in one's own country – even so, years ago I bought into a shipping business, trading round our coasts. Sound at the time, but now goods go by train – dirty, noisy things. Do you know they can travel at sixty miles an hour? Coastal shipping has been badly hit and I've lost a deal of money, probably have to sell this house.'

'Sell it? But where would you live? Not at Plummers, surely?'

Lord Randolph shuddered. 'Not if I can help it. I suppose I shall have to find some miserable lodgings with just room enough for me and Harper.'

George could not keep back a laugh. 'What a prophet of gloom and doom you are. I don't believe it is as bad as that. You must let me look into it all. I'll see Warburton tomorrow.'

'It's just as I say,' his father reiterated. 'There's precious little money. Perhaps I'll sell Plummers.'

'You can't. It's entailed.'

'So it is, I'd forgotten.' The old man sat staring into the fire, while George watched him.

At last George spoke again. 'I can see it is high time I was here to try to set matters right.'

'Oh? Have you brought a fortune with you? That would surprise me considerably.'

'No, I have not.'

Lord Randolph looked him up and down, taking in the brown cut-away coat, fawn waistcoat, check trousers, and fine lawn shirt showing at the neck and cuffs. 'You don't look penniless. You pockets must be adequately lined if you can dress well and buy no doubt very expensive horses.'

George shrugged. 'I'm not on the breadline, if that's what you want to know, but neither am I particularly flush at the moment.'

21

'Well, if you've not come home with a fortune, then we are in Queer Street. The only way out is for you to marry an heiress. Oh, you may well laugh, but it is one solution.'

'Indeed? I think you are fantasising. How should I know any heiresses?'

'Unlikely, I admit – but I do.' The old man regarded his astonished son. 'I mean it. You won't know that your Great-Aunt Adela is dead.'

'No, I didn't. She was as I remember a fearsome old hag who lived in a house stuffed with curios, and had a tongue dipped in vinegar.'

'Only for those she had no time for. She has left a fortune that will bring in twenty thousand a year. Reminds me of King Jog, old Lord Lampton who died near ten years ago; he said he could jog along nicely on forty thousand. I imagine you could jog along comfortably enough on twenty?'

George's jaw had dropped. 'Good God! I'd no idea. Who on earth has she left it to? And where did it come from?'

'Old Crabtree made a fortune in India, invested it wisely – more than I did – and then made another.'

'Then who – not to me, surely?'

'Certainly not. She remembers you as an impertinent boy who caught frogs in her garden and released them in her drawing room when she had guests.'

'Maurice then?'

'He was as bad.'

He paused and George said, 'For God's sake, tell me, sir.'

'She has left the entire inheritance to Miss Sophie Sterling.'

'And who the devil is she?' George's face was a mask of blank astonishment.

'Dr Sterling, her father, is a second cousin of mine. My grandfather and his were brothers, Adela being their sister. Another sister Aunt Mary married a Sterling – good Northumbrian family, some relations still living there, I believe. Their son David went to Edinburgh University for his medical training. After he came south for a post in, I think, St Bartholomew's hospital, he married – beneath him, the family thought – and never went back north. I'd not seen him for many years, until recently. He has two daughters and a son, Sophie being the eldest. Apparently he kept in touch with Adela Crabtree and Sophie visited her quite regularly. It seems the old lady took a great fancy to her. Anyway, there it is – the whole goes to that girl, except the Crabtree collection of Indian curios, which is given to the British Museum.'

George had flushed with sudden anger. 'I call that monstrous. Was the old girl in her right mind?'

'Apparently very much so.'

'Then this girl must have prejudiced her, worked on her. It's beyond belief – there's myself, Maurice, Uncle Joseph's brood – oh, all the cousinage. It isn't right that one should be singled out, especially not one less connected and about whom we know nothing. Did you say her father is a physician?'

'I did.'

'And do you know her?'

'I called on them a few days ago.'

'Then where do they live, these Sterlings?'

'Clapham.'

George looked at him in exasperation. 'And where the devil is Clapham?'

'South of town.' His father waved a vague hand. 'I know Robert drove me over Vauxhall Bridge. It's become a respectable suburb.'

'Never heard of it. It doesn't sound at all the sort of place to amount to anything.'

'Well, I suppose the people in Clapham need a doctor as well as anyone. My glass is empty, George.'

His son refilled it. 'I'm trying to grasp what you are saying. Are you really proposing that one of us, and I presume you mean me, should marry this girl for Great-Aunt Adela's money?'

'Exactly so,' his lordship said plainly. 'At least it's to be considered, don't you think? Keep it in the family?'

George gave a bark of laughter. 'You think it would solve all our problems? But if I put my mind to it, I might find a more congenial heiress in better society.'

'You might, but this is one to hand. I want an heir, George, and time is running out for me.'

23

His son's face darkened. 'Oh, I see. I am to be put out to stud — like my Arabs!'

'Now you are being coarse. Isn't it natural for a man to want to see his grandchildren, to safeguard the family inheritance?'

'What inheritance? Impoverished coffers and an old house in bad repair. I gather Plummers is near falling down.'

'And our name, George, an old and honourable one, and that counts for a great deal.'

'A rabble of border reivers,' George muttered. 'And this girl — who is to say we should find each other even tolerable? Why should she consider me? She doesn't know me, nor I her, and with all this money she won't lack for suitors.'

'The world is the same as it always was. People marry for other things than love, and you will be Randolph of Redesdale one day, maybe sooner than later — a title any scheming mother would jump at. David Sterling has connections while Mrs Sterling has pretensions — one visit told me that!'

'What? You can't have broached the subject already?'

'I most certainly have. When I heard you were coming I drove to Clapham to sound out the doctor's opinion, and at the same time take a look at the girl.'

George was really angry and for a moment searched for adequate words. 'Sir, I consider that high-handed in the extreme. I wish you will not talk to me as if I was eighteen instead of all but twenty-eight. I believe I am capable of choosing a wife for myself, always supposing I want one, without your interference.'

Lord Randolph shrugged off this outburst. 'If you are planning to set up at Plummers, surely a wife, and a wife with money, would be an advantage?'

'I hadn't got as far as considering that aspect of it. Are you really saying you want me to offer for a physician's daughter who lives in some ghastly suburb with obviously a harridan for a mother?'

'I dislike snobbery, George. It is vulgar.'

George banged his fist on the mantelshelf, where he had returned to confront his father, causing one china dog to fall on its face. 'You wouldn't commend the match if

24

she hadn't been left Adela Crabtree's money. I call that hypocrisy, which is as bad.'

'Certainly not. It is a proper sense of the social state. Your aunt Louisa thinks − '

'She is worse than you are. I never saw the like of her scheming to get a duke for Amabel, albeit she had to settle for a viscount. It's no more than market-place bargaining.'

'Don't take that tone with me, sir,' his lordship said, equally angry now. 'We have no need to strike an attitude about our antecedents and when you have offspring of your own you will, if you've any family feeling at all, want equally well for them. And Amabel's marriage appears to be very happy. She has two boys and another on the way.'

At this moment George could not interest himself in his cousin's marital affairs. He was silent, his mind racing. He saw Plummers, which he had loved as a boy, put to rights, his stable set up, his horses thriving on the fresh grass of Oxfordshire, himself wealthy and with considerable standing in the county. It could not but be an appealing prospect. And a wife and children would in due course be a necessary part of that. Rousing himself he asked sharply, 'And what was the result of your call?'

'I wanted to see David and at least make sure the girl was not already promised.'

George flushed darkly, his anger now barely under control. 'To do it without speaking to me first − really, that is going too far.'

His father gave him a tired glance. 'When one gets to my age there is a need to see matters arranged. I have the family interests at heart and I only made a very tentative approach, privately, to David himself. I stayed to luncheon and met the girl.'

'You stayed to − I can see you wasted no time! Then what is she like, this cousin of mine?'

'A quiet, sensible girl, well bred, and just the one to bring you to a more ordered way of life.'

'My God!' George said with considerable feeling. 'Are you determined I shall be bored to death?'

'That remark was quite unnecessary. I had hoped your

years away would have brought you to a better frame of mind.'

'Because I won't be manipulated by you? And, if you will forgive me, sir, you have hardly seen enough of me to formulate a judgement as to what the years have done to me.' He paused and set the china dog on its feet before asking abruptly, 'Is she pretty, this girl?'

'No, I would not say so. The younger sister is the beauty, but Miss Sophie has a very pleasing countenance.'

'You mean she is plain.' There was a long moment of silence, which extended itself into another. Lord Randolph stared into the fire, while his son reached for his cigar case and then changed his mind, remembering that smoking had never been permitted in this room. Instead he looked out of the window at the steadily falling rain, the street outside awash, people hurrying by under umbrellas. At last he said, 'I'd forgotten what an English winter was like.' He brought his gaze back to his father. 'It is a pity we dislike each other so much, isn't it? I in my turn had hoped you would have received me in a more forgiving manner. I am not the youth who went away.'

A man of deep reserve, possessing an iron will that saw no need to explain itself to anyone, Lord Randolph said nothing, aware that George to some extent had inherited both these traits. Outside a carriage splashed past, sending showers of water over passers-by, an errand boy whistled and a man trundled past with his hand-truck covered in tarpaulin.

At last Lord Randolph, making what was for him a great effort, spoke slowly. 'My boy, I don't dislike you. We have not got on in the past and I must admit that court case tried me beyond measure. My main feeling was one of thankfulness that your mother wasn't alive to face the scandal.'

Through tight lips George said, 'So you told me at the time. I don't think it was necessary to say it again.'

Another pause, and then the old man conceded, 'No, it wasn't. I beg your pardon, George. You are both older and wiser now, I'm sure, and as for me − I don't know how much longer I shall grace this world. Shall we call a truce and make a fresh beginning? I want to hear about your travels and talk over the financial state we are in. We have much to occupy us and I, — ' with an even greater effort — 'I feel my strength drained. I need your support, my dear boy.'

It would have been a hard heart that could have resisted this olive branch. George leaned forward and took his father's outstretched hand. 'Believe me, sir, nothing would please me more than to do anything I may for you. It's true we've never got on well, but perhaps now — six years is a long time.'

'A long time,' Lord Randolph repeated. 'There have been many times when I wished — ' He broke off. Not for anything would he have admitted how much he had regretted the bitter words, the blistering quarrels of the days when Captain Lawrence Horton had filed for a separation and sued George for the seduction of his wife, a case that had been the scandal of the season of 1844. The culmination of all this had been George's banishment abroad, father and son implacable enemies. Now he knew that this was his last chance to be on better terms with his heir. 'Another brandy, if you please, George. That old fool of a doctor tried to tell me that it would be injurious for me to take more than one glass. Injurious to what, I wonder? If he meant it might rob me of a few more months of life, I can only say that seems to me to be neither here nor there. Perhaps I'll consult David Sterling — a younger man with maybe some new ideas. Which brings me back to his daughter.'

'Must it, sir?'

'At least meet her, if only out of the courtesies.'

For a moment their eyes met, and two strong wills contested for the ascendancy. Then George gave a shrug. 'If I must, I must. I will admit I could do a great deal with such a fortune — jog along very nicely, as you pointed out. But I won't be paraded as a prospective husband.'

'Of course not,' his father said smoothly, satisfied to have achieved at least this first step in his plan. 'I have arranged an easy way of meeting her.' He did not add that he had had to overcome some reluctance on Dr Sterling's part. 'There's a gentleman by the name of Willsher in Wandsworth, pleasant house up on the hill, and it so happens Sterling is his

27

physician. The families are apparently on intimate terms, and as he gives a ball every New Year I have procured you an invitation to the one that is to take place in two weeks' time.'

'What a conspirator you are,' George said sarcastically.

His father received this as a compliment. 'It was not too difficult, particularly as Mrs Willsher is a relative of Warburton's. If I am well enough I shall accompany you and take advantage of the meeting to talk to David about my condition. You will come?'

But it was hardly a question and George gave in with as good a grace as possible. 'I suppose I must, but I won't give any assurances, still less a promise.'

'That's fair enough. And there's the dinner bell. You must be hungry after your journey.' Lord Randolph stood up and with his stick in one hand and the other resting on George's arm he walked into his dining room where he ate a better meal than he had done for some time.

That evening, when Lord Randolph had retired, his son, despite having had a very long day, stayed over his wine, enjoying a cigar. It was strange to be in this room again, after so many years. Nothing had changed – the sombre panelled walls, the heavy mahogany sideboard on which stood gleaming silver dishes and a magnificent epergne, the same framed hunting scenes decorating the walls – and it seemed as if the years between had hardly impinged on its solidity. For it was here, with the dishes on the table, that they had had their final quarrel. A wretched, unhappy business, and he hoped it was far behind him. But his father had had to mention it, to clear the air perhaps, to tell him that Mrs Horton was dead. Poor Emily, she could not have been more than in her late thirties. Younger than her by some twelve years he had been swept away by her beauty, her charm, her sheer vitality. They had fallen overwhelmingly in love and she had revealed a depth of passion that still sent a tremor through him, caution thrown to the wind, wild love-making that had inevitably gone to the head of the untried George. There had been other women since, of course, in St Petersburg, Paris, Rome, though he had been careful never to get entangled with one of Emily's standing, nor one with a madly jealous husband. None of them had touched his heart. And now Emily, passionate Emily, the lover of that amazing summer, was dead, lying buried somewhere in the unchanging earth. It was horrible to contemplate. He had thought he had got over his love for her, but the news of her death brought it all to the surface again. The miserable court case, the revenge of the cuckolded husband, the damages his father had had to pay out — he wanted to forget it all. The shame of it, the ignominy, the shock when Emily refused flatly to go abroad with him, to live on the small wage he would have at the embassy, still haunted him. No doubt his father had been right, the years abroad, alone, had been the only, the best thing for him.

Now, however, to come back to find family affairs in a bad way, with no cash for his new project, was tiresome to say the least. He poured himself another glass of his father's excellent claret — at least the cellar was not empty. But it was annoying to find the old man as truculent as ever, even illness failing to rob him of his desire to arrange everything for everyone. Still, it was doubtless a good thing to be on terms again. And now there was Great-Aunt Adela's money. If he married this girl — she sounded dull, prim and missish, and he backed away from the idea. Remembering the days with Emily, it would not, could not surely be like that! Nor was he any longer a callow twenty-one. He had had only too much experience of the fickleness of life. On the other hand, twenty thousand a year would sweeten his coffee more than somewhat. He would be comfortable, free to pursue what he liked, repair Plummers, set up his stable, enjoy the multifarious occupations of a country gentleman. It was a great temptation. He would have to meet Miss Sterling and see if she was remotely appealing. But innate pride made him shy away from the whole business and he was still angry, with Adela Crabtree, with his father, even with Miss Sterling.

It was a damnable thing to be faced with on the first day of his return.

Chapter Three

The ball given by the Willshers to usher in the year 1850 was one of the highlights of the winter for all who secured a much prized invitation. Wandsworth, with its large houses encircling the Common, was considered a very good address for gentlemen of the city now that they were served by the excellent train service from Clapham Junction.

The Sterlings arrived to find lanterns slung across the branches of the leafless trees, windows lit up and carriages encircling the gravel drive as guests were delivered. Alighting, the doctor could not help but be proud of his girls. Alethea was quite stunning in a pink ruched gown, a gauze scarf about her bare shoulders, her mass of fair hair elegantly dressed, a pink silk rose set in it, matching the corsage at her waist. Perhaps a little overdressed for a girl of her age, he thought, but there was no interfering with his forceful wife over such matters. To his mind Sophie, who had her own opinion when it came to clothes, looked very well in her familiar blue gown, the skirt layered and billowing out over several petticoats. She wore her hair as usual with ringlets to either side of her face, the rest in a knot behind. He wondered if he should have told her the Randolphs were coming, that Lord Randolph had proposed a match between her and his son? No, better not. Let the child meet them merely as relations and see if the young man was at all to her taste. He had given no more response to his titled cousin than that he was agreeable to a meeting, not wanting to have any pressure put upon his Sophie. She was his favourite, the companion he loved most, and he had no desire to lose her except to a man she could love. Certainly he had not mentioned it to his wife, whose behaviour would have changed dramatically and might embarrass them all.

As yet the Randolphs did not seem to be among the gaily dressed crowd. There was dancing in the long saloon, while a buffet had been set up in the dining room for the supper to be served at eleven o'clock. Boughs of holly and evergreens decorated the rooms and there was a festival atmosphere as the servants brought round trays with silver cups of steaming punch. Sophie and Alethea were prepared as ever to enjoy themselves, especially Alethea, whose first year it was as a grown-up young lady, and inevitably she was captured at once by an acquaintance and led on to the floor. A gentleman who was a city broker came to beg Sophie for the first set; she had known him for several years and took his arm, prepared to enjoy the quadrille and what idle chatter could be had between the movements. In half an hour Alethea's card was full while Sophie's, dangling from her wrist, had a respectable number of dances promised.

Later, in a pause in the dancing, George Randolph entered the room. His father had no sooner arrived than he had immediately engaged Dr Sterling in conversation, the pair of them disappearing into the library, so that for a moment George stood alone. He had had a tiresome morning in Mr Warburton's office, faced with balance sheets and accounts which brought home to him rather starkly the pressing straits to which they were reduced. Afterwards he had tried to look up one or two old friends, but had drawn a blank. Life, and people, had moved on in six years. His anger still simmered. He hated the whole business of being driven to marry for money and his dark eyes swept over the crowd, wondering which was Miss Sterling. However, Mr Warburton, soberly immaculate in black evening clothes, came over to speak to him, offering to introduce him to the Sterlings.

George looked down at him with no very pleasant expression on his face. He had had enough of the lawyer for one day. 'You are well aware, Warburton, whom my father wishes me to meet. My own having nothing to do with it.'

Used to dealing with the difficult Randolphs, Mr

31

Warburton made no comment, merely allowing his gaze to look intently about the long room. 'Ah, there they are, Miss Sophie and Miss Alethea, standing by their mother, the lady in purple sitting near that gilt mirror. Allow me to – '

But George waved away the introduction. If it had to be done he would rather do it without Warburton's fulsome overtures, and he walked purposefully across the saloon.

'Mrs Sterling? May I be so forward as to introduce myself? My father, I believe, is engaged with your husband and as you will know are related. My only regret is that I have been abroad and not yet had the felicity of meeting you or your charming daughters. I am George Randolph.'

It was the sort of polished speech one might expect of a man who had spent many years in diplomatic circles and it put Mrs Sterling instantly in a flutter. Ever since Lord John's visit, and despite her husband's elusiveness over the matter, she had been determined they should meet the heir to Randolph of Redesdale.

'How do you do, sir. It is very pleasant – indeed I had hoped – connected as we are – may I present my daughters, Miss Sophie and Miss Alethea.'

He had glanced at once at Alethea and a sudden guarded appreciation was instantly apparent, combined with a gleam of hope. His mistake realized, the flash of interest receded. There was no doubt which was the elder and he turned to her. 'Miss Sterling, it is a great pleasure to make your acquaintance. Miss Alethea, good evening.' It was all perfectly polite and he had long ago learned to mask his reactions to people, which were always strong and often irrevocable.

Sophie, however, was so used to young men being swept away by her sister's looks that she was inclined to smile, taking his hand, but keeping her gaze at about the level of his top waistcoat button. For a moment he and her mother made desultory conversation, then he asked her to take the floor with him. Sure that only etiquette prevented him from first asking Thea if there was a spare dance on her card, she nevertheless laid her hand lightly on the crook of his proferred arm and walked away with him, while Alethea was immediately claimed by a young officer. Loving dancing, and aware that it was one thing she was rather good at, Sophie said nothing at first but moved smoothly with him, finding him equally proficient. But she was quite unable to help wondering what view Lord Randolph and his son took of her. Had she not snatched the Crabtree inheritance from under their noses? No, not snatched, for she had never once, during the pleasant days spent talking or reading to the old lady, even considered herself in the running for that wealth, having no idea it existed. The old lady had lived frugally enough to prevent anyone guessing at its extent.

Her father had told her after Lord John's call and the shared luncheon that his lordship wanted the two families to take up friendly intercourse again, and that he had no objection to that, but had said no more. Intelligent enough to see that her change of fortune had something to do with his lordship's overtures, Sophie felt distinctly uncomfortable. To what end was all this leading? A nasty suspicion had early crossed her mind but she had thrust it away. Now here was this cousin, whom she remembered only dimly meeting once as a child, waltzing with her in his arms. At last she brought herself to look up at him.

Dark hair was brushed back to either side of his face, and under straight, well-defined brows, his eyes were of a rich brown that one might expect to be warm — but they were not. They seemed hard with a hint of — what was it? Wariness, a deep distrust of life perhaps? Olive skin tanned darker by the southern sun gave a sense of good looks that might not have been there with a pallid complexion. His mouth was his real appeal, not too full; a habit of pressing his lips together, as if to restrain his words, kept a withdrawn look there, but if coaxed into a smile it could redeem his face. It was his manner that was not endearing; he had the misfortune to make people feel he would rather be elsewhere — at this moment elsewhere was dancing with Alethea, Sophie thought resignedly. Conversely, when he did deign to smile he could achieve just the opposite. However he was not smiling at the moment.

'I have only just returned from abroad,' was his opening remark. 'It seems a pity our families have not been on terms before, living as we do only a carriage drive apart.'

33

'Perhaps,' she said drily, 'but I fear Lord Randolph moves in a very different sphere from us.'

His brows went up. 'When you know my father better you will know he would not consider that of any importance. Nor, I gather, did our shared great-aunt. She frightened the life out of me when I was a child, but didn't intimidate you, or so I gather.'

'I liked her so much.' Aware that she had sounded prickly, Sophie spoke more warmly. 'We didn't really know her until a few years ago when she dismissed her physician and Mr Warburton reminded her that Papa was a medical man and not far away. So she sent for him. I enjoyed visiting her, but I never saw your father there.'

'I believe he did call occasionally. We saw more of her as children, when Uncle Crabtree was alive, but then we went away to school and after that my brother Maurice went to sea and I to Oxford. She became something of a recluse and my father not much better after −' He broke off. He had been going to say 'after the scandal' but it was a phrase on which he at once pressed his lips together.

Wondering what he had been going to say, Sophie could only remark that it had taken Great-Aunt's death to bring them all together.

'And her legacy,' he said, and would have given anything to withdraw that lapse of restraint, for the girl had stiffened in his arms.

'I see,' she said. 'Now I understand. Believe me, the whole business is quite odious to me. Pray take me back to my mother.'

The set was not over so he ignored the request. 'I beg your pardon. That was an abominable thing to say. I didn't intend to imply −'

'It doesn't matter what you intended to imply,' she broke in. 'I don't think, sir, it is a subject I should discuss with you.'

'No? Don't you think it is what our respective fathers intend?' And then, somewhat shaken by the revulsion on her face, he added, 'I beg your pardon again, Miss Sterling. I really had no intention of offending you. I have been abroad so long and only recently come back to the most difficult of situations that I fear my manners are astray. But we are cousins, and therefore not subject to the same restrictions of etiquette.'

'Perhaps not.' She wished the dance would end so that she could escape, but, not wanting to cause an incident by releasing herself and stalking off the floor, she added coolly, 'I will accept, Mr Randolph, that you meant no offence. If I could give the money to − to the British Museum I would, but I'm sure no one would allow that.'

He gave a brief laugh. 'No, I believe not. It is a very strange turn of affairs for you, for us all, none of us having the faintest idea that the old girl was so fabulously wealthy. Had you not thought that as such it should draw the families concerned closer together?'

'As to that,' she said frankly, 'I think it is more often the other way about. It has already caused arguments in my own and it feels like an albatross about my neck.'

'I'm sorry. Your sister −'

'Oh, she sees a vision of new gowns and heaven knows what else! She is only just eighteen. But that isn't what I meant.'

'No,' he answered. They moved apart in the dance. When they were together again he added, 'I'm quite sure it isn't. What is necessary is for you and the legacy to be in safe hands.' And that wasn't what he meant to say either, for instantly her brows went up and she asked bluntly, 'Yours?'

Now she really had brought him up short! Trying to amend the blunder, he began, 'I didn't say that, Miss Sterling, but −'

However, before he could qualify what he did mean, she went on, 'I think I had rather stay a spinster than be the subject of so much interest.'

'That would be a great pity. But London is full of fortune-hunters, you know. Family need not be put in that class.'

'They can often be worse.'

The logic of this struck home. At once he said, 'I can see it is painful for you to discuss it, though I'm sure our parents are doing so at this moment. I saw them disappear

35

together. I am finding, you know, that after six years my father still wants to arrange my future, and maybe yours too.' Driven by his anger, his annoyance with the whole affair, he saw that he had again said too much, for she had flushed from her neck to the roots of her hair and was looking so distressed that he felt instantly sorry for her. In a gentler voice, he added, 'Miss Sterling, I'm behaving like an oaf and a tactless one at that. My father and I have agreed on a fresh beginning − I went away estranged from him, you understand − so we are trying to put the past away, bridge the gap of six years if you like. May I not beg you to put aside the past ten minutes?'

Did he dislike this buiness of the inheritance as much as she did, or was he pursuing the acquaintance with the obvious end in mind? She wanted to run away, be taken home, forget what Great-Aunt Adela had done to her, but the hand holding hers was firm and warm. She was very much aware of him as a man, of strength, of an overwhelming personality. Trying to keep her voice light, she glanced at the large gilt clock above the fireplace which showed twenty minutes after the hour. 'As far as I am concerned, Mr Randolph, it is still only ten past eleven,' and as she spoke she looked up at him.

The music ceased and he chose this moment to respond with his slow smile, which had conquered many in the past and now had its effect on Sophie. Something inside her seemed to contract and then explode into the oddest sensation. Surely it could only be because of the strange situation in which they found themselves that this odd feeling had seized her? I am being stupid, she told herself, and walked off the floor with him.

As they did so he said, 'Will you not show you have forgiven my clumsiness by riding with me one day?'

'I'm sorry,' she said in a low voice, 'I'm afraid I don't ride.'

'Oh.' It seemed extraordinary to him that a lady should not ride. 'Perhaps you will let me teach you?'

'I − find horses rather alarming creatures, sir, unless safely between the shafts.'

He laughed. 'Then perhaps a drive?'

She inclined her head and as they had reached her mother's chair, set companionably with other matrons, he said no more, merely bowing and walking away.

'You look over-heated, my love,' Mrs Sterling remarked. 'I must say the crush in here makes one feel warm,' and she beckoned to a waiter to bring them some lemonade.

The rest of the evening passed in something of a daze. Dancing with other young men, every now and again Sophie's gaze would wander across the floor to see if he was there. Once he led Alethea into a polka. Her sister was laughing up at him, eyes sparkling, lips parted, as she bounced through the dance − it could almost be said that she romped − coaxing a laugh out of her partner. Little minx, Sophie thought, she can't help but flirt, and was aware that for the first time in her life she was jealous of Thea's ability to sparkle − which she could not.

George returned that young lady to Mrs Sterling at the end of the dance and after receiving a favourable answer to his request that he might call on them before too long, he went away to find somewhere where he might smoke a quiet cigar. A small room behind the stairs that was almost filled by a desk on which lay a number of account books served the purpose, and leaning against the desk, he extracted a cigar from his case and proceeded to light it. Thus occupied he heard himself addressed as he had not been for a long time.

'Randy! *Randy!* I can't believe it. How in thunder do you come to be here?'

'Jack! My dear fellow, I never expected to see you of all people.' He was off the desk, his hand held out.' What on earth are you doing at this suburban set-to?'

'I'm here because I know the Willshers well, but you! When did you get back?'

'Last Tuesday, with an Arab stallion, two mares, a great deal of luggage and very little money. I thought my father was dying.'

'I'm so sorry − '

George said crisply 'You can take that consternation off your face. He is very much still with us, while apologizing for being so − and enjoying it, the old hypocrite.'

'What a way to speak of him! Yes, I will have one of your cigars. But seriously, would you not have come back if you had known he had recovered?'

George shrugged. 'I don't know. I'd begun to have enough of chasing round Europe – North Africa these last two months. I mean to breed Arabs, which made me think of Plummers. I'll be the first here to do it.'

'I've not seen the breed.' Jack accepted the proffered cigar.

'I'm not surprised. You never were a judge of horse-flesh.'

'Well, as long as they can carry me – '

'Philistine! You won't know perhaps that my great-aunt Crabtree has died and left a very substantial fortune?'

'By Jove, has she? To you?'

'No, confound it. To Miss Sophie Sterling.'

Jack looked dumbfounded, his amiable freckled countenance all surprise. 'I can't believe it. I didn't even know the old girl had gone. Well, well. I'm hardly in court circles, you know, and I don't often read the obits in the paper. Wasn't she at one time a friend of the last Queen, Adelaide? I thought so. She's left all of it – *all* of it – to Miss Sterling?'

'Every last penny, except for certain sums to her servants.'

'Good God!' Jack drew deeply on his cigar and let blue smoke curl from his mouth. 'I'm sure that has put some noses out of joint. What a very odd thing to do. Do you know how it came about?'

George explained, painstakingly. 'So the devil is in it, my father wants me to marry the girl. We're only third cousins, so there's no barrier there. And if I'm any judge Mrs Sterling would like the title for her daughter, and the entrée into London society. Do you know her?'

'Indeed I do, and the family, though not well, but I'm sure you're right about Mrs Sterling. What a poser for you. What does Dr Sterling think about it? He is not at all like his wife, you know.'

'I've not had any conversation with him yet, though my father has – interfering as always. I've no idea what to do. But I suppose it will do no harm to get to know Miss Sterling better. Jack, only think what I could do with twenty thousand a year!'

'Whew! What couldn't anyone do with it? So you're after Miss Sophie? I suppose you would be if she were cross-eyed and bad-tempered, only she isn't. A thought quiet perhaps, but a very pleasant girl, and more to her than one first supposes.'

'One dance has told me that she is no milksop miss. She set about me with no hesitation.'

'Oh?' Jack laughed at him. 'Have you been crossing swords with her already? That's no way to go about securing the twenty thousand.'

'Are you looking in that direction?'

'Good heavens, no. But others will be.'

George blew out a cloud of smoke. 'Well, I never was so glad to see an old friend. I've tried to dig up one or two but without luck so far. Is there any decent wine to be had here?'

Still laughing, Jack admonished him. 'One day you'll look down that long nose of yours once too often. The Willshers are a very decent sort of people. Of course I would think so – you see, I am pledged to their daughter, Verity. The odd thing is, Sophie Sterling is her best friend.'

George's brows went up, but he did not comment on this, merely saying, 'And what do your people think of the match?'

'My mother has quite taken my lovely Verity to her heart, bless her. My future father-in-law may not have blue blood but he's a dashed nice fellow. He advised my father over an investment and the old man made a tidy profit. That put the thing in a good light.'

'It would do. When do you marry?'

'Next month. I'm still with the Foreign Office, by the way, a nice little post in Whitehall. You'll stand up with me?'

'Of course, but had you not arranged it with anyone else?'

'Only my cousin Timothy and he'll step down, amiable fellow. So if you are to be my groomsman and Sophie is one of Verity's bridesmaids, it may smooth the way for you – a fortunate coincidence, one might say.'

George gazed moodily at a very dull painting of a duck. Well, he was not going to rush into the thing, despite the appeal of the twenty thousand. What couldn't he do with Plummers and his horses with that? But it was a distasteful bargain. Too early yet to say if he could like the girl, or she him. That would hardly be expected either by his own father or Dr Sterling. And did the Sterlings know of the six-year-old scandal? It would be much better if that never came to light again. Pride would surely have kept his father from talking of it? And it was hardly a matter Dr Sterling would have discussed with his wife and daughters. Apart from all this, why on earth should Miss Sophie accept him? The title could be the only inducement that he could see, and as far as that was concerned her mother would be favourable. He'd made a bad beginning with a reprehensible lack of tact, and embarrassed the girl. He was not a man to fall into rages or lose his temper; he relied on his tongue for a weapon with sometimes cruel wit, which to his mind was the more useful. Only he had not meant to turn it on her.

'Randy,' Jack begged, 'at least put yourself out to be amiable. I know you can be, if you choose.'

This drew a reluctant smile from George. 'I suppose I must — which is a bore.'

'Nonsense. I'm not far off thirty now so you must be near twenty-eight. One can't go on playing japes and chasing the girls for ever! You'll come to my wedding as my groomsman?'

'I wouldn't miss it for the world. How are the rest of your family, your parents? Your sisters?'

'All well, though my father complains of rheumatism these days. Mary is married to a member of Parliament, and Helena is the mother of three children now — one a year since she wed John Turnbull, Sir Harvey's son. I'm the last to go. February isn't the best of months for a wedding, but I shall whisk my bride away to Italy, courtesy of my prospective father-in-law, his wedding present to us, among others. He's a most generous man.'

George felt a momentary twinge of envy. Jack was so obviously in love with his Verity that he made matrimony seem attractive. A marriage of convenience would be entirely different. It often happened — men married for money, and what would he not do for the sum dangling in front of him? But it was a distasteful business. He must get to know Miss Sophie and find out if they could even like each other, without pretending to deeper feelings — that would hardly be expected by anyone. But he had made a bad start. Why had he talked to her as he had? Tactless and stupid! Venting his annoyance on her had indeed been both. Probably she would not give him another thought, and yet — she had allowed him to put the clock back ten minutes!

While these thoughts chased in his head, Jack considered him, noting the changes in him since that time six years ago when George had arrived in Paris, breaking his journey to St Petersburg. Bitter and morose, scarred by the miserable court case and even more by the defection of the beautiful Emily Horton, it was to Jack that he had gone, and Jack alone who had steered him through the first months and restored at least some reason to his days. It was odd that they should have found each other again when George was facing another turning point in his life.

At last Jack said, 'Take a little time, Randy. This has all been sprung on you. But I think you could get to like Sophie — if you took the trouble.'

'Could I? Well, I made an abysmal start with none of my diplomatic tact.' His voice held a sardonic note. 'You see, I assumed, wrongly, that her father had already mentioned the proposition.'

'That was not the wisest thing to do.'

'Apparently not. I arrived here depressed after a morning with Warburton and being confronted by the bad state of our affairs. There are debts I must try to clear so that my father can die in peace when his time comes. But none of that was any excuse.'

'It must be difficult to come home to such a situation and I can see the appeal of a rich bride. If you behave yourself you'll find the doctor an excellent fellow to deal with, Sterling by name and sterling by nature. You won't care for his wife, I'm afraid.'

George groaned. 'I saw that much in the first moment I spoke to her, a dragon in purple. And the younger sister, a flirtatious chit but a beauty, eh?'

'Undeniably, and set on an advantageous marriage, but she is not the heiress. Anyway, she would drive you mad in a week.' Jack laughed at his friend's expression. 'Come, it isn't as bad a prospect as all that. But don't pursue the business solely for the money. Even twenty thousand a year will not make up for a loveless marriage.'

'Others will be after her — it's a common enough situation.'

From his own happy position, Jack could not help feeling a certain pity for his friend, wishing, as he had done many times before, that the lovely Emily had not turned her eyes on the youthful George. 'I suppose,' he said slowly, 'that if the matter proceeds you will tell Sophie about the past?'

'Good God, no. Why should I? It's a long dead story.'

'You'll be making a great mistake if you don't. Be sure some busybody will, even if her parents don't know about it already. Play fair, Randy.'

'You have become very moral,' George said caustically. 'I see no need to rake up ancient history.'

'Well, you must know from experience that living a pretence can be intolerable.'

A shaft of anger lit the dark eyes. 'You needn't remind me. Lawrence Horton was a possessive, malicious devil, and life with him must have been hell for Emily. You know she is dead?'

'No, I didn't. I'm sorry, but perhaps it's for the best as far as you are concerned. Put your mind to getting to know Sophie — and if you exert yourself no doubt you can persuade her you are a halfway decent fellow.'

George gave a reluctant laugh. 'I doubt it, after this evening.'

'I wonder what you said?'

'More than I should.'

Jack gave a sigh bordering on a laugh and George went on, 'I did at least beg her pardon. Now let's go and find some champagne before you ask too much of me.'

They left the room and in the ballroom he saw his friend instantly seeking out his betrothed, his love lying openly on his freckled face. Would he himself, George wondered, ever look at anyone like that — let alone Miss Sophie Sterling?

Chapter Four

Despite all Dr Sterling's efforts, word of the legacy was out and the vultures descended. People who barely knew the Sterlings but who had marriageable sons began calling, tradesmen delivered leaflets, advertisements for expensive dressmakers appeared, and they were showered with invitations to dances and parties.

Sophie hated it all, hid herself in her room and tried to avoid callers; there was one she would have wished to see but for two weeks he did not come, despite his promise. What was he doing? Had she made so bad an impression on him that he didn't want to see her? Well, she told herself with spirit, *he* hadn't exactly been the soul of good manners. Yet every time the bell rang, her heart gave a lurch in case it should be him. How stupid she was being! Going on with her ordered days as normally as possible, beneath the surface she was aware that nothing was as it had been before the Willshers' ball. She was quite unable to put from her mind a dark head, a stern face, the rare slow smile. Her appetite seemed affected, and she was apt to go into a daze and not hear what people said. Verity called to talk about the final arrangements for her wedding and Sophie was abstracted. Only Verity's remark that Mr Randolph had gone into the country brought her to instant alertness.

'Oh,' she murmured in deep relief. 'I thought — he'd said he would call, and I wondered — '

'Sophie!' Verity exclaimed. 'Do you really like him? I found him inclined to be stiff, manners all on the surface, but an impression of boredom underneath. Of course he is your cousin, but — '

'I don't know,' Sophie said honestly, 'whether I actually like him. Half the time at your ball I was thinking how impertinent he was, overbearing perhaps, and how he presumed on the fact that we are cousins. Did you know his father wants us to marry — I mean, did Jack say anything?'

'Something to that effect, but, darling Sophie, don't let anyone urge you into the match if it would be repugnant to you. Oh dear, how prosy that sounded. I want you to marry for love — as I am.'

They were in the cosy small sitting room, one each side of the fire on this bitter winter day, toasting their toes companionably, and Sophie hoped it was the heat from the flames that was responsible for her reddening cheeks. 'I would like that too, but I think now I'm an heiress, it will be that much more difficult to find someone who cares at least a little for *me*. As for love, I don't think I have your romantic nature.'

Verity laughed and clasped her hands about her knees in a manner that her mother told her was unladylike. 'You will be surprised when you do fall in love. I was at a very boring reception and I looked at Jack and he looked at me and that was that. It was weeks, no, two months, before he declared himself, but we both knew it in our hearts. I told you all about it at the time.'

'Oh dear.'

Sophie sounded so stricken that Verity laughed. 'Now what's wrong? Jack told me after our ball that George appeared interested in you.' Actually her betrothed had said a great deal more than that, but she was not going to repeat it. For there was no getting away from the fact that the legacy had instigated the meeting and clearly both families would approve of the match. But at what cost to Sophie, had been Verity's first thought.

Sophie was staring into the fire. 'You don't think one should marry to oblige one's family?'

'Well,' her friend said honestly, 'it often happens, I know, and sometimes turns out well, but oh, I do want the best for you and Jack has shown me what that is.'

'I think you are very fortunate,' Sophie said in a low voice. She had always thought of herself as the sensible, practical one of the family, leaving Thea to wallow in romances from the library, and could not see herself glowing as Verity glowed with love. 'I must admit that Mr Randolph did rub me up the wrong way, even if we did part on a better note, and I thought perhaps – I'm not making sense. Only you see I can't help knowing all the time that Aunt Adela's legacy colours everything.'

'I could wish you hadn't got it,' Verity said. 'It seems on the way to spoiling things for you.' She leaned forward and kissed Sophie's hot cheek. 'One thing to be thankful for, other people will manage it for you. As for George, don't let yourself be hurried into making any decision. Jack is very fond of him, you know. He says George had a bad experience in his youth that has made him as he is.'

'What was it?'

'I don't know. He wouldn't tell me. He said that he couldn't blab George's private affairs, even to me. Men can be very touchy over what they call their sense of honour, can't they?'

'I suppose so,' Sophie agreed. 'Dear Verity, thank goodness I have you to talk to.' But when her friend had gone Sophie sat on alone, pondering the enigma of the man who had walked into her life at the Willshers' ball. If it had not been for the money, would he have come at all?

Eventually, the day before Verity's wedding, George called and with a great effort Sophie schooled herself to appear her usual calm and collected self, thankful that he had no chance to speak to her alone. The last few weeks had been like no others in her life, and while he made himself pleasant to her mother and talked to Dr Sterling of the poor state in which he had found Plummers, she sat quietly, watching and listening. Dr Sterling recollected some boyhood days there, but he could not linger after luncheon, leaving the female members of his family to entertain the guest, and George stayed on until an engagement in the evening sent him home.

Mrs Sterling was full of praise for him, chiding Sophie for barely joining in the conversation, and later, in the privacy of their bedroom, she told her husband archly that if he did offer for Sophie it would be an excellent thing. Dr Sterling turned sternly on her. 'Rose, I'll not have you push this forward. We have no idea yet whether George is the sort of man Sophie would care for as a husband. I'll not have her sacrificed for the sake of a title.'

'Sacrificed! My dear, surely it would be an excellent thing for her? Only think, she would be Countess of Redesdale one day, a day not too far off from what Mr Randolph says of his father's health.'

'No, she would not. My cousin John is a baron not an earl, and anyway I am more concerned with her happiness,' the doctor retorted drily. 'I'd rather see her married to Douglas Patterson and be happy, than be miserable as Lady Randolph.'

His wife was aghast. 'Douglas Patterson? Why, he's nothing but a clerk in a tea merchant's.'

'I'm quite sure she's never considered him,' he said. 'I merely used him as an example. I won't have Sophie forced into marriage because you or Lord Randolph wish it. The money plays too big a part in this.'

'Very well, my dear,' Mrs Sterling murmured obligingly, but her thoughts were far different. Men didn't understand these things. One had to marry one's daughters for position and advancement, and an alliance with the Randolphs would put Sophie among the cream of Society, which would reflect most profitably on them all. Having no doubt she could achieve this ambition and bring her husband to a proper awareness of his duty in the matter, she wisely said no more for the moment.

The wedding of Jack and Verity brought a further meeting. Sophie talked with her many friends who were there, carried out her duties as bridesmaid to a glowing Verity, and with George groomsman to Jack, they were naturally thrown together. As the carriage bearing the bridal couple away to Dover finally disappeared down the drive George murmured, 'A besotted pair, don't you think?' To which Sophie replied,

'It can't be anything but good to see two people so happy,' which seemed to her a far different thing.

'Of course,' he conceded, and turned to speak to Jack's mother, while Sophie, wondering if George was trying to make her dislike him, went to talk to Verity's younger sister who seemed disposed to burst into tears.

An invitation to dine at the house in Mount Street, however, put Mrs Sterling in a flutter and she overrode the doctor's objection that it was a long way to go for a good dinner. His wife barely listened to such a comment, only rejoicing that in anticipation of such a card arriving in the post, she should have ordered two new dinner gowns for her girls. Alethea was in transports and chiding Sophie on what seemed her lack of excitement, to which Sophie replied that she was sure it would be very pleasant.

'Pleasant! How prosaic you are,' Alethea teased, and Sophie wondered if George thought her prosaic.

The house in Mount Street could not but be impressive. Lord Randolph had asked his sister − she who had once schemed for a duke for her daughter Amabel − to act as hostess for him, and the sheer elegance of her dress, lorgnettes hanging about her neck amid strings of pearls, quite overwhelmed Mrs Sterling, who tended to gush. Amabel and her Viscount were there, both of them assets to any dinner table, and the talk ranged from politics to the Royal Family, the expansion of the railways and the proposed Exhibition. Now that a Royal Commission had been set up, it looked certain to take place next year, and Lord Randolph, forgetting his ills, treated them to witty anecdotes and comments on the people concerned.

'Lord Brougham is against it, though heaven knows why,' he told them, 'except that he grows more and more eccentric with the years − I feel sorry for anyone up before him in the Court of Appeal. And at the moment a member of Parliament, a certain Colonel Sibthorpe, who has hitherto scarcely rippled the waters at Westminster, has come out in his support, protesting that it would mean cutting down some elms on the south side of the Park where it is proposed the building should be set up.'

'Are there no other sites?' the doctor asked.

'None so central or so suitable,' his cousin told him, 'and as the whole weight of the Prince and his committee are for it, so I believe they will succeed. Sibthorpe causes nothing more than a great deal of laughter in the House, or so I'm told, a choleric little man bristling with indignation – *Punch* did an excellent cartoon of him last week.'

Sophie of course listened more than she spoke. Never having attended a dinner with so many side dishes, she wished she could do justice to more, but Lady Louisa, determined that her nephew should marry the Crabtree inheritance, had seated her next to George and his presence seemed to rob her of her appetite.

Remarking that it should be a fascinating affair, he told her of the similar exhibition in France two years ago. 'Which I had the luck to visit,' he added. 'The exhibits made one realise how much talent there is in the world.'

'It would be a tremendous project, if ever people can be got to agree about it,' she murmured.

'That's what committees are for, to air all the odd notions, while the people who matter get on with the job.'

She gave him a little smile. 'Is that really all committees are for?'

'I think so, to expel the hot air, like a balloon coming in to land. Have you ever seen a balloon, Cousin Sophie?' He had evidently decided this was the less formal address, and when she admitted she had not, he went on to tell of a flight he had seen taking off from the Champs de Mars in Paris. 'That particular one landed on the roof of some poor fellow's house and caused a deal of damage. The pilot was lucky to escape with a few broken bones.'

'It sounds extremely hazardous.'

'Well, so it is, but one or two ladies have even tried it. Do you think you could be so adventurous, Cousin Sophie?'

Thinking it a silly question, she shook her head. 'I doubt it, to the extent of going up in a balloon, anyway.'

In the drawing room afterwards, Amabel confided to Sophie that she was 'expanding' again. A plump little person and full of good nature, she added, 'Children are my delight, and I'm sure you will find them so when your turn comes.'

Marriage being the last thing she wanted to discuss, Sophie wondered if they all knew of Lord Randolph's wishes. Was it talked of in the family? She felt she was being inspected and was painfully embarrassed.

Amabel was at once aware of the awkwardness. 'I want us to be friends. Won't you and your sister come to spend a day with me? Henry and I have a house in Knightsbridge as well as such a pretty place in Wiltshire. Do come. It is so delightful to find new cousins.'

It was impossible to resist Amabel, especially since Alethea overheard and exclaimed how much they would enjoy it. They chattered on, Amabel making a point of drawing Sophie into the conversation. Lady Louisa interjected to ask Sophie if she knew London well and if she was familiar with the pleasure of driving in the Park. On hearing that she was not, the rather formidable lady proposed at once that she might like to stay a few days in South Street and be shown the sights. There was nothing for Sophie to do but accept gracefully.

The gentlemen had joined them and George said at once, 'Well, I shall claim some part in that. Don't forget, Aunt Louisa, a great many things will be fresh to me too. In the brief time I've been here I can see London has been growing.'

He looked across at Sophie and she murmured that she was sure there would be much to see, but on the way home in their carriage, while her Mama was extolling his lordship, his sister, his house and his dinner, Sophie slipped her hand into the crook of her father's arm and whispered, 'Everything is changing, isn't it, Papa?'

'I'm afraid change is inevitable,' he agreed, 'but I admit I had not foreseen this particular one. Do you mind so much, my love?'

'Oh, no, not really. It's just that — to stay with Lady Louisa, and to spend time with Amabel, whom I do like very much, will disrupt our usual quiet way of going on. Indeed I would rather — '

He patted her arm. 'Don't let yourself be too quiet, dearest. All your life is in front of you and it is a chance for you to move out into the wider world.'

'I think it's exciting,' Alethea interrupted, sitting upright on the seat, her eyes bright. 'Don't be a spoilsport, Sophie. If you refuse, they won't ask me later on and oh, I do so want to be taken into Society. It's what I've always longed for − London, a great house, balls and dinner parties and who knows − Lord Randolph or his sister may take you to Court, and then I could go in my turn. Only think of it! Mama, maybe *I* will find a duke!'

Her mother pinched her cheek. 'A title anyway, I'm sure, given such an opportunity. Don't you agree, my dear, this will be a quite wonderful chance for our girls?'

He sighed. 'You are probably right.' But despite his encouragement to Sophie he was far from happy about the changed situation and worried for her. At the same time he could see the advantages. Louisa meant well, and would no doubt be an excellent chaperone, able to do far more than he could in the way of worldly advancement. Only he did not want them spoilt. He had few fears for Sophie, it was Alethea's head that could easily be turned. But there seemed to be something inexorable about the tide that had started rolling. And at the back of his mind was the memory of the unhappy business of years ago. He knew very little about it, only what he had read in the paper, and had never mentioned to his wife or children, for it was particularly unpleasant. However, he was a fair man. If everyone, he thought, was made to pay permanently for the sins of their youth, where would any of them stand?

On his first visit to the house in Clapham, John Randolph had briefly brought the subject up. 'That old affair, water under the bridge, eh? Best forgotten.' And it *was* best forgotten. The doctor was prepared to wait and see how his cousin's son had turned out.

As spring approached, George became a regular visitor to the house on Clapham Common. He was courteous though a little distant with Mrs Sterling, talked of his travels with the doctor, thereby impressing him with the maturity they provided, and walked the dog with the two girls. He suggested they should call him Cousin George, adopting the same form of address with them, and teasing Alethea in a brotherly fashion which Sophie thought over familiar. Alethea, of course, responded to the extent of wishing herself in Sophie's shoes.

'He's so good-looking,' she sighed one evening. 'I do envy you, Sophie.'

'Why?' her sister asked bluntly. 'Don't you see it is the inheritance that brings him here?'

'Oh, fiddle. He likes us, you can see he does.'

'Does he indeed? Well perhaps – certainly Papa. But when Mama was talking the other day about Court circles and presentations, and being so – so pushy, I could see Mr Randolph's face, his mouth drawn in, as it is sometimes, when he doesn't like the conversation. No, Thea, he suffers some things because he wants something else.' Wracked by the knowledge that if he did make an offer for her, it could only be for the wrong reasons, she had no idea what answer she should make.

'Even so,' – Alethea insisted on pursuing the subject, far more interesting than the embroidery she had thrown aside – 'don't you see what an advantageous marriage it would be for you? Think what you could do for *me*. And you do like him too, I know you do. When he admired that watercolour of the garden that you did for Papa last year, not knowing you had done it, you blushed when Mama said so. I saw you.'

Wondering what one could do to stop telltale flushes creeping into one's cheeks, Sophie concentrated for a moment on the sketch she was copying from a book of travels in Switzerland. Did she like him at all? He could be reserved, sometimes almost to the point of rudeness, which Mama never seemed to notice; he was inclined to be cynical in his comments on what they read in the newspapers; arrogance obvious in much of his talk. Oh, there were plenty of things to dislike, so how could it be that when he entered the room he seemed to fill it with his presence, the feel of his warm fingers when he shook her hand so disturbing? And when he was gone she began to wait for the next time he should ring the doorbell. He was fortune-hunting, of course he was, and if he did ask her, well, she should snub him, send him away with a flea in his ear. Only – could she do it?

The promised visit to Lady Louisa arranged for April, Sophie was not sure if she wanted to go or would rather not. So the days drifted by, subtly changing. One morning, at Alethea's less than subtle hint, George took her riding. He had arrived to find her in her habit and when she said she was waiting to go out with the groom asked laughingly how he could refuse such an invitation, adding that he was sorry Cousin Sophie would not be joining them.

Sophie smiled and said she had plenty to do, but was glad when, on his return from the ride, he accepted the invitation to stay to luncheon. Thea ran upstairs to change, calling for Sophie to come to her room.

'Well?' her sister asked. 'Did you enjoy your ride?'

'Oh, he is a splendid horseman. It is a thousand pities you didn't see him.'

'I've seen him ride up the drive many times now.'

Thea went into a fit of laughter. 'Oh, Sophie! That's nothing like a full gallop. That big mare of his is a tremendous goer. My Stella was hard put to keep up. Once she stumbled, and George caught the reins at once, making sure I was all right. If he thought I'd tumble off he was disappointed! Only, Sophie, he got off to look at Stella's hock and he was so gentle with her, in a way that only someone who loves horses could be. You must try to learn.'

'I can live my life perfectly well without being a horsewoman,' Sophie said calmly. 'People must take me as I am.'

'You mean George must?'

'I suppose so.'

'It would please him though if you —'

'Oh Thea, don't harp on about it.' Sophie's patience was wearing a little thin. 'And do hurry up, there's the gong.'

But she thought of her sister's talk about George's care for her horse. It seemed to put him in a new light. And this she saw for herself the next week. George was with them, and as he often did, accompanied them when they took Dash for his usual walk. There were some fields about half a mile off and a copse of trees that Dash particularly liked for nosing about. Generally he was an obedient dog but this morning he suddenly took it into his head to live up to his name and tore off across the field.

'Here, sir,' Sophie called. 'Come back at once.'

'He's probably seen a rabbit,' George suggested and Thea added, 'He's always seeing them, generally imaginary.'

Hearing a sudden loud yelp and seeing Dash sitting on the ground near the path into the woods they hurried across, and it was George who went down on one knee by the panting, frightened animal.

After a quick examination he said, 'Look! There's a trap and he's caught a paw in it. My God, how I hate these things.' He set both hands to either side of the vicious teeth to force the metal apart while Sophie knelt beside him to pull the paw clear.

'Oh, it's bleeding,' her sister exclaimed and Sophie added, 'I've never seen a trap here before.'

'Some wretched poacher, no doubt.' George had whipped out his handkerchief and was binding the paw. 'I swear I'll never have one of these things on my land.'

'This is common land,' Sophie murmured. 'I suppose it was set by a poor man wanting to feed his family.'

George glanced up. 'Do you think that excuses this?'

'No, oh no.' She got to her feet. 'Only I always try to see a reason for things.'

George tied the makeshift bandage and Dash, who had sat quietly through this operation, gave only a small yelp as his rescuer lifted him into his arms.

'Let me,' Sophie said quickly. 'I've carried him before. You might get blood on your clothes.'

He gave her a brief smile. 'And you might get blood on your dress. He's quite heavy too, but he's settled down with me, haven't you, old fellow?'

Back at the house, Alethea said, 'There's some balm Papa made up, in the tackroom. Do you think – '

'I'll have a look.' There George set down the dog on the rough table. The room was hung with spare harness and other necessities, smelled of straw and horses, and Sophie seldom came here. But she watched as George filled a bowl with water, washed the wound and smeared it with balm while Thea ran into the house for a bandage. Observing his gentleness, his soothing of poor Dash, his careful bandaging, he seemed to bear little resemblance to the man who had been so sarcastic on their first meeting. Then he carried Dash to his basket in the library, where the doctor said he would report the matter to the local policeman.

'You have got blood on your waistcoat,' Sophie exclaimed. 'Do let me sponge it.'

'My man will see to it when I get home,' was George's casual answer. Sophie said firmly blood mustn't be allowed to dry and the doctor settled it by taking George away to his surgery and doing it himself.

Sophie was quietly thoughtful during lunch and when George had gone and Thea was sitting on the rug feeding Dash with little pieces of meat, she went upstairs to the old schoolroom where she kept her painting materials. But she was not inclined to work and sat instead looking out at the laurel bushes, the leafless laburnums. Thinking of George's hands, so careful not to increase the animal's pain, it occurred to her that Dash seemed to trust him. He was obviously good with animals; perhaps, she thought wryly, it was only to his fellow man that he showed up in a lesser light. Nevertheless it coloured her thinking of him and so she told Verity. Her friend laughed and said, 'I think I know what your answer will be when he asks you.'

'If,' Sophie said soberly and wished it was not all quite so unsettling. But it was a new picture of George that would stay in her mind.

At the end of March, when spring was in the air and daffodils pushing through the hard soil in the garden, George arrived one day in his curricle, pronounced the day mild and asked Mrs Sterling if he might take Cousin Sophie for a drive. He had caught the three ladies in the act of parcelling up discarded clothes for the poor and Mrs Sterling said at once, 'What a capital idea. Wrap up well, Sophie. You may take my large cashmere shawl and then there'll be no danger of your catching cold.'

Sophie murmured something about Alethea coming too, but despite that young lady's eagerness, her mother overrode her. 'I need your sister to help me this morning. And as you

55

are cousins, it's quite all right, my dear. There's no room for a third in a curricle, is there?'

'None,' George said firmly. He had recovered somewhat from the gloom of his arrival home, having spent as much time as he could in Jack's exhilarating company, and as he drove out into the Surrey countryside, trying to get some speed out of his father's horses, the thought absently crossed his mind that when he had money they should be replaced.

Sophie directed him towards Brixton Hill where there was a windmill that would make a target for their drive, and then was quiet. He made one or two attempts at conversation, but he had the sense to realise she was shy at this, their first time of being really alone − which was exactly his purpose in setting out this morning.

It was not until they were passing a wood of wild daffodils that with sudden animation she exclaimed, 'Oh, how beautiful. I would like to paint that little scene.'

Without turning his head he said, 'You would find delightful views worthy of your brush at Plummers. It is surrounded by woodland and meadows, and there's a lake one can boat on. The gardens are lacking care but could be got into shape under a wise hand. I saw much that needed doing, though the purpose for my visit was to be sure my horses were being well cared for. Thankfully I can trust my groom, Hedges, implicitly. Did I tell you I had brought three fine Arab horses home?'

'You mentioned it, sir.'

'Several times, I shouldn't wonder! I found them enjoying the fresh grass in the paddock, but the stables and their stalls are in need of repair and the roof leaks − I've set that in train, for I can't have them getting chilled at night. Hedges needs a stable-boy and the tackroom is a disgrace. My father has had no interest in the place for years and though I couldn't stay long, and slept with friends nearby, it was long enough to see that an enormous amount of work needs to be done.'

Now we're back to the legacy, Sophie thought bitterly, and lapsed into silence until they reached the mill. The sails were still on this windless day, the miller being nowhere in sight, only a few chickens scuffing in the dirt, waiting for the wind and a few ears of corn to blow their way.

George remarked that he hadn't been in a mill since he was a boy. 'We have a water mill at Plummers, like everything else in sad need of attention.'

Ignoring this, she said she was sure Mr Jones, the miller, would not mind if they went in. It was a tower mill, tall and brick built, and George pushed the door open, so that he could give her his arm up the wooden steps. Once inside he inspected the wheel, the grinder and the chute with considerable interest, Plummers in his mind.

She went across to look out of the tiny and very dirty window, the smell of corn and flour and dust filling the air. After several remarks on the different style of mills he had seen on the continent, he came across to her, rested one hand against the wall, and suddenly leaned towards her. With her back to the window there was no way of retreat, and turning her head aside, she murmured, 'Cousin George — if you go up the ladder you will find — '

He gave her an amused glance. 'Did you think I meant to kiss you? I do beg your pardon, but there is a very large spider exploring your left shoulder. There!' He brushed the offending insect to the ground where it scuttled for cover and Sophie sprang away, her cheeks turned scarlet by what he thought her assumption to be. 'Oh! Of all things I do dislike spiders — well, the large ones, anyway.'

He was still amused. 'Do you have a general dislike of the animal world, I wonder? You don't care for horses or spiders. What else?'

A reluctant smile was drawn from her. 'You mistake me. I don't dislike horses and our own two serve us very well, it's only that I've no desire to sit on one. And I'm very fond of Dash, as you must know from our walks.'

'Indeed. At first he was inclined to take a piece out of my trousers, if not my leg, but since the business with the trap he seems to have decided I am a persona grata. I was only teasing, you know.'

Thinking how much he had relaxed in the last weeks, that he could tease, rather faintly she added, 'You must think me very foolish, but large spiders, the ones with hairy legs, they run so fast and I really do dislike them.'

He moved to where she was standing. 'Your shawl is all over flour dust, let me shake it clean.' He took it from her, brushed it with one hand, shook it, and put it back about her shoulders, before letting both hands rest on them. 'But a kiss is not such a bad thing, you know. Look at me, Sophie.' And when she did raise her eyes to his face, he thought briefly – this is the moment, I have to do it. Yet over the last weeks he had come to see that though Sophie might not have her sister's beauty, she had twice the character. Ease of conversation, whatever society she was in, and much natural common sense coupled no doubt with other qualities were well suited to a wife – and a wife, a rich wife, he must take. He took a deep breath, rather in mind than body, and went on, 'I know I should speak to your father first, but I wanted to save myself a pointless exercise if you won't consider me. But will you? We know each other better now, don't we? Do you think we could live companionably together?'

She was taken by surprise, not thinking he would ask her directly, schooling herself to be quiet and patient until one day Papa would call her into the study to tell her, ask her what answer she would like him to make. It would give her time – but this frontal approach took her breath away. His motives were plain enough, but was it only the inheritance that prompted him? Did he care for her at all?

At last, in a low, troubled voice, she murmured, 'I don't know what to say. Yes, in the last three months we have all had a very pleasant time, but you don't, you can't love me. I've never thought – '

He began to walk up and down the confined space, his talent for polite speeches warring with honesty. 'No,' he said at last, 'I can't pretend I'm in love with you, Sophie, any more than you can be with me – '

Shaken by this further assumption, she kept her eyes on the floor and he went on, 'Only I do think we can like each other reasonably well, which cannot but be a good basis for a marriage. But before you answer I think I must be quite open with you. If I'm not, some gossip-monger will surely enlighten you.' Seeing sudden alarm in her face, he wondered if Jack was wrong to insist on openness. But having begun he went on, painful though it was. 'Six, no nearly seven years ago now, I was involved with a lady, a married lady. It was all very reprehensible and I was a foolish youth of twenty-one. The matter unfortunately came to court and my father, understandably, banished me abroad.'

It was a shock, something her father had never mentioned, though surely he must be aware of it. She knew little of litigation and could not imagine what such a matter involved, nor it seemed had George any intention of going into details. But the fact remained that he had been entangled with another woman, years ago though it was. 'Is she — ' she was beginning tentatively, bringing him at once to a halt.

'I have learned since I came home that she died a year or two ago,' his voice was toneless, 'so there's an end of it. Not, I assure you, that I would have gone down that road again.'

She laid a hesitant hand on his arm. 'I'm so sorry. It must have made you very unhappy.'

'At the time, yes, but it's far in the past now. Still, I thought you should understand why I stayed away so long. My father and I were never on the best of terms, though I think we get on better now. He would welcome you as a daughter-in-law, and not just because of the legacy. But perhaps what I've told you has changed your mind about me — that is, if you have been thinking about me at all.' He looked down at her, no smile on his face, but searching hers, the brown eyes sombre.

'I don't see why it should change anything now,' she said carefully, measuring her words, not to say too much or too little. 'As you point out, it was all over long ago. But I haven't said — '

'No, you haven't. Do you like me at all, Sophie?'

A murmured, 'Yes, oh yes, indeed. We have all come to — ' caused him to brush aside the rest of the family.

'It is you I'm concerned with. Will you consider my offer? I won't cheat you by saying our Great-Aunt's money is neither here nor there, because it wouldn't be true. Of course I want it, I'm desperately in need of it, but we are family, you and I, and if we marry we can keep it in the family, do a great deal of good with it and provide for future Randolphs.' She did not answer at once, looking out of the window. 'Well?' he asked, almost harshly.

She had flushed of course, and kept her gaze away from his face. At last she said to the floor, 'I think, sir — Cousin George — you must apply to my father.'

He was suddenly impatient. 'Come, you are not Alethea — that's the sort of coy answer I'd expect from her. But you can at least be honest with me, as I have been with you.'

How hard it was to give him a sensible answer, the sort of answer her mother said girls must give to all importunate young men. One must never show 'feelings', which could only come later, after marriage, but at the same time an utterly new sensation was crying out, yes, yes, I'd marry you tomorrow, take you on any terms — and she was aghast at the thought! At last she made herself speak. 'Thank you, sir. I am sensible of your offer, and in light of what you say — '

'Sophie! You dreadful girl, yes or no?'

Sudden laughter between them eased the tension. This was the way for them, humour, laughter, the light touch. 'Then it must be yes.' Ignoring the sudden look of satisfaction on his face, she went on hurriedly, 'I do like you very well and I do think I would enjoy helping you to put Plummers to rights. Though I've never seen it, I've heard a great deal about it from Papa.'

'I'm glad,' he said simply, 'And I think it's time for that kiss now, don't you?'

It was the lightest of salutations, but it sent a tremor through the as yet unkissed Sophie. It seemed to her all that a kiss should be.

Then he held her away. 'Now I will speak to your father. What answer shall I get, do you think?'

'He only wants my happiness, and — I will tell him I believe I can entrust that to you, Cousin George.' Her eyes were glowing with a new light, her face warmed into a new attractiveness.

Misgiving shook him, but he had at least played fair with her, as Jack had told him to do, and it struck him that it was satisfactory to have done the right thing. Emily belonged far in the past. The future looked brighter, his ugly mood of last December dispelled. Plummers would wreak its magic and there surely they would grow close, do so much together.

'I will do my best to make you happy,' he answered, and taking her hand led her out of the dusty mill into the brightness of the spring day. For Sophie the world had never looked so beautiful.

Chapter Five

The wedding was arranged for the end of June. 'The perfect month for brides,' Mrs Sterling remarked, and soon had her daughter immersed in preparations. 'We must visit that paper pattern house in St Paul's churchyard,' she announced, 'and then into Nicholsons for the dress,' by this meaning the length of material required by the pattern. 'And Swan and Edgar for all the accessories, as well as underwear. Regent Street of course for the lacemakers and for bonnets and hats. Oh, we shall set you up famously.'

'Not too much fuss, Mama, please,' Sophie begged, to which her mother replied, 'My dear, you are moving into the aristocracy, of course you must have everything of the best. As a married lady you will be able to wear adornments not fitting for a single girl. And there's not only yourself to dress, but the bridesmaids and a new gown for me.'

'Oh,' Alethea sighed. 'I wish it was me. I wouldn't mind any amount of fuss.'

'You will have your turn,' her mother said. 'I think you and Daisy and those two young cousins of George's will look best in pink. We'll choose materials when we are at Nicholsons. And not made up by Mrs Sedley either. We will find someone far better.'

'My dear, you will hurt her feelings sadly if you go to a smart London dressmaker,' her husband remarked, but he recognized that particular look of determination on his wife's face and gave a resigned shrug.

Lord Randolph requested that the marriage should take place at St George's in Hanover Square, where he had been married himself more than thirty years ago. 'Of course it is a journey for you,' he said to Sophie, 'but I have asked my sister and she would be delighted if you would all stay in South Street the night before.'

Slightly taken aback, Sophie hesitated before answering. Then she said simply, 'It is very kind of you to suggest it, and kind of Lady Louisa, but I would prefer to be married from my father's house and in my own parish church.'

Lord Randolph was not used to such a firm rebuttal and joined battle at once. 'Well, I suppose it is your wedding day, but there will be a great number of guests, you know, and Clapham is a long way out.'

'I hope I haven't given offence.' She gave him a quick smile. 'I'm sure you understand, sir. We do live quietly in Clapham, but I've known the Vicar of Holy Trinity all my life. I'd much prefer to be married there.'

'You would, eh? And you mean to do as you wish?'

'I think, sir, this is one occasion when I may.'

'And what does George say to it?'

A little diffidently she said, 'He agrees it must be my choice.'

He reached out and took her hand in his. 'Which is not St George's, eh? Not even to please an old man?'

Sophie covered their clasped hands with her free one. 'My lord, I'm afraid you will think me very stubborn. I hope I can find other ways to please you, but – '

'I'm answered then. It was just a whim, I suppose.'

'Don't you really think a bride should come from her father's house? I know Papa wouldn't think of anything else. And, you know, we shall have relations staying. Mama has a great many of them.' He was tempted to shudder at the thought and she added, 'I'm quite fond of some of them.'

Unable to resist the little laugh that accompanied this statement, he said, 'I yield, my dear. Of course it must be as you wish,' and was regarded by a warm kiss on the cheek. It occurred to him that Adela Crabtree had known what she was doing.

Over another matter, however, Sophie was forced to yield. She would have liked to see her new home before the wedding, but a visit to Plummers seemed almost impossible to arrange. A hostess and chaperone would be needed and there was no one available on George's side, except his aunt Louisa who gave a little shriek of horror at the mere idea, being too immersed in the London season to wish to leave it. Mrs Sterling, when Sophie mentioned her wish, said firmly, 'Oh, my dear, there's far too much to be done here without travelling into the country, even for a week, nor could I be expected to play hostess in a house I've never seen. And your Papa can't spare the time with this outbreak of smallpox in Brixton.'

So there was nothing for Sophie to do but look forward to seeing Plummers when she arrived as a bride, George's comment being merely that it would present too many problems to go sooner. There was much bustle in the doctor's house, much coming and going, hours spent over catalogues and samples of material. George was there sometimes, but he seemed to have a great deal of business concerning Warburton and the doctor's man of business, Mr Trant, as settlements were drawn up. Mrs Crabtree's house was put up for sale, and all the Indian curios packed up and sent off to the British Museum, except for one ivory elephant with a howdah on its back, which Sophie fancied as a keepsake.

'When we are in London I think we should stay in Mount Street,' George suggested. 'My father would like it very much.'

And having disappointed the old man over the matter of the wedding venue, Sophie agreed. The idea of living in Mrs Crabtree's house had never appealed, whereas the house in Mount Street was central, near the Park where she envisaged George taking her for pleasant drives. In these weeks of preparation he was attentive, courteous to everybody, but a little withdrawn at times and his bride was coming to see he was a man of deep reserve. Her secret doubt and regret was that he said and did nothing of an affectionate nature to her, apart from a peck on the cheek when arriving or leaving, though now and then he did smile at her as if acknowledging their new relationship. No doubt, as Mama said, 'that sort of thing' came with marriage. At times, however, she felt herself very ignorant.

As far as her future father-in-law was concerned, he

seemed to have taken her to his heart. He had achieved his object, secured the heiress for his son, and after the first brush with Sophie, was more pleased than otherwise that she had stood up for her own wishes. He was constantly sending her little notes, asking her to lunch with him, or take tea, and these meetings cemented their relationship. Sophie had a talent for getting on with and understanding older people so that they were soon on excellent terms. This surprised him, for he had lived since George's departure in gloomy seclusion, bitter, disappointed, lonely − his only bright days during his younger son's periods of leave. But here was this child − one soon forgot she was not beautiful − paying him attention, reading paragraphs out of the paper, pouring his tea, teasing him in a manner that no one had dared to for years. She persuaded him to take a turn in the park with her, holding his arm as if it was she who needed assistance, and when they went for a drive it was she who wrapped a rug about his knees. He began to brighten up, waited impatiently when it was a few days between her visits. Sometimes her mother or sister came with her but he liked it better when she came alone with her new maid to attend her.

Mrs Sterling had decided her daughter must have a personal maid at once and three women came from the agency to be interviewed. Mrs Sterling considered the woman in her thirties to be the most suitable and once again Sophie asserted herself. 'No, Mama, thank you. Mrs Philpot seemed to be very − what Papa would call dour. I didn't care for her at all. My choice is Phoebe Watson.'

'But she can't be more than sixteen.'

'That pleases me. I can train her to my ways, and I liked her, so bright and cheerful but perfectly respectful.'

'Very well, my dear, if you insist,' Mrs Sterling was surprised, having been used to making decisions for her daughters. 'I merely thought Mrs Philpot, being a widow, would take better care of you.'

'Between us, I believe Phoebe and I will manage very well,' Sophie assured her and so it was settled. Phoebe moved in and Sophie was sure she had made the right choice.

With his son about to marry and his prospective daughter-in-law so much to his taste, Lord Randolph began to think he might disappoint George by living a good deal longer than expected. His sister said bluntly, 'Well, John, it was your own fault you went into a decline. We must be thankful that you are come out of it now.'

To her nephew she remarked, 'You appear to have landed on your feet, George. Since Sophie's visit to me, I have discovered what an admirable wife she will make you.'

George replied that it appeared likely, which his aunt thought very unenthusiastic. Privately he wished they had more in common. It would be too much, he supposed, to hope that she should be a woman who could match him in the saddle, love horses as he did.

The visit to Lady Louisa in South Street had been a great success. She escorted Sophie to two balls, as well as making a number of visits with her to people of some consequence; they had gone shopping in Piccadilly and Regent Street, Amabel often joining them. One ball to which they all went was at Cavendish House, the London home of the Duke of Devonshire, and proved to be quite an occasion, chandeliers glistening, flowers everywhere, the best musicians hired for the evening.

Sophie's first spontaneous remark to George was, 'How Thea would have enjoyed this.'

'The sooner that girl is safely married the better,' was his rather dry answer, in his new position of brother. They were circling the floor in a waltz. 'In my opinion, Sophie, you put her forward above yourself. You seem to think because she has exceptional looks and has something, trivial usually, to say about everything, that she is your superior. It isn't so, I assure you.'

'Oh,' she turned in his arms. 'Don't you like her?'

'She has her own brand of appeal, I suppose, and I hope some man will turn her into a passable woman, but she will probably always be a butterfly.'

'Is that such a bad thing?'

George looked down at his betrothed. 'I think it is. I've discovered that a man wants more than beauty in a wife − and don't say money, for you know I didn't mean that. I think we will be companionable, which is worth a great deal more. These last months have shown us that, haven't they?'

She had flushed of course at the compliment. 'I'm glad you think so,' she said quietly. 'I hope as a brother you will be a good influence on Thea.'

'Well, so do I. Being with her is rather like playing with a puppy. But if we take her in hand next spring, bring her out for the London season, who knows what we will achieve.'

'Thank you, George, thank you so much.'

'Don't thank me,' he said. 'It's only a form of self-protection for us to see her safely married off,' which made Sophie laugh and she went on to say how sorry she was that Frank would still be away at sea at the time of the wedding. 'He's a good boy at heart, if a thought wild,' she told him. 'Another member of the family for you to take in hand.'

'That sounds like a task for Maurice. I've every hope he will be home soon.'

When the music ceased Lady Louisa took her off to present her to a number of people – Mr Carlisle, the author, who rather overawed her, though she found his wife pleasant, and Mr Disraeli, the leader of the Tory party in the House of Commons, whom she thought fulsome. Miss Angela Burdett-Coutts, daughter of a wealthy banker, a great philanthropist and friend of the Duke of Wellington, she found overpowering but kind. The highlight of the evening for her was when George took her to be introduced to the great man himself. Now eighty, with white hair, his eyes were still keen, and she thought him quite splendid. He pinched her cheek and said, 'Well done, Mr Randolph, you have secured a charming bride,' which gave Sophie a pardonable blush. There were a great many uniforms there and she danced with a captain from the Life Guards, a connection of the Duke's, and she also took a turn with Lord Seaton's son, wishing it was with his lordship himself. He was there with his bright, pretty wife, a tall, dignified man with the kindest smile who, as Sir John Colborne, had led one of the foremost charges at the battle of Waterloo. She asked her partner about this, but Graham Colborne merely said his father preferred not to talk of it these days. Dancing next with a Mr Pelham-Clinton, a relation of the Duke of Newcastle, she thought she had never heard, let alone met, so many titles and connections of titles and was somewhat daunted to find where her marriage to George was leading her.

After supper she and other ladies slipped upstairs to freshen themselves, and coming down she encountered her host. The sixth Duke, now over sixty, had never married and seemed totally absorbed in making Chatsworth in Derbyshire and Chiswick House just out of town places of great beauty. He told her that his head gardener, and friend, he added, had built him a huge and spectacular glasshouse at Chatsworth and he was going to invite him to try a design for the building to house the Great Exhibition, now a fact indeed, Lord Brougham and Colonel Sibthorpe having been routed.

'Sir Robert Peel is all for the scheme and of course he carries a great deal of weight,' he told her. 'Do you know anything of the plans, Miss Sterling?'

'Only what I have read in the papers,' she said, 'but my father, who is very mechanically minded as well as being a doctor, is all for it.'

'I'm told you are to marry Randolph's eldest son. When is it to be?'

'At the end of June, my lord.'

'Then I wish you happy. I've known John Randolph these forty years.'

When they were gathering up cloaks to go home, George said, 'Well, did you enjoy yourself?'

'I found it all somewhat overwhelming,' she said honestly, 'but oh yes, so enjoyable. And actually to meet the Duke of Wellington! I can still hardly believe it.'

'My aunt, as you are no doubt beginning to discover, knows everyone worth knowing in London. My late uncle was a member of the Privy Council and my aunt at one time a lady-in-waiting to Queen Adelaide. If there is anyone you wish to meet or anything you want to do just ask her.'

Sophie gave him a rueful glance. 'I think I shall have indigestion of the brain if I do any more. I have enjoyed it all a great deal but I shall be glad to go home tomorrow.'

On the morning after the ball, she called in at Mount Street and was sitting over a late breakfast with Lord Randolph when there was a bang on the front door and a cheery greeting.

'Hello there, Beveridge. I hope I see you well. No, don't announce me, you idiot, I want to surprise 'em.'

As his voice carried the length and height of the house there was not much surprise when Captain Maurice Randolph entered the room. His father sat upright in his chair, a look of both surprise and satisfaction on his face, but all he said was, 'Well, Maurice, you are come most appropriately.'

'Do you say so, sir? What's to do then?' He took his father's outstretched hand. 'How are you? Better, I hope?' Then he glanced at Sophie.

'As you see. And you are in time for your brother's wedding,' Lord Randolph told him. 'This is Miss Sophie Sterling, George's bride, to be a sister for you.'

Maurice strode to her place and took her hand. 'I didn't even know the dear fellow was home. May I felicitate you, Miss Sterling?'

'You may,' she said smiling. There was something irresistible about this exuberant sailor.

At that moment George was heard coming down the stairs three at a time to burst into the room and seize his brother's hand. 'Well!' he said. 'Well! Why didn't you let us know you were coming?'

'I got into Portsmouth yesterday and decided if I came up on the mail train, it would be as quick as sending a letter.' Maurice was taller than his brother, smart in his naval uniform and not in the least like him, for George favoured their father, whereas Maurice took his looks from the lady who gazed down from her portrait on this family reunion. His hair was light brown and curling, his eyes hazel and keen as they surveyed his elder brother. 'You old landlubber,' he added. 'It's good to see you home too and about to be married, I hear. I've not yet had time to become properly acquainted with my future sister-in-law, but I congratulate you.'

'Sit down,' Lord Randolph said testily. 'I can't conduct a conversation with a maypole. Ah, thank you, Beveridge,' as the butler brought another coffee cup and plate from the sideboard where dishes of bacon and scrambled eggs, sausages and grilled kidneys lay under silver covers.

Maurice helped himself to a gargantuan breakfast and

appropriated the seat next to Sophie, waving George away to the opposite chair. 'Now tell me,' he said, 'how all this came about? When did you and my brother meet? I'm delighted with the news. The dear old boy has been rolling about like a loose cannon for far too long.'

'I hardly know where to start,' Sophie began in some confusion in the face of this whirlwind, and it was Lord Randolph who came to her rescue. In the most tactful terms he told his younger son of the reunion between himself and Dr Sterling, throwing in the Crabtree inheritance as a secondary thing, and remarking on how well everything had worked out. Maurice was delighted, quizzed Sophie about her family and laughed uproariously when she told him of her brother Frank, who, as a mere midshipman, would not dare address a post-captain.

'I'm afraid he is at sea,' she added, 'and won't be here for the wedding, though we have written to him at Gibraltar.'

'Ship letters chase one around the seas,' he said, 'but when we get out of uniform, perhaps I can be an elder brother to him. What ship is he on?'

'The *Vesuvius*.'

'That leaky old tub? I thought it had drawn its last water. I'll put in a word at the Admiralty, maybe I can get him on to my *Triumph* when she's seaworthy — perhaps get him promoted to ensign. How does he do with his mathematical studies?'

'Well, I think,' Sophie said, 'it would be very good of you to take an interest in him.' There was something very attractive about Maurice Randolph.

After breakfast he changed, and took his brother off for a visit to various gentlemen's clubs to look up old friends. George apologized for abandoning Sophie, but as she was not going until the afternoon, he promised to be back in time. She and Lord Randolph retired to his study where he sat with the paper in the mornings and shared matters of interest, but today neither of them could concentrate.

Sophie said, 'Sir, you must be so glad to see them together again and at home, though I gather they did contrive to meet in Naples.'

'Yes, about two years ago, I think. Certainly, a brush

70

with death sharpens one's sense of the priorities in life. I thought I was going to leave this earth without seeing either of my sons again.'

Sitting opposite his large winged chair she could not help saying warmly, 'Captain Randolph seems very different from George, so — so easy-going and full of life.'

The old man was lost in a reminiscence. 'Ah, when they were boys it was always Maurice who conceived every piece of mischief.'

'And George?'

'Difficult to know. But I've a shrewd idea you will be the making of him.'

Pleased at this compliment she murmured that she hoped to be all he wanted, but his thoughts were back with his younger son as he went on. 'I would like to see him settled, for I think it's he now who's like the proverbial loose cannon he called his brother. But he never seems to want a home and family of his own.'

'I suppose that time will come,' she said, 'but it must be difficult when he's away for such long spells, difficult for a wife too.'

'Part of the lot of all naval wives,' he commented. 'You are right in that he is a different sort of fellow from his brother. He does not have George's reserve.'

Wanting to ask more, to know if George had been like Maurice in his youth, if the reserve had only come after that disastrous affair of seven years ago, nevertheless she did not feel she could probe and his lordship said no more. It was easy to see, however, how glad he was to have his sailor back and she guessed that Maurice had always been his favourite. George, she thought, was far too like his father in temperament for them to get on.

In the afternoon she returned home, laden with gifts — gloves and lace and a length of pretty summer muslin from Lady Louisa. The best gift of all was a small box which Lord Randolph produced when she came to say goodbye to him. Opening it she found a brooch made up of opals in the most exquisite design.

'It belonged to my late wife,' he said, 'and I put it

71

aside until I should have a daughter-in-law. It was her favourite piece.'

She kissed him and whispered, 'You are so very kind to me. I will try to be a good wife to George.'

He returned in time to drive her to Clapham in his open curricle, and his first remark was to hope that she would like his brother, adding, 'I can't tell you what it means to me to have him here for our wedding.'

'Could anyone not like him?' she countered lightly.

'True enough, but you have to understand Maurice. He is all breezy and easy-going, on the surface, but his first love is the Navy. Nothing else counts with him and I know he's highly thought of at the Admiralty. On shore is a different matter. It's as if he lets all restraint go and enjoys himself like a lad of eighteen. At least that is how it seems to me. He may have changed since I last saw him, but I doubt it.'

'Surely you can have seen little of him over the last few years?'

He conceded that. 'Don't misunderstand me. I love him dearly, – as you say, who could not? – but that doesn't prevent me knowing him. On the quarter deck, or so I've been told by the first lieutenant on his last ship, he is precise, meticulous even, and will have instant obedience from his crew. He's also a first-class seaman. The result is he runs a tight ship; indeed, I expect to see him an admiral before he's done. On leave, however – ' He left the sentence unfinished.

'In what way is he different?' she asked.

'Well, when I saw him in Naples, I discovered that his addiction to the female sex still runs riot ashore, his affairs pursued ardently but without substance. And he gambles, mainly on the horses – so do I when I can afford it, so I can't fault him there. But I sometimes wonder how much of his pay actually finds its way into his bank account. And knowing him, I am concerned that when he sees Alethea he will find her beauty irresistible, and probably turn her head to no good purpose.'

'Oh,' Sophie digested this. She could see them together, Maurice all life and charm, Thea with her lovely looks and her head full of romantic nonsense, and a sense of unease crept over her. 'I hope — oh, I do hope — ' and was not sure what she hoped.

He drew in to the side of the road, letting the horse crop some tufts of grass, while he reached for her hand. 'They could make us seem a very sober pair, couldn't they? But I doubt if it will come to that. Maurice is not yet ready to settle down, and Alethea will probably have her heart broken a dozen times before she accepts anyone.'

'Do you really think Maurice will turn her head? He is very attractive.'

'Don't you think it's likely?'

'I'm afraid I do. Oh dear. I can imagine him sweeping any girl off her feet. And if he's unlikely to mean it — I suppose it is too much to hope they will act like brother and sister?'

George's mouth twitched. 'Far too much! Now you are not to worry about it,' he added firmly. 'If they make a match of it, well and good, but I think we are looking too far ahead. What is more likely is that they will flirt outrageously during Maurice's leave. In any case, his frigate will be sea-worthy before too long.'

This seemed a very small crumb of comfort. But perhaps she was imagining too much. She gave George a little smile and said, 'I would so much rather marry an oak tree than a whirlwind.'

He laughed and put the hand he held to his lips, before gathering up the reins and driving on, while Sophie forgot her sister and his brother in the thought that in less than a week she would be George's wife.

Chapter Six

Two days before the wedding and walking through the newly developed Belgravia, to head home through the Park, George was feeling optimistic about his forthcoming nuptials. The three months of engagement had made him see Sophie in a better light — he liked her practicality, her occasional impish sense of humour, and the fact that she could hold her own with quiet dignity in the society into which her marriage would bring her. He hoped she would get absorbed in Plummers and in due course in their children, leaving him to pursue his own plans for the place, for the Arab stud, and the hunting.

He was just considering whether to go to Tattersalls for the horse sale tomorrow when he paused to allow a woman to go up the shallow steps to a front door. She was tall and with a mass of auburn hair half hidden under a shady straw bonnet. The face beneath the brim was both beautiful and tremendously attractive. She turned her head and then came to a sudden halt as she saw him.

At the same time George was standing rigid with shock. He caught hold of the railings.

'Emily? *Emily!* Great God, I thought — I was told — is it really you?'

She too had been startled, but far less so. 'Yes, it's me. Dear George, what a pleasant surprise. But you look as if you'd seen a ghost.'

'I have — you are. My father told me you had died, a notice in *The Times.*' He had not moved, still gripping his railing, oblivious of passers-by. 'My God, I can't believe it. But he said he'd seen it — '

She gave a low laugh. 'Oh! The paper was mistaken. He wouldn't have known and perhaps you don't recall my husband's maiden aunt was also Emily Horton. It was she who died.'

He transferred his grip from the railings to her free hand. 'I thought I'd never see you again − all these months, thinking you dead −' speech failed him.

'Well, here I am. Let me go, George, we can't talk in the street. Come inside, these are my lodgings.'

Dumbly, his mind in a whirl, trying to accept the incredible, he followed her. At the top of the first flight of stairs, she led him through her own door into a small entrance hall and then into a large room, comfortably furnished and with high windows looking out into the street.

'There,' she said and removed her bonnet. 'Let me look at you.'

For answer, he seized her hand again. 'Emily − you are more beautiful than even I remember.'

'Come, sit down.' She indicated a winged chair. 'We have so much to say to each other. I'll ring for my maid to make us some tea.'

'I don't want tea. *Emily* −'

'Nevertheless, tea is what you shall have.' She freed herself, pulled the bell sash and by the time her maid came she had pushed him into a chair and taken the one opposite.

Tea was brought with sweet biscuits, and as soon as they were alone again, he began, 'Tell me − where have you been, what have you done since we parted so wretchedly? If only you had come with me!'

'To do what? Life in a garret was not for me, George, and your father would not have got you that diplomatic post if you had proposed taking your mistress with you. He would more likely have washed his hands of you, wouldn't he?'

Restlessly he set his cup down on the table beside him. 'We need not have cared for that. I'd have found something in Paris, tutoring perhaps, I don't know, but we would have managed together.'

She was shaking her head. 'Dear me, no. The scandal would have been prolonged. Anyway, it would not have answered. I was over thirty and you hardly more than a boy. No, it would have been the greatest mistake.'

'You broke my heart.'

She smiled teasingly at him. 'Oh, I think that organ is a great deal stronger than most people believe. Neither of our hearts was broken, though we did love each other very much.'

'My God, how much! I've never felt for any woman what I felt for you.' Taut with the intensity of the moment, he went on, 'Your face has haunted me all these years.' He gazed at that face, seeing at first only the astonishing beauty that had captivated the impressionable youth he had been, but now he detected a few signs of what all the trouble had done to her — a line here and there, a certain twist to her mouth, as if she saw the world through hardened eyes. Even so, the beauty was still there. 'When I was lonely and, I must say it, very bitter in St Petersburg, and other places, you haunted me. I could see you, smiling as you used to do. I don't know how I endured it. I might have blown out my brains if it hadn't been for Jack Fleming.'

She poured him another cup of tea. 'I remember him. But I wouldn't have been worth that. I did find it equally hard to get you out of my head, only the odds were stacked against us. That court case,' she gave a little shudder, 'it was dreadful — dreadful. I could never forgive Lawrence for that. There was never any question of divorce, of course. You remember both our families are Catholic? And a civil application for an Act of Parliament would have been unthinkable. But for him to bring a case for separation and damages — we hurt his pride, you see; his anger ate into him, turned his mind, I think.'

'He's a devil. What he put you through!' George's voice shook, the tea forgotten as once again all the brooding hatred for the man who had wrecked her life, and his, rose up in him, refusing to give room to the knowledge that he himself was at least partly responsible for that. But they had been so in love. With an effort he asked, 'What did you do afterwards? Surely you didn't go back to him?'

'No, indeed I didn't, though his lawyer suggested a reconciliation. No, I ran away to Ireland. Wasn't it cowardly of me? But it was for the best. I went to an aunt and uncle who were kindness itself. My parents were dead by then, not

76

that I think my father would have received me back into the family, which he considered I had disgraced. But my aunt was a wonderful woman, forgiving and warm-hearted, and I stayed a long time. Then my uncle died and my aunt went to live in a convent. She was a deeply religious woman. Perhaps that is what I should have done.' She gave a little laugh. 'But that was not in my nature, was it? Anyway, my uncle had left me a comfortable sum and I was in the throes of looking for an apartment in Dublin when I received a letter from Major Bryce. Do you remember him?'

'Bryce? No, I don't think so.' And then, searching the recesses of his mind, 'Wait a moment — wasn't he that damned army officer who gave evidence for Horton, said he had seen me leave your house at three in the morning?'

'That's right,' she said, the twist to her mouth more pronounced. 'Edgar Bryce. You haven't heard of Bryce's Balloons? No, well perhaps you would not have, as you've been away so long, but he has left the Army and turned showman with two or three assistants and several of the brightly coloured things. He puts on entertainments all over the country.'

'What an odd thing to do.' For a moment he recalled having talked to Sophie about balloons, but the last few months seemed to have receded in the face of Emily's reappearance.

'Perhaps, but profitable. People flock to see his displays and even take a flight with him. He was Lawrence's closest friend, so I suppose he couldn't help but support him. He went to America last summer and saw him. I received a letter from Major Bryce forwarded from my brother's house. Lawrence is dead.'

'Dead?' George exclaimed. 'I didn't know. But how should I?'

'He'd gone to New York several years ago. I believe there was a brief notice in one of the morning papers here, bringing up the scandal of course, though I didn't see it. You see, he had committed suicide, shot himself. Oh,' seeing George's stunned expression, 'not because of me, nor of us, not altogether. He had been suffering from gout and the pain was driving him mad. I think he *was* half mad and perhaps I should feel responsible for that.'

'You should not,' George broke in, almost roughly. 'The man was always unstable. Jack told me he had to resign his commission because of some row or other.'

'That's true, and I suppose that was why he went to America. Major Bryce says in the letter that his mind was unhinged. Poor Lawrence. He was once so – so different.'

'Damn him,' George muttered. 'I'm glad he's dead. He put you through unpardonable suffering. I remember one day finding you with your arm all bruised. That was him, wasn't it? Though you wouldn't admit it at the time. Emily!' as a thought struck him, 'then you are free?'

'A widow, yes. Tell me, my dear, what did you do when it was all over? You went abroad, I think.'

Briefly he told her, explaining finally what had brought him home and she exclaimed, 'I am so glad you are reconciled with your father. I always blamed myself for that quarrel. And you – you have a wife?'

He sprang up, knocking over the little table beside him and the half drunk cup of tea. 'No – yes!' Ignoring the resultant mess, he rushed on, 'To see you again – now! Oh God, Emily, I'm to be married the day after tomorrow!'

She sat very still. 'How – how very strange. All those years ago you were free and I was not – now I am free and you are not.'

He gave a groan, leaning one elbow on the mantelpiece. 'It is too damnable to bear. Emily, my love, my love.' He caught her hands, pulling her to her feet and into his arms, to sink his mouth on hers in a kiss such as Sophie would not have recognized. All the old fire was returning, and the kissing deepened. He could feel her body responding in a manner he well remembered.

But at last she freed herself and turned her head away. 'This – this is absurd. George, let me go. Now – please. Sit down again and tell me about – about your bride. Are you in love?'

'Good heavens, no,' he exclaimed. 'I'd have thought the last few minutes would have told you that.' Busying himself retrieving the cup and saucer, setting the table on its legs again, he added, 'No, it's a matter of convenience. The Randolphs need money, and the Sterlings, from a back-of-beyond place called Clapham, are cousins and would be glad of the title. At least, Sophie's mother would. Her father is a much better sort of person and I like him very well.'

'Is the family wealthy then?'

Briefly he explained about the Crabtree inheritance, about his father's scheming and Mrs Sterling's determination. Then he lapsed into silence and Emily, moving away, studied his face. 'And this girl, what is she like? Do you care for her at all?'

'I like her well enough,' he said in a goaded voice. 'She is educated, well read, I suppose one would call it − sensible, my father said, which was enough to put anyone off. I think we do get on. She's no beauty, but pleasant enough to face across a table. Her sister is, devastatingly so, only she's not the heiress.' He glanced at Emily. 'Do I sound callous? Perhaps I am, but we do desperately need the Crabtree money, what with debts and Plummers in a bad state, and Sophie seemed willing to take me − not for the title, I'm sure of that − but because we are family and we can do much with Plummers, which is after all the family home. Yes, I do like her and I was pretty well content, until − Emily, Emily, it's the most cruel turn of fate that I should find you again − too late. If it had been three months ago, before I offered, but now − if I begged you to marry me we would hurt so many people. And without the Crabtree money, I've very little; Plummers will probably fall down and my father die in debt − the shock would probably kill him!'

'How could you even consider it?' she retorted swiftly. 'This poor girl − within two days of her wedding! You can't do such a thing. Your father, her people − no, no, it would be quite dreadful, and I doubt if I'd accept you anyway.'

His mouth twisted into a smile. 'I believe I could win you again.'

She surveyed him, remembering the slender youth, dark eyes bright and fiery with love for her; he had turned into this assured, well-dressed man with an air about him, a touch of arrogance. But oh, the eyes were the same. Only she was not the woman of nearly seven years ago. 'Perhaps you could,'

79

she said a little shakily, 'but for what? I am too old to be swept into another disaster.'

'You think marriage to me would be a disaster.'

'Undoubtedly. You've said that without this girl, the Randolphs are in financial trouble. I've only a modest income. Marriage to you and the world well lost? No, George, that is not what I want.'

Uneasily he asked what she did want.

'Well,' she sank back in her chair. 'It is only a few weeks since I came to take up life in London again, seeing old friends and starting to go about. A woman separated from her husband is not marketable, you know — a widow is! Like you, I shall look for a rich spouse, and you, I'm afraid, certainly would not fit into that category, nor can I have you disrupting all my plans. Anyway, it would be quite wrong under the circumstances. Marry your Sophie and try to be happy.'

'Happy!' He sank down into his chair, his head in his hands.

She did not move. 'I feel sorry for your bride if you marry her thinking of me.'

'Oh my God, my bride!'

There was a knock on the door and she called, 'Come in. Yes, Millie, what is it?'

'Excuse me, madam, but shall I lay an extra cover for dinner?'

She was about to say that her visitor would not be staying when she saw the intense pleading in George's eyes. 'Yes,' she said quietly. 'Mr Randolph will take dinner with me.'

'Thank you,' he said in a low voice when the door had closed. 'There's so little time left. Afterwards — we go to the Hague for a week or two, maybe to Amsterdam — not long, I want to get settled at Plummers — or I did. But — everything is arranged. Maurice is back to stand up with me.'

'Dear Maurice. How is he?'

'Well, and a post-captain now, waiting for his ship. My Aunt Louisa's daughter Amabel is married to Viscount Storrington and they've two children. You remember Amabel?'

'Of course. She was a dear girl. And your father, is he well now?'

'I came back because our man of business wrote that he was dying, but he has taken a new lease on life — Sophie's doing. Our quarrel is patched up but we are badly in debt, which is why he engineered this marriage. That was his doing.' He paused, his fingers clenched on the arm of his chair. 'Emily, I would walk away from it if I could, but — two hundred guests, a great marquee in the Sterlings' garden, Sophie with her bridal gown and trousseau for our honeymoon —' For a moment his mind revolted against the thought of the coming weeks alone with Sophie. 'What can I do?'

'Nothing,' she said firmly, 'nothing.'

Dinner was served in the small adjoining room and over it they both tried to make desultory conversation. George barely touched the food set before him. He was trying to assimilate the fact that he was dining with Emily Horton. After all the years of longing and frustration, after the shock of hearing last winter that she was dead, here she was opposite him. She had changed out of her walking dress into a gown of bronze-coloured silk, almost the shade of her hair, a long string of amber beads hanging about her neck, the whole effect simple but in the height of fashion, her lovely mobile face betraying the emotion that stirred her too. No, he thought wretchedly, Emily could not live on a pittance. Neither of them spoke of the court case; it was too painful and buried deep. Instead they talked of the years between, of old friends, of the halcyon days when they had first known each other.

'My fault,' she said. 'I should never have let you take me to Richmond that day, but I was already wretchedly unhappy with Lawrence. Nor take me out on the river in that boat. Do you remember the little island we found? I've thought of that so many times. But I should never have gone with you, never let you fall in love with me.'

'I don't see how you could have stopped me. When I think of that night, the hotel in Richmond — and other places —'

For a moment memory briefly softened her expression. 'I don't think we'd better talk of that. Maybe there was too

81

much passion between us. It might have burned away as quickly.'

'I'll not believe that,' he said sharply and then pressed his lips together as the maid came in.

Coffee was brought to them in the drawing room and the maid departed, for she only came in by day. Darkness fell and Emily got up to draw the curtains. 'You must go home too. It's getting late, past ten already. I didn't mean for you to stay so long.'

'Didn't you?' He got up, crossed the room, took her in his arms. 'Didn't you, Emily?'

'No, I did not, though after all this time your arrival has quite taken my breath away. But you're to be married the day after tomorrow − I've no place in your life now. It would have been better, would it not, if you hadn't come down the street today?'

'You can't believe that, and neither can I. Nothing can change the fact that you've come back into my life. You are free, alone.' He began kissing her in a manner few women could resist, her eyes, her cheeks, her neck, her mouth, all the pent-up longing of the years overwhelming them both. Emily Horton was not an immoral woman but she had strong passions and had lived without love for too long. And George, a man now in place of the youth, she was not strong enough to resist. He felt her yielding, old longings rising, a new desire, and they stayed thus for many minutes.

Then she collected herself enough to remove her arms from about his neck, set her hands against his shoulders. 'I've lived like the nun I refused to be for too long − well, almost, and to be in your arms − ' She left the sentence unfinished. 'But this is quite pointless. It was over, long ago, it is over now.'

'It's not over,' he said in a low voice, shaking with the strength of his desire. 'How can it be over? Emily, let me stay, at least for tonight. If you send me away − oh my love, my love, don't − don't.' And as his mouth came down on hers once more, he felt the moment's resistance yielding to a passion that matched his own.

At six o'clock the next morning George walked across the

Park to Mount Street, turning his face into the fresh morning breeze, his mind in torment. After such a night as he had had with Emily, how could he walk down the aisle with Sophie tomorrow? He thought of their most recent talk in the carriage when he had driven her home, and how he had reached a sense of surprising optimism. He had even said, when telling her of the past, that he would not go down that road again. It was easy to mean it with Emily dead, but now − now it was all shattered, everything wrecked, himself in an agony of heartbreak for the second time. It was cruel, a wickedly cruel twist of fate. And Sophie did not deserve a bridegroom in the state he was in now. Yet what could he do? He would have to, must go through with it. The settlements were signed, everything ready, but the thought of his honeymoon in Holland brought him to a halt beside a tree, one of Colonel Sibthorpe's elms, with a desire to batter his head against it. What was he going to do, what could he do? Emily was alive, disturbingly close, and nothing could change that. He had held her in his arms all night, his desire, and hers as well, increased by the years apart, by maturity. Passion had once more swept them away, given them a night such as they had hardly known even at the height of their affair. A youth then, experience had taught him much about women. And his dreams of her, over the years, had fed his imagination, never daring to believe they could culminate in such a night.

But half an hour ago, seeing him out of the door, she had said, 'This is goodbye, my dear.'

And he had denied it. 'It can't be, it's not possible. After last night, how can I stay away? I'll come again, when I'm home after −' He could not bring out the word 'honeymoon.'

'Unwise' she said, 'but then we never were very wise, were we? Only this time I am going to be sensible for both of us. Goodbye, George.' She almost pushed him through the door, saying her maid would be there any minute. He groaned aloud, thankful it was too early for many people to be about. Reluctantly he moved on. Two riders came towards him but he barely heeded them, until one of them called out, 'Have a care, sir.' He walked on, round the Park not heeding where he went, for more than an hour, until at last, wearily, he turned for home. At the house in Mount Street, Beveridge let him in, betraying no surprise, merely saying, 'His lordship has been asking for you, sir.'

'I stayed at my club,' George lied. He hated lying and it occurred to him that he was going to have to do a good deal of it. 'Tell him I am home. I'm going to my room.'

Once there, dismissing Morgan, his newly acquired valet, he threw himself on his bed. Exhaustion, emotional and physical, overcame him and though he thought it impossible, he slept the whole morning. At midday his valet knocked a little nervously. Morgan was somewhat in awe of his new master, aware of that sharp tongue, and he was painfully eager to please.

'Excuse me, sir, but will you be taking luncheon? I understand his lordship is having a day in bed to prepare for tomorrow and will be served a tray there.'

'Did I ring for you?' George snapped and sat up, aware of his dishevelled appearance. 'No, I don't want luncheon. You can prepare a bath for me.' Soon after, sitting in the hot water brought up two flights of stairs by perspiring servants, he thought in a desultory way that he would have a bathroom installed at Plummers. The house seemed singularly quiet, and he remembered his brother had to attend the Admiralty this morning. His wedding clothes were ready, hung up and carefully prepared by his valet, and trickling hot water down his back he gazed broodingly at them. Morgan was tidying away the linen he had taken off, putting out a fresh shirt, clean socks. He would do, George thought, a willing enough young fellow who would soon learn his master's ways, one of which was not to talk too much. Tomorrow he would be helping him into those smart clothes: black coat, fawn waistcoat and trousers, perfectly tailored by Heath of Oxford Street. Having felt justified in spending freely, George had set himself up with an entirely new wardrobe, and enjoyed doing it. It was an odd experience, being able to spend freely. All these thoughts trickled through his head like the water down his back, because he must not think of anything else.

Out of the bath and towelled dry by Morgan, he dressed and went to see his father, thankful the curtains were half drawn against the bright sunlight. Surely last night must have set its mark on his countenance and he didn't want to be seen until time had passed and he had himself in hand again.

Lord Randolph was dozing and merely said, 'I mean to be at my best tomorrow, my boy. It will be the happiest day I've had for a long time — that dear child for a daughter will brighten as many more days as I'm permitted on this earth. Where's Maurice?'

'Gone to the Admiralty, sir.'

'Oh, to be sure. Well, dine together. I'll not come down tonight.'

George left him and walked slowly downstairs to the study. There he found Warburton busy at the desk.

'Mr George, good afternoon. Did you want me? I think all is in order, a few bills to pay but no need for us to worry any more, eh?'

'I've letters to write,' George said pointedly and Warburton got up at once, gathering a few papers.

'I can finish these at home.' Reaching out to grasp George's reluctant hand, he added, 'Tomorrow will be a great day for us all. I do wish you well, sir.'

When he had trotted off George sat down, drawing a sheet of paper towards him, choosing a pen, but had got no further than 'My darling Emily,' when he came to an abrupt halt. What was he going to say? Beg her, plead with her to let him visit her when he was home again, say that they would find ways to be together, lovers again? But the thought of the next few weeks, the trip he had planned to The Hague, Amsterdam, Brussels and perhaps going on into Italy caused him to put down the pen and sink his head into his hands. His honeymoon! Dear God, he had meant to try to make Sophie happy, be content himself, no stinting any more with money, the future full of hope — perhaps in time, a son. It had all begun to seem so good, but now! Emily had said this morning that he must put her and last night out of his head, but how could he? Seeing her there, her wonderful hair loose, in a pale blue dressing gown, the tantalizing lover he had dreamed of through the lonely years, how could it be goodbye? Only there was no going back, nor going forward. It was too late, and for a brief moment he shook with dry sobs.

Then, controlling himself, he began to write, tore up the letter, began again, consigned this also to the wastepaper basket, but the third effort he signed. Only twenty-four hours ago he had been looking forward eagerly to living at Plummers; now he wanted to be in London, to be near her. Begging her at least to allow him to visit occasionally, his language was so urgent that he thought she must, she could only concede. He had just sealed it when Maurice came in, followed by Jack Fleming.

'There you are!' the captain exclaimed. 'What the devil were you doing sleeping on your bed in all your clothes? I wanted you to come to the Admiralty with me.' Without waiting for an answer, he went on 'I ran into Jack in the Mall and we've come to take you out for a splendiferous dinner to celebrate.' Then he did come to an abrupt stop. 'George! What's the matter? You look ghastly. Don't tell me that Sophie has cried off, for I'll not believe it.'

Jack said more quietly, 'Dear old fellow, has something gone wrong? Your father — '

He looked from one to the other, his face grey and drawn. 'The report in the paper was quite wrong. Emily Horton is not dead.'

'Good God!' Maurice was astounded. 'Do you mean you've seen her? Where?'

'In a street, off Knightsbridge. She has lodgings and I went there last night.'

Something in his tone caused Maurice to raise his eyebrows, and Jack to look sharply at him. Maurice said, 'George, you three times idiot, it's no great matter to have a last fling at freedom before matrimony, but not for God's sake with Emily Horton! Are you crazy?'

It was Jack who, in amazed tones, put the ultimate question that he neither wanted to ask, nor to know the answer. 'You can't mean — you didn't — '

But they both knew that undoubtedly he had.

Chapter Seven

On her last evening at home Sophie felt, as she was sure most brides must, a sense of apprehension, fear of the unknown future, of a wholly new state of living, her girlhood over. But she only had to look at Jack and Verity to see what married happiness could be. A marriage of convenience of course might be different. George was not in love with her — at least he had never given any sign of it — but he did like her now, she was sure of that, remembering how a few days ago, before driving her home, he had smiled at her and put her fingers to his lips. Surely, surely, in time love would come? On her side it was there already.

The last of her packing done and alone with her mother she said tentatively, 'Being married will be such a change, won't it, Mama? I do want it to be a success.'

'What an odd word to use!' Her mother gave a quick laugh, shying away from what might be embarrassing questions — dear Sophie could be too outspoken at times. 'Well, my love, marriage is marriage and has good and bad in it like everything else.'

'But — to share so much — I mean —'

'My dear, you will learn that some things are a necessity for gentlemen while for us women, well, we have to put up with their ways. For us, our home and children are our portion in life. Now, where did I put your white gloves? Ah, there they are. I must say, I'm glad we went to London to have your bridal gown made. Mrs Sedley could never have achieved such finish.'

She rattled on and Sophie only half listened, gazing at the

gown hung up so carefully. It was beautiful, gleaming white satin, rosebuds of the same material about the hem, a quantity of lace decorating the bodice, while the sleeves ended in a series of little points. Her headdress was of floating gauze, a knot of artificial orange blossom at each side, holding it in place and she thought how beautiful Alethea had looked this morning when she had set it on her own fair head.

Mrs Sterling bustled away and Sophie, glad of the quiet, sat down to write a few more letters of thanks for the gifts she and George had received, all lying spread out in the parlour for the guests to see, but after only one she set aside the pen and went downstairs. Her father was in the act of discussing the order of the hired carriages to take the whole party to Holy Trinity church, only he and Sophie travelling last in their own, but he dismissed the coachman and held out his hand.

'You look very serious, my darling.'

She came down the last step. 'I feel it, Papa. It — it is such a big step.'

He led her into the study and closed the door. 'It is not too late, even now, if you feel you cannot marry George.'

She gave a little laugh. 'Oh no, Papa. Imagine what Mama would say, with all these preparations. She would have an apoplexy!'

'You are probably right.' He smiled back at her. 'But you are happy, aren't you? You have seemed so.'

'Indeed yes, really. It is what I want and I do care very much for him, Papa. It is just that — there are some things I am so ignorant of and Mama will only say that the home and children are what a woman should look for in marriage.'

He laughed out loud at this. 'Well, perhaps, yet I think if pressed your Mama would put love for a husband on the list. But seriously, my dear child, being a doctor makes me understand a great many things that are not generally discussed. I would just reassure you that marriage, which results we hope in children of your own, is a union between you and your husband and is the most natural thing in the world. There's nothing to fear in that.'

Only having the mistiest idea of how this happened, she leaned her head against his shoulder. 'I wish I had not to leave you, Papa.'

88

Stroking her hair, he murmured, 'Yes, we have always been very happy in each other's company, haven't we? But this is the right step for you, as I shall not always be here and I want to see you safely settled with a good husband. Remember what the Bible says — *"For this reason shall a man leave his parents and cleave to his wife, and they shall become one flesh ..."* and it applies as much to a woman. George will take care of you and Aunt Adela has seen to it that neither of you will want for anything. I hope I am not wrong in believing your marriage will be crowned with love.'

'Oh, I hope so,' she whispered into his coat. 'I thought — I thought George was coming down today. He did say — '

Dr Sterling smiled. 'I doubt if your Mama would have welcomed him! And I'm sure he must have many things to do and relatives to deal with, as we have.'

Sophie was quite unable to suppress a giggle. 'I must say, I always find Uncle Mayfield quite overwhelming and poor Aunt Mary is such a mouse and so afraid of him. I don't think that I shall be afraid of George.'

'Of course not.' He patted her cheek. 'Don't worry about anything, dearest. Your happiness is all I care about and tomorrow I shall give you to him in that hope.'

'You and Mama will come often to stay at Plummers, won't you? Now there's something I *am* quite frightened of — it sounds so big!'

'I'm sure you need not let it worry you. When your aunt was ill last year and Mama away, you managed capitally.'

'I think Plummers will be a little different from this dear old house. But you will come?'

'When my patients let me. As your brother had no calling to follow my profession I think I shall have to set about finding a young assistant. Yes, Perks, what is it?'

'It's the wine for tonight's dinner, sir. You did say — '

'Poor Papa,' Sophie teased, 'there'll be no peace for you until it is over. And you'll have it all to do again with Alethea.'

'Not yet,' he said, 'not yet, I hope.'

It seemed likely that rest would be impossible tonight, but to her surprise Sophie slept soundly and didn't wake until

Phoebe was drawing her curtains and Alethea bending over her, calling, 'Wake up! Wake up, it's your wedding day and the sun is shining.'

'What's the time?'

'Half past seven and Phoebe's brought your tea-tray.'

She would have liked a few minutes' quiet to begin the day, but there was no hope of that. Her mother came in, resplendent in a rose-pink peignoir, followed by a manservant bearing the hip bath, and a maid with a large can of hot water, who then scuttled away to fetch more. After that it was all activity, excitement and preparation. And at nine o'clock, bathed and with her hair arranged before being helped into the beautiful gown, Sophie was ready.

'I'm so glad the dear Queen set the fashion for white,' Mrs Sterling said, arranging the folds at the shoulders. 'This lace really is exquisite.'

Alethea had gone to dress with Daisy Patterson and the other bridesmaids, but now everyone assembled in the hall, Aunt Mayfield showing a tendency to begin her tears even before they got to the church, and being severely admonished by her husband to 'buck up, m'dear'.

Gradually they filed out to the carriages, Sophie took her father's arm and they drove the short distance to Holy Trinity. The church seemed full of guests and local well-wishers, for Dr Sterling was known for miles around, and many heads turned to see the bride. Having come here Sunday after Sunday all her life she was glad she had insisted on being married in this familiar place, despite its drawbacks, such as the huge three-decker pulpit that almost obscured the altar and was definitely in the way, and with an encouraging press of the hand and a 'God bless you, my darling,' from her father, she walked steadily up the aisle. Two figures awaited her by the altar steps, the brothers a great contrast, Maurice's taller figure in full dress uniform, George so much darker but looking very distinguished in his wedding clothes. He turned his head slightly as she came, but Maurice swung round to give her a broad welcoming smile. Doubts the sailor might have, but he brushed them aside in his usual cheerful manner, confident his brother would heed his advice to 'pull himself about and consign the past to the bottom of the sea'.

Jack, far more perceptive, was relatively more anxious but he had said nothing to his wife, not wanting to spoil her vicarious happiness in this wedding so soon after her own. Standing in his place in the third pew, he put little faith in George's ability to thrust away the happenings of the last forty-eight hours and to return to the optimism of recent months. One had only to look at his face to see how profoundly he had been affected.

Sophie, on reaching the steps, and her hand being given into George's, glanced quickly up at him. She was shocked at what she saw. He looked tired and drawn, and though he managed a brief smile, it did not reach his eyes. She knew a moment of panic. Oh no, could he be regretting it already? He hadn't come yesterday — had he wanted to call it off? Terror seized her briefly, but then common sense took over. Surely it was merely that he was taking the ceremony with the gravity it deserved? Oh, if only she was at home in her own room, far from being the centre of this momentous and crowded occasion!

But George was holding her hand, no one came forward with any just cause or impediment, and then he was making his vows in a low voice. She recovered, repeated the words, felt the gold ring slide easily on to her finger. For better or worse, it was done! In the vestry she signed her maiden name for the last time and the Vicar, who had known her for many years, offered his congratulations. Then, as Sophie Randolph, she walked down the aisle on her husband's arm.

In the open carriage returning to the house, there were waves and more good wishes from many of the doctor's patients, who had come to see his daughter married. 'That'll be the one to go next,' one elderly woman prophesied, nodding towards Alethea. ''Tis a wonder she didn't go first.'

In the carriage on the short journey, it was Sophie who broke the silence to say, 'It was a beautiful service, wasn't it?'

'I suppose it was the same as all weddings,' was his not very promising reply and after a moment he added, 'I thought your aunt would never stop crying.'

To which Sophie retorted, 'If I was married to Uncle

Mayfield I think a wedding might make me cry,' and had the satisfaction of drawing a brief smile from him. But the conviction that something was wrong, above the solemnity of the occasion, remained.

The reception passed in a haze of greetings, speeches, circulating among the guests, trying to talk to everyone, to remember who had given her what. Lord Randolph took her hand and kissed her cheek.

'No day could be happier for me,' he said affectionately, 'nor could I ask for a daughter I could love more. I trust, dear child, you will let me be a second father to you.'

It was all so hopeful, so propitious, and she felt a corresponding warmth, clinging to him for a moment and whispering, 'Oh yes, please,' before being captured by Lady Louisa, who proposed a visit to Plummers as soon as Sophie felt able to entertain − a prospect that terrified her. Moving on among the crowd, only occasionally glancing at George, who was mingling with other guests, it was impossible not to sense his change of manner, as if he was trying to distance himself from what was happening. How little she really knew him. The prospect of the coming weeks alone with him suddenly seemed daunting, rousing an indefinable fear within her.

Maurice proposed their health in an amusing speech that made everyone laugh, George steadied her hand to cut the three-tiered snowy cake, and then it was all over. Changed into a pretty muslin walking dress of soft blue, she took her place in the carriage that would bear them to the station and the train for Dover, Phoebe and Morgan accompanying them on the box. There was one last glimpse of the waving crowd, Alethea laughing up at Maurice as he made some comment, Mrs Sterling almost as tearful as her sister-in-law, the small figure of the doctor receding as the carriage moved away, leaving Sophie with a sudden desire to jump out and run back. But that was childish; she was Mrs Randolph now. Turning to George she said lightly, 'Did you remark it − Maurice and Alethea?'

'I did indeed,' he answered. 'It was like tinder to touchpaper, wasn't it? She could hardly take her eyes off him.'

'I know. She kept saying how nice it was to have another brother, but she didn't look at him as if that was how she regarded him!'

'Well, I hope she won't get her hopes up in that direction.'

'Why? You could see he was attracted to her – and no wonder. She was looking very beautiful, and he so very handsome in his uniform, too.'

'Maurice has been attracted by and to many girls, but to my knowledge he has no intention of settling down.'

'As to that,' she answered, 'I fear Mama is looking higher for Alethea. She's only just eighteen and a great deal of patience might be required to bring Mama round. Though of course one could point out that Maurice might be an Admiral of the Fleet one day.'

'You misunderstand.' George was not looking at her, but staring out of the window at the streets sliding by. 'I know Maurice. He cares for nothing but the Navy, wants nothing to distract him. He does mean to be an admiral one day.'

'But if they should fall in love? It might change his mind, don't you think? It would be quite delightful, the four of us ...' Her voice trailed away as there was no responding smile.

'It is never wise to start matchmaking,' was his dry comment. 'I doubt we'll see anything more than a flirtation there, in which practice Maurice is accomplished and Alethea not far behind.'

Sophie withdrew a little. This was no way to start a honeymoon, arguing over his brother and her sister. And George, though she could see only part of his face, was wearing a grim look. When he spoke again, seeming to make an effort, it was to remark on Amabel's little boy having, as a pageboy, behaved himself better than usual.

By the time they reached Dover it was getting late in the day. There, boarding the Admiralty mail packet for Ostend, she was in a state of confusion, unable to understand him. He was quite unlike the companion who had set his ring on her finger three months ago. The pleasant conversation and growing ease of manner were quite gone, and he was more like the man she had first met, who had given her

93

the impression of wishing to be elsewhere. Had he wished it today? Did he wish it now as they walked up the gangway in the fresh evening breeze? The sky was clear, turning pink and gold as the sun sank over the horizon.

'You'll have a calm crossing, ma'am,' a young officer greeted her as she stepped aboard, 'though the wind may get up later.'

Never having been on a ship before, Sophie held tightly to George's arm as she walked across the deck. The expanse of sea, the light in the sky above reflected in the water below, the sturdy little ship, the crew about their work, all took her breath away.

'I've only been to the sea once,' she said. 'We had a holiday with Mama at Hastings after Alethea and I had had the measles, Papa thinking it would be beneficial for us, which it was. But to actually travel on the sea is very exciting.'

Her enthusiasm touched him. For good or ill he had married her while deep in desire for another woman, and he began to see he had done her a great wrong. Yet what else could he have done? Either way he had probably wrecked her happiness and his own and must make what he could of it. The last thing Jack had said to him was, 'Be kind to her, George. Kindness is what counts.' Well, he would do his best. She should never know what it was costing him to appear normal, to behave as if Emily Horton had not returned from the dead. Unable as yet to realize how corrosive that effort would be. Managing a smile, he asked her if she thought she would be a good sailor, at which she laughed, remarking that time would tell.

Taking one look at the tiny cabin allotted to them, he said, 'I think I shall leave this rabbit hutch to you and Phoebe and stretch myself out in the saloon.'

Secretly relieved, Sophie agreed and thought it tactful of him to realise how embarrassing it could be for a bride in such tight quarters. She slept well, the gentle swell of the waves a pleasantly rocking motion, and in the morning dismissed all the doubts and forebodings of the previous day. Of course George just felt the solemnity of it all, as she did, wondering naively if he was as shy of her as she was of him. Walking off the ship and on to the soil of the first foreign country that she had ever visited, she felt her spirits rise, and could hardly know that at this beginning of their life together, her husband's sank proportionately.

Within a few days Sophie was quite certain that a profound change had taken place. George was trying to be companionable, she could see that, but thinking of him as he had been a few days before the wedding – relaxed, teasing Alethea, talking amiably with her father – it was impossible not to face the fact that something radical must have occurred. She wanted to cry out, 'Oh, what is it, what's wrong?' But that this would have been a mistake she had no doubt. All she could do was to try to recapture the easy companionship they had achieved during the last few months. Bravely, she made cheerful conversation as they travelled by land from Ostend to the Hague, to the comfortable hotel near the Groenmarkt where George had bespoken rooms for them.

There was no difficulty in enjoying the places they visited, the St Jacobskerk with its spectacular tower and large carillon of bells, the ancient Kloosterkert dating from the early fifteenth century, the old buildings of the Binnenhof. The Huis ten Bosch – the House in the Woods, beloved home of the Princes of Orange fascinated her, as did the museum in the Buitenhof with its walls covered with paintings; and there were other museums specialising in porcelain, furniture, old manuscripts, sculpture. George was never anything but courteous, and telling herself that whatever had upset him it would probably pass, Sophie gave herself up to enjoying it all, every outing full of interest. In the shops they bought a few items for Plummers – a little folding lap desk for Sophie, some china and a dessert service that took her fancy. George remarked they would need a crate to ship all their purchases home.

Trying not to notice that he was often abstracted and seemed not to hear what she said, she found it impossible not to be aware that at times he looked intensely bored, and after a second visit to the Buitenhof she said, 'I'm sorry. I don't think you like this as much as I do, but art, especialy the antiquities, has always fascinated me.'

'It's I who should be sorry,' he answered. 'See as much as you wish, my dear, though this afternoon if you would care to walk in the gardens near the hotel there's a horse sale I've a mind to go to. Take Phoebe with you and look at the Orangery again. You won't need me for that.'

She had discovered that he was an accomplished linguist, fluent in French and German, and with a modest knowledge of both Dutch and Russian. This was hardly surprising after his years abroad, but it was another thing about him that she had not known. Sometimes his sophistication alarmed her, for she had not been aware of it in Clapham, but she was acutely aware of it now as they went about the Hague and he dealt with hotels, waiters, drivers and porters.

'Would you not like me to come with you?' she asked tentatively.

'To a horse sale? Good heavens, no.'

'Oh, I thought perhaps I should − '

'It's no place for women,' was his uncompromising answer, 'and certainly not for someone who doesn't care for horses.'

'But,' she was hesitant, 'I do want to begin to share your interests, as you've been so patient over mine.'

'Pray don't put yourself about,' he said lightly. 'I think we should each follow our own bent and not interfere with each other too much, don't you?'

'I don't know − I hadn't considered − '

'I believe it's better to agree to go our own ways in such matters. In any case, when I took my early walk this morning, I met up with an old acquaintance from my days here, and he invited me to go with him. We may well dine together, so I suggest you have a tray in our room.'

A little crushed, she spent the afternoon wandering in the gardens with Phoebe, admiring the flowers massed in the sunshine, but only half listening to Phoebe's chatter. She didn't expect George to dance attendance on her every minute, but it was their honeymoon and the evening seemed long. Trying to read *The Tenant of Wildfell Hall,* she eventually went to bed and lay there in the candlelight, wondering when he would come. It was near midnight when he returned. She thought he sounded a little drunk, not being used to gentlemen in their cups, but in fact he was only pleasantly inebriated.

'I thought you'd be asleep,' was his first remark as he pulled off his stock. 'You shouldn't have waited for me, I could have slept in the dressing room.'

'I didn't know how long you would be,' she murmured. 'Did you buy a horse?'

'Two. Too good a bargan to miss. I'm not only going to breed Arabs, you know, and must build up my stable.' He disappeared into the adjoining room, calling through the door, 'I shall send for Hedges to take them home. We can't go trundling about Europe with extra horses in tow.'

Perhaps the Hollands he had drunk had impaired his judgement, but there was a moment's silence while he fought a battle with himself. The honeymoon was a strain, the prospect of several more weeks alone with Sophie something he found hard to face, and though aware it was despicable of him, nevertheless he seized the opportunity to shorten it. 'The fact is, I don't want to be away too long. Shall we give Italy a miss and go home at the end of the month? No doubt we can visit there another time.' He added guiltily, 'Maybe next year.'

'Oh − I did want −' She bit back the words. She was not going to beg, in view of what he had said about following their own bent, but it was a great disappointment to be deprived of the Uffizzi Gallery and the wonderful churches in Milan and Florence and Rome.

From his dressing room came the sound of drawers and cupboards being opened, and then he appeared in his night-shirt and rolled into bed, where, settling on his side, he was almost instantly asleep, without even blowing out the candle. About to repair that omission, his wife leaned on one elbow to look at him, dark lashes down on his cheeks, his mouth a little pouted in sleep, his hair untidy.

A sudden, new and totally unexpected desire to kiss his closed lids, his mouth, came over her. Was this very immodest of her? She didn't know. It seemed it was only in sleep that he was really hers. The sharing of a bed and what happened there was very strange. George seemed to want nothing more than to get it over. There was no tenderness, no warmth, no caressing, nothing for her to respond to, and it bewildered her. Having seen so much to hope for before their marriage, this seemed an odd reversal, inexplicable, especially in the light of Verity's confidences of how kind and loving Jack was, accompanied by blushing hints of how happy he made her. Sophie was sure that was how it should be – but for her it was not. Her relationship with George seemed more distant now, instead of closer. Only occasionally did he kiss her and often it was no more than a peck on the cheek.

She thought back to his talk before the horse sale, more or less telling her that he wanted to pursue his own pleasures, to the exclusion of hers! She shouldn't let it hurt, but it did. Blowing out the candle, she crept back into bed, very conscious of him beside her. Perhaps she had expected too much of a marriage of convenience. Yet the question remained – why had he changed? Why was he so cold when she wanted him to love her, to really love her? Though she was seldom given to tears, she could not stop a few trickling down her cheeks.

At breakfast the next morning George picked up a day-old paper and reading it over his coffee, suddenly exclaimed, 'Good God!'

'Whatever has happened?'

'It's Sir Robert Peel. Apparently he had a fall from his horse, on our wedding day, and has died of the consequences. Poor old Peel, he'll be sadly missed, especially by my father.'

'Is his death likely to affect the government, do you think?'

'No. Lord Russell will stay on as Prime Minister until the next election, though I think we may see some changes then. Palmerston seems the likeliest candidate to succeed him, but he's heavy-handed and my father told me the Queen dislikes him. Lord Russell was a more diplomatic choice. "Pam", on the other hand has been better as Foreign Secretary.'

This knowledgeable talk surprised her, for she had not thought George much interested in politics, until she remembered his years in the diplomatic service. Changing the conversation to the satisfactory results of yesterday's sale, he sent off a letter to Hedges. 'And I must see about stabling until he comes. We had planned to move on soon, hadn't we? But I'd really rather we stayed here a few more days to wait for him. I can − ' he hastily changed the first word, 'we can occupy ourselves well enough, I expect.' And aware that his behaviour the previous day had not been all it might, he added, 'Another museum, eh? What would you like to do?'

Responding at once she smiled and said, 'No, I'll not subject you to that. It's such a lovely day after yesterday's showers. Could we not hire a carriage and drive out into the countryside?'

'I'll see about it,' he said at once. 'By the way, I'm dining on Thursday with my friend of last night and some companions of his.'

'I see. Are wives invited?'

'No, my dear. This is strictly for racing talk, brandy and cigars, and not at all the thing for the gentler sex. You don't mind?'

She did, but what could she say? As they drove out into the countryside she pushed it to the back of her mind and gave herself up to the enjoyment of the moment, beside George in the open curricle. The wide, flat scene, the windmills turning in the breeze, the dykes full of water, the little bridges, the Dutch folk about their daily business − all fascinated her. He took her to the old fishing port of Scheveningen and then on to Voorburg with its Roman past where, stopping at an inn, they sat outside under a shady tree and ate delicious Dutch cheese with fresh baked bread and a wine George said was not bad by half. A boy of about three came up to watch them and Sophie smiled and rolled his ball for him while George sat watching her.

Utterly unable to banish his longing for Emily, remembering her on that last morning, her wonderful hair falling loose over the shoulders of her blue dressing gown, he found his marriage an intrusion. Would Emily permit him to visit her? Would she consider being his mistress on a permanent basis? But though there was nothing unusual about such an arrangement, neither was there anything permanent about it. Had he any right to ask it? Suppose Sophie found out?

It was not fair to make her pay for his warring emotions. But the stirring of hope, the growing ease with her over the last months was all gone and he asked himself, how can I live with this? Not, how can Sophie live with it? She knew nothing of it − yet. Quiet, yet not so quiet as he had first imagined; practical, with intellectual interests he did not share; he could only hope, watching her with the child, that she would become pregnant soon, leaving him free to go up to London from Plummers now and again, to indulge his passion for Emily Horton.

It was in this mood that a quarrel flared on the way back. Sophie made the innocent remark that she wished she had brought her sketching materials.

'No doubt we can purchase whatever you need,' he answered, 'but if you propose to spend hours sketching, pray excuse me, my dear. I shall hire a horse and take a ride to Delft.'

'Oh!' she said blankly. 'I didn't intend − I mean − I won't spend too long on it. An hour or so would suffice and then I can work up the sketches at home. That wouldn't bore you too much, would it?'

'Take all the time you want. I'm sure you don't wish me to offer totally useless comments. I once had friends living in Delft and I thought I might call.'

'Without me? On our honeymoon? Wouldn't they think that odd?'

'I don't see why. You will be occupied.'

'I think you are using my wish to sketch as an excuse.' She was surprised at the tart tone to her own voice.

With raised brows he countered, 'Now why should I do that? We have already decided not to live in each other's pockets, haven't we?'

'You have. I don't recall entertaining any such wish.'

'Indeed? I was under the impression it was a mutual decision. You can hardly have expected us to be moonstruck like the Flemings, God help them.' The moment he had said this, he regretted it, and the sneer that went with it. 'Pray, Sophie, don't let us make a mountain out of a molehill.'

'You *will* talk in clichés,' she said with rare petulance. 'It really is worse than gentlemen who make puns all the time, like Uncle Mayfield.'

'My goodness, you are on your high horse today — there's another for you! I hadn't expected it of you, Sophie.'

In sudden annoyance she turned on him. 'What did you expect? A miss-ish sort of wife who would hardly open her mouth? If so, you misjudged me.'

'If you had been like that, I doubt I'd have offered for you,' he retorted. 'Good God, Sophie, I thought we understood each other, agreed we could like each other with enough respect to allow for some latitude, without making too many demands. If you are going to be quarrelling with me on every possible occasion —' he paused, checking the horse by some rocks, 'it is hardly going to make for congenial living.'

Stung, she retorted, 'I'm not quarrelling, but you had no cause to be annoyed over the sketching.'

'I wasn't annoyed — only contemplating a day of boredom.'

'Then by all means do what you want — I'm sure you will. Go and buy some more horses.'

'A sensible idea,' he said coolly. 'At least I am now in a position to do so.'

Her mouth shut hard on an indignant retort. To make the Crabtree money a further cause for sniping at each other would be unpardonable, and after a silent drive home, she hurried upstairs to her bedroom. Standing trembling by the window which opened on to a charming iron balcony, she heard him in his dressing room. Shortly after he knocked and came in, dressed for the evening and expressing surprise that she was not. She rang then for Phoebe and he went down to await her in the saloon.

Alone, she sank down in a chair, covering her face with her hands. Now it was out. His last words on their drive had told her plainly enough that he had married her for the inheritance, wanted it for Plummers and for his horses, needing nothing in return from her but a willingness to leave him to his own pursuits. All that talk of being comfortable together was nothing but a means to an end. How foolish, how tragically foolish she had been! Blinded by her growing love for him, closing her eyes to his lack of response, she

101

saw now that he had been nothing but one of the fortune hunters Papa had warned her about. And in fairness she had to admit that he had never hidden his need for money. Yet she had thought, hoped, seen what she must have mistakenly read as a stirring of something warmer on his side, if only he had been willing to give it a chance. But once the ring was on her finger, all that was gone − oh, it was not fair, it was cruel! She wept, unable to control her sobs. Loving him so much, to be quarrelling so soon hurt almost unbearably.

Springing up when Phoebe came to help her dress, she said, 'I think I have a cold coming. I will go to bed with a book.'

'Yes, ma'am. Shall I ask them to send dinner up?'

'No,' Sophie said, her stomach in revolt. 'Just some soup. Ask Morgan to tell Mr Randolph.'

During the long, lonely evening she tried to read but couldn't concentrate. At last, heavy-eyed and wondering what George was doing, she fell into a sound sleep so that she had no idea when he came up.

Waking alone in the morning, it was obvious that, no doubt out of consideration for her, he had slept in the dressing room. When he came in soon after to ask after her cold, she replied that it didn't seem to have come to anything, though she would be glad of a quiet day. Thus released, George went off to Delft, but not before he took her to a nearby shop and bought her all the sketching materials she needed, and when he returned presenting her with a beautiful pair of Delft candlesticks. A sop to his conscience, she wondered? And then berated herself for such an unkind thought. Pleased with the gift and determined to put yesterday's unpleasantness behind her, she responded at once to his suggestion that as soon as Hedges arrived they should go on to Bruges for a week before returning home.

'A delightful place,' he told her, 'certainly for an artist, full of charming squares and canal walks and quaint houses.'

'Thank you. I would like that very much,' she said at once, 'though I'm sorry if my sketching is tiresome for you.'

'Not at all,' he answered politely and concentrated on his breakfast of ham and Gouda cheese, for which he had a passion.

That evening he took her to dine at an excellent restaurant and she enjoyed her dinner. He seemed to be putting himself out to be his old, pleasanter self and she was glad. Perhaps he felt as she did, that to lay the foundations of their future together with arguments could hardly be fruitful.

But over coffee he ill-advisedly made the remark that he had bought the gentlest little mare, 'Which would suit you admirably. Once we get to Plummers I am determined to teach you to ride, Sophie.'

'I thought you understood my feelings. I really would rather not.'

He made an impatient gesture. 'Can't I persuade you even to try? I did think that under that timid exterior there might be a woman of spirit.'

Colour flooded into her cheeks. 'Timid! I am not timid. What a perfectly horrid word. But I don't see why I have to get on the back of a horse to prove it.'

Abruptly he said, 'I thought you might want to please me in this.'

She struggled with herself, surprised at her own irritation and searching for the right words. At last she managed to say, 'You are my husband, George, and of course I want to please you, but I don't see why you are so intent on forcing me into something I don't feel the least need to do.'

'It will be expected of you at Plummers.'

'Why?'

'It is hunting country and even if you are not brave — ' he hastily changed the word, 'proficient enough for that, you will be expected to attend the meet, and act as hostess if it assembles at Plummers. Horses are part of the country scene.'

'I'm sure,' she retorted vigorously, 'that not all ladies in Oxfordshire ride.'

'Most learn as children.'

'Well, I did not. I would remind you of what you said about us following out own ways, and I won't be bullied into this.'

'Bullied! Good God, girl, I am not bullying you. I am only trying to enable you to enjoy life at Plummers, and riding will be part of that. Really, Sophie, I had no idea you could be so obdurate.'

'No doubt I have a number of other hidden traits that will displease you!'

'That wasn't worthy of you,' he said, which was no more palatable for being true.

She laid down her napkin, glancing round the dining room. They had been talking in low voices but even so the exchange between them and her heightened colour were, she was sure, noticed by the people at the next table. 'Do you not think we should continue this elsewhere?'

'If there's more to be said.' He paid the bill, ordered a cab. But when they were sitting in the dark interior neither spoke. Driving the short distance to the hotel in silence, they went up to their room, where Phoebe was awaiting her mistress.

George disappeared into his dressing room, and when Phoebe had gone came into their room, blowing out the candle before climbing in beside his wife. Wishing her goodnight he settled himself for sleep. Sophie murmured 'goodnight', but sleep was far from her and she was more unhappy than she had ever been in her life, longing for him to take her in his arms and heal the quarrel. But he did not.

In the morning the phlegmatic Hedges arrived, never one to be surprised at anything his master did, and before going off with him to the livery, George thrust a roll of bills into Sophie's little bead bag. 'There, my dear, go out and have a last orgy of shopping. I have told Morgan to accompany you and Phoebe. Presents for the family, eh? I'll be back for luncheon.' He kissed her cheek and took his share of the guilt off to the serious business of dealing with his horses.

He was going to be absorbed in Plummers, in a life she could not altogether share, but she didn't believe she had to give in over the matter of riding lessons in order to win his liking, let alone approval. Having thought, wrongly it seemed, that she had already won it, a streak of obstinacy, obduracy he had called it, made her dig her heels in over this. It was illogical and she knew it, but Plummers surely would offer her other things. At least if she became pregnant quickly that would settle the matter.

But her love for George had received a blow and she withdrew into herself, the warmth and eagerness with which she had become his wife, if not dying, at least buried deep. Her hurt and anger at his jibe rankled. Somehow, someday she would make him take back that unfortunate word.

Not having the remotest idea that his obsession with horseflesh was partly an outlet to hide his own wretched unhappiness, Sophie was aware that the space between them was widening. Conversation was never allowed to become too personal again, and courtesy on both sides was a cool replacement for the forging of new bonds. After Bruges, which Sophie loved enough to enjoy, they turned for home. Neither wished to prolong the time of being alone together and so the honeymoon ended.

Chapter Eight

Her first sight of Plummers was on a hot August evening, several weeks earlier than they were expected. Hedges had brought the horses home, neither his master nor his new mistress having hinted that their return was imminent. The open carriage, hired at Oxford, passed through fields ripe with corn where cutting had already begun, men, women and children lending a hand in the serious business of harvest, and the hot, warm scent of cut grain filled the air. Passing through the gates, hastily opened by the surprised lodge-keeper, they came through an avenue of limes, casting deep shade. The end of the drive opened out into a large circular gravel approach and there the house stood – a long, solid building of grey Cotswold stone with mullioned windows, made striking by the parapet encircling the roof, for into this and over the porch had been woven the letters A.E.R. On one side of the house was a shrubbery, while on the other lay a terrace with steps leading down to sloping lawns and beyond these a lake, shimmering in the sunshine.

'Oh,' Sophie breathed, 'It's beautiful. I had no idea it would be quite so large, so old.'

'Antiquity is not always an advantage,' George said. 'I happen to think good plumbing is more important.'

'You Philistine,' she laughed at him. 'But George, I am quite overwhelmed. To be the mistress of such a place! I never dreamed –'

'I'm afraid it may overwhelm you in other ways,' he answered, with a wry smile at her reaction. 'When you come to look more closely you will observe it is in need of a great deal of renovation. See, the stones have fallen away above the porch, and look at that cornice, quite broken off. I imagine every window will need attention − my father always complained of the draughts.'

'How long have the Randolphs been here?' she asked. 'I see their initials up there in the stonework, and the date, 1617.'

'They aren't ours, but by a lucky coincidence the first owner was a Russell, the initials standing for Arthur and Elizabeth Russell. The house passed through other hands until my grandfather bought it some sixty years ago, intending to live in the south − I think he wanted to found a dynasty! My father brought my mother here as a bride.'

'I can't imagine how he ever left it,' she murmured as they drew up before the porch. To her surprise a maidservant was idling on the steps of the terrace; the girl got an even greater surprise and fled to the rear of the house.

George's brows drew together. The door was open and unattended, for no footman appeared to deal with the vast amount of luggage, and it was he who handed down his wife, offering his arm to lead her into the house. There an astonishing sight met their eyes. The hall was wide and high, a magnificent carved staircase parting at a small landing to lead to either side of a gallery. A fine stone fireplace almost filled one wall and a long table stood before it; on this was a jug of ale and in a large chair sat a footman, his livery undone to reveal his shirt, and nursing on his knee another maidservant, without apron or cap. They were laughing and drinking and had clearly not heard the arrival.

George came to an abrupt halt in the entrance. 'What the devil − '

The footman sprang to his feet, tumbling the girl to the floor, to stand aghast at the sight of a personage who was obviously the master of the house. Fumbling to do up his jacket, he stammered, 'Sir − sir − we didn't expect − Mr Hedges said not for a few weeks − '

'Your business is to expect me at any time I choose to arrive,' George said with such withering sarcasm that the man took an involuntary step backwards. 'What do you mean by sitting there drinking? Where is Mr Watkins?'

'G-gone to the village, sir, to see his s-sister.'

'And Mrs Bodiley?'

'In her room, sir.'

'I see. And you thought you could do as you pleased — what's your damned name?'

'Robert, sir.'

'And what sort of welcome do you call this for your new mistress? How dare you use this part of the house?'

Robert was quaking, seeing dismissal staring him in the face. The girl had scrambled up and begun to cry.

'And what the devil was that female doing on the terrace?'

'I b-believe she'd taken some chicken to the gardener's m-mother.'

'By the front drive? Why wasn't she using the back lane? By God!' By this time George's rage was towering and Sophie, waiting shocked by the door, was in full sympathy with him. How he must hate this! A quick glance round showed her the cobwebs trailing from one picture to another, dust everywhere, candle grease on the floor.

George strode forward. 'Get this mess cleaned up and get out of here. Find Mrs Bodiley and send her to me in the library at once. Stop snivelling, girl. Somebody had better send to the village for Mr Watkins. And is it possible that out of the shambles my house appears to be in we should get some dinner?'

'I'll see to it, sir, I'll see to it all.'

'And fetch me up a bottle of the best claret, no, better make it two. I presume,' the enraged master added with further heavy sarcasm, 'you know your way about the wine cellar?'

Robert's face was scarlet. 'But — but the key will be in Mr Watkins' cupboard, sir, and that's always locked when he's out.'

'Then at least someone has a little sense left. Hasn't Mrs Bodiley a spare key?'

'I believe she may have — '

'Then get it.'

Robert fled, the girl running after him, and in silence George crossed the hall and opened a door for Sophie to enter. The library was a large room, well stocked, and she was distracted for a moment by the thought of the pleasure she would have in browsing through these shelves of books. The windows went almost from floor to ceiling, looking out on the terrace and the ragged lawn, like everything else in need of attention. 'What a delightful room,' she exclaimed in an effort to mitigate George's wrath, but all he had seen were the ashes of a long dead fire in the grate, a small table with a broken leg, a crooked picture.

'I'll have their hides for this,' he muttered, and to Sophie, stiffly, 'To bring you to such a homecoming! I should have seen when I first came down the state everything was in. I am to blame and I am sorry – I'm afraid my horses were my first thought.'

'Please don't distress yourself,' she said quietly. 'We can soon begin to put all to rights. Was it like this when you came down in the winter?'

He shrugged. 'I don't really know. I'd no mind to stay here alone, so I visited my friends the Laytons, who live about four miles away, and I was really only interested in the stables. I saw enough to tell me the place needed a great deal done to it, but the domestic details escaped me.'

There was a knock on the door and it opened to admit the housekeeper, flustered and flushed. She had been having a nap in her room when the horrifying news was brought to her by an almost incoherent Robert, and hastily abandoning her dressing gown, she had struggled into corsets and black bombazine. Mrs Bodiley had been at Plummers since she was twelve, having come as a scullery maid, and now in her fifties considered herself entitled to take life easily. When she saw George's face, however, all comfort fled.

'Sir, good evening. Ma'am,' dropping Sophie a curtsey. 'I do beg your pardon for not seeming ready for you but Mr Hedges never said –'

'Yes, we've already established all that,' George broke in. 'Mrs Bodiley, how could you let the place get like this? When was a fire last lit here – or the grate cleaned?'

'I'm sorry, sir, but jackdaws nested in the chimney last spring –'

'That's no reason for this.' He waved an encompassing hand. 'As for that fellow – Robert, I think – drinking in

109

the hall with a stupid girl on his knee, I am astounded. You and Watkins have been with us long enough to keep better order.'

'Yes, sir, yes indeed, but I didn't know what Robert was up to — I swear I didn't. Simmons left and Robert has not been here that long — '

'And won't be any longer.'

'No, sir, if you say so. The thing is — it's years since his lordship came, or you, Mr George, apart from when you rode over from Mr Layton's last January, and if there's no master or mistress to a house it's all to sixes and sevens. In the old days when her ladyship was alive — '

'Ah,' George said, and his face softened a little, 'the old days. Maurice and I were a pair of scoundrels, weren't we?'

'You were boys, sir.' Her hands were still tightly clasped together. 'I hope you will forgive me and Mr Watkins. He's getting old, poor body, and with never a soul here we haven't kept up the standards as we should.'

'Well, everything will change now. This is your new mistress, Mrs Randolph.'

Mrs Bodiley bobbed again, but Sophie came over and insisted on shaking her by the hand, Dr Sterling having instilled into her that servants should be treated as people, not slaves to do one's bidding, and she was sorry for the woman who was obviously near to tears. 'How do you do, Mrs Bodiley. I'm sure we shall get on very well, and tomorrow you can tell me about all the domestic things I need to know.'

George put his hand on the housekeeper's shoulder. 'My wife is right. Matters can be set in train again. We are here to stay and Plummers won't be neglected again. We even hope to persuade my father to spend a little time with us.'

'Oh, sir — to hear that — to have the family here again, you that I've known since you were born — '

'Don't upset yourself, there's a good woman,' he said hastily, with all the male horror of tears. 'We mean to do great things for Plummers. In the meantime, send the maids up to get the west suite ready for us. I doubt if it's been used

110

for years. And see about dinner. Did you have a key to the cellar?'

'I did, sir, and Robert's gone for your wine, the stairs down there being too much for me now.' She walked to the door and hesitated there for a moment. 'We planned a proper homecoming for you, the servants lined up to greet you – like the old days – but – Mr Watkins'll be that upset – ' She made a helpless gesture. 'I'll set the maids to getting your rooms ready at once, ma'am. As for dinner, we'll do the best we can.'

'I'm sure you will,' Sophie said encouragingly. However it was not a good best. Robert brought up the wrong wine and the master of the house was forced to go down to the cellar himself where everything was dust and cobwebs. Hoping Watkins had kept the wine ledger in order, he found a claret and told Robert to open it and let it breathe while he changed.

Mr Watkins, coming hastily from his sister's cottage where he had been about to sit down to a plate of her stew, arrived to take charge in the dining room. Old and breathless, his trembling joy at seeing 'Mr George' was touching. He nearly wept at hearing they were here to stay and promised miracles in the morning.

'You see, sir, we hadn't expected – '

'I've been made only too well aware of that.' George was struggling through tough lamb chops and poorly cooked potatoes and carrots. 'Now tell me what servants you have.'

'Well, sir,' Mr Watkins filled his empty glass, 'there's Robert, and the maid you saw – '

'Who are both to go in the morning.'

'If you say so, sir. And then there's Cook and a scullery maid, with a boot boy who does the fires – '

'Or doesn't!'

Mr Watkins was wishing he had not lived to see this day. 'I do beg your pardon, Mr George. The fact is, I'm getting old. I'm that pleased to see you back, but you need a younger man for butler. I don't seem able to keep order as I did, and my memory – that's not all it was neither. If you would let me retire, live with my sister, I'd be nearby if you needed me when you've company or such, but of course not until you have someone else in my place.'

George melted a little. 'Of course I'll agree to that, though I'll be sorry to let you go. Like Mrs Bodiley, I've known you all my life. You shall live with your sister – Mrs Box? I remember her well, she used to come in when we had a house party. I promise you, you will live very comfortably.'

'You're very good, sir. After such a return ...' Poor Watkins was overcome and his voice trailed away.

'Well, we'll try to forget about that,' George said, and Sophie added, 'I'm sure I shall need your advice, Mr Watkins.'

George gave him the first vestige of a smile since he had come home. 'And I'm sure you will agree we need a new cook, as soon as maybe! Don't you think so, my dear?' Sophie was forced to agree and he added, pushing away the remains of an indifferent pudding, 'We'll not put up with dinners like this. Yes, I know it was sent up in a hurry, but it won't do. I'll write to Lady Louisa tomorrow and see if she can find me a London cook.'

'I trust her ladyship is well, sir? I remember her being married from this house.'

'So she was, when I was still in my cradle. She is adept at searching out excellent servants and I'll ask her to find us a first-class butler, though you will be hard to replace, Watkins. Footmen – perhaps you can find two in Woodstock or Oxford. As for maids, no doubt they will be forthcoming from the village or nearby – I'll leave that to you, my dear Sophie. You'll know how many we need.' Another thought struck him and he added, 'Do I have a game-keeper?'

'No, sir,' Watkins said apologetically. 'There's been no need and Mr Kidwell died two years ago.'

'Old Kidwell gone? Well, well, he taught me how to handle a gun. That will mean the coverts are all to pot.'

'But there's some good men about, Mr George, only too eager for work. If I may be so bold, my sister's grandson, Henry Box – he's only a lad of twenty odd, but he's a hard worker and sensible and he knows the woods round here.'

'Poaching, no doubt?'

'As to that, sir, I must admit he's been up before the

112

magistrate now and then, but if he has work − '

'That will put a stop to it,' George said firmly. 'Send him to me tomorrow and I'll see what I think. My dear, have you finished that really execrable pudding?'

They sat in the gloomy little parlour for the evening, the vast drawing room still under Holland covers. Sophie found a Boule writing table with paper and ink and began to make a list of the things she wanted to know and check over in the morning, while George drank several brandies and continued to simmer over their disastrous return. On going up to bed they found that the master bedroom had been adequately prepared, with fresh sheets on the large bed, the dressing table polished. Sophie's luggage had been unpacked and her brushes and toiletries set out, Phoebe hovering in her white apron and cap, ready to attend her.

'It's so big, ma'am,' Phoebe was obviously in a state of awe. 'I'm sure I'll never learn to find me way about.' She began to brush her mistress's hair with long, soothing strokes.

'I feel the same,' Sophie answered, 'but I expect we'll get used to it. Has Mrs Bodiley shown you where to sleep?'

'Yes, ma'am, at the top of the house, a room all to myself, being as I'm a lady's maid. I'm that pleased.'

Sophie smiled at her enthusiasm as she chattered on. George's voice and Morgan's sounded from the dressing room next door. Through the arrival and the evening she had felt desperately sorry for him. His pride was wounded and she didn't wonder at it. All she could do was to talk encouragingly of the future. On the long journey home she had thought a great deal about that. Whatever had happened, and even if George had only married her for the money − which she was still reluctant to believe − they were together for the rest of their lives, and it seemed to her that the only way to make the situation endurable for both of them was for her to be cheerful, practical, efficient in the running of his house and in time, hopefully, bear his children. He had seemed to be making an effort to be co-operative, to make impersonal conversation, and this, she thought, was how they must build their lives together, never deluding herself that it would be easy. But here she was, George's wife and the

113

mistress of a great mansion, and when he came to bed, she began, 'There's so much to do. I wonder where we should start tomorrow.'

'The house is your domain,' he said. 'I've to see to the stables, hire a gamekeeper, God knows what else. I wanted to ask the Laytons to dinner to meet you — I think Monica Layton might be a good friend for you, and I've known Charlie all my life — but we can't do that until we have a decent cook. My God, what a shambles to come home to!'

'Please don't let it worry you on my account,' she was beginning, but he hardly heard her.

'When I think what it used to be like! We never came home but someone would have been watching for us, a groom to hold the horses, footmen to open carriage doors, Mrs Bodiley in the hall with the maids lined up.'

'I'm rather glad I escaped that,' Sophie murmured, but he went on, 'I'll have every servant off the place, except Mrs Bodily and Watkins, and a fresh start with people who know their work. When I think of Robert and that girl — by God!' He threw himself into the bed, punched savagely at the pillows and with a muttered goodnight, blew out the candle.

Sophie tried to settle. The bed was very comfortable, but her mind was too alert for sleep after the unfortunate scenes downstairs. She would not have said so to George in his present mood, but she was daunted by the state of everything. How was she to manage such a large domestic scene? Mrs Bodiley would be some support, but she was past her prime. If Lady Louisa sent down a good cook and butler it would help, but she still saw a formidable task in front of her. As for entertaining George's friends, or anyone else, that would have to wait. It would take some time merely to learn the geography of the house ... Eventually she fell asleep to dream she was wandering through vast rooms and endless corridors, unable to find her way out.

In the morning, with the sun shining again, she got up with renewed vigour, and an eagerness to begin.

Over breakfast George told her, 'I'll probably be out all day. I mean to ride over the estate and see what's what.

We own a great deal of land, good hunting country,' he added pointedly and for the second time. 'And I must make my arrival known. I've tenants with small holdings who are probably in arrears and I have to see Jardine, our steward, who is conspicuous by his absence. Watkins tells me he only comes over from Woodstock once a month now, which certainly is not good enough.' He waited while Sophie filled his coffee cup. 'And what about you, my dear? What do you want to do?'

'It's more a question of where to begin,' she said, smiling, 'Mrs Bodiley is going to take me on a tour of the house this morning, and I want to see every nook and cranny.'

'Change anything you want,' he said. 'New curtains, carpets — Jardine will get in touch with a firm of decorators in Oxford that we've always used, when you know what you want done. Probably only the library need escape because of its panelling. Spend as much as you like.'

'Thank you,' Sophie murmured. 'I wonder if this is what Aunt Adela meant me to do with her wealth.'

He threw down his napkin. 'What an odd thing to say. It is ours now, isn't it? And perhaps she would have been glad to see some of it spent on Plummers. I must go.'

Sophie sat on alone for a while with her coffee, wishing she had not made that last remark. But loving George with no hope of return — she did wish he would not always call her 'my dear' — seemed to be making her touchy, which was unusual. Turning her mind from this she contemplated the parlour. The wallpaper was badly faded, the curtains old and too dark for the room, which was north-facing anyway, and the paint was a sad blue.

Ringing the bell for the housekeeper, she then spent the whole morning with her, throwing back curtains, choking on the dust, one rail collapsing where the wood was rotten. On inspecting the magnificent dining room, with its leaved table that could seat thirty people, she found the Turkey carpet in reasonably good condition, but the flock wallpaper was hanging in shreds. She remembered once seeing some in Heal's and determined to send for a catalogue. There was a fine array of silver which Watkins had hastily produced last night, having at least kept it in immaculate condition —

candelabra and sweet dishes, and a great silver épergne on the sideboard. Mrs Bodiley explained that there was a great deal more, 'But with no one here, ma'am, Mr Watkins put all the entrée dishes and such safely away wrapped in green baize. He's getting out what you need at this moment.'

Beside the dining room there was a long drawing room opening at the far end into a neglected conservatory; the small parlour where they had breakfasted; the library; a gun room, steward's room and a music room with a fine piano – probably out of tune, Sophie thought – and, hanging from the stuccoed ceiling, a beautiful and unusual candelabra of painted china.

'This is a lovely room,' she said, 'and facing south, but not much used, I should think. Do you know, Mrs Bodiley, I think I'll change things round, make this the parlour for Mr Randolph and myself when we are alone, and have the piano moved to the present parlour, which is so dark with all those trees and shrubs outside. We can always use lamps if we have music.'

'As you wish, ma'am.' Mrs Bodiley did not like change, nor want to see the place she had known all her life turned upside down, but neither did she want to fall foul of her new mistress, especially after last night. Unlike Mr Watkins, she did not have a sister in the village with whom she could retire!

Sophie ate a lonely luncheon as George was nowhere to be seen and in the afternoon turned her attention to the bedrooms on the first floor. There was scarcely one that did not need renovation and she enquired into the amount of linen, having no doubt the house would soon be filled with visitors, adding, 'We have a great many wedding presents to arrive by the carter, including some beautiful linen. We must make a room especially comfortable for my father-in-law, as I'm sure I can persuade him to come down, for a little while anyway,' and Mrs Bodiley, seeing a mountain of work ahead of her, nevertheless agreed it would be good to see his lordship again.

Mr Jardine, apprised of their arrival, appeared in the late afternoon. Employed as an assistant steward by the Duke of Marlborough at Blenheim Palace in Woodstock, he tried to

116

fit in Plummers as well, with only occasional visits.

'That will have to change,' was George's comment, coming in to find Jardine at work in the steward's office. 'I'm not going to spend half my time sitting at my desk paying bills and doing the accounts. What's it to be, Jardine? Let me know tomorrow,' – and left the disconcerted man to his books. It was settled eventually that the steward should return full time, and George wrote a courteous letter to the Duke, explaining matters, the upshot of which was an invitation to dine at the palace.

Within a week the transformation began. The house was full of workmen, the noise of sawing and hammering echoing through the place from morning to night as broken window frames were mended, a new door fitted to the stable yard, gun racks replaced, and furniture moved. New servants were engaged – a senior footman named James, who quickly got the measure of the house and seemed both efficient and reliable, with an under-footman to assist him. However, the lad who did the fires and carried wood was retained, as being too simple to have given offence, Mr Watkins taking the blame for the state of the grates and chimneys. Two new housemaids were brought in, as well as an under-maid and a scullery girl. The cook was given notice after a particularly bad dinner and Mrs Bodiley had to turn to and cook for her master and mistress, pending the arrival of a replacement.

Only one maid was saved from the wholesale dismissal. Sophie found her weeping over the drawing-room Holland covers as she removed them. She was not the girl who had sat on Robert's knee, but she had used the front entrance and George had wanted her to be sent packing. Sophie spoke to her, and her repentance, and her desire to keep her place, both seemed very genuine. Telling George that she would like to give Mary a second chance, she was sure that her gratitude would win them a loyal servant.

'As you wish,' George said, his first towering anger gone. 'The maids are your affair.'

So Mary stayed and did nothing further to offend, only saying, 'Yes, ma'am ... thank you, ma'am ... at once ma'am ...' if Sophie addressed her.

The house was a rambling maze of rooms, of small, unexpected flights of two and three stairs; there was even a long gallery, running the length of the front of the house just under the parapet, hung with a fine collection of landscape pictures, family portraits being kept for the hall and staircase. Slowly Sophie began to find her way about, and as she searched in old books and manuscripts, she found out the history of the house — how the owner during the Civil War had held it for the King before being forced into surrender and sent off to jail. Surviving this, he had returned at the Restoration to put his house in order again. It was not until the middle of the next century that Plummers passed into the hands of a wealthy Oxford man. Sophie found it all fascinating, the portraits particularly interesting her, and she made George walk round with her, explaining who they were. One in particular in scarlet uniform particularly caught her attention for the face and form were so like Maurice, and she asked who it was.

'My father's brother,' George said. 'Maurice has a look of him, though with our mother's colouring. The poor fellow was killed at Waterloo.'

'What a shame,' she murmured, 'he must have been so young. George, you must have a likeness done, to hang here with your forbears.'

'You too,' he said. 'We must do the thing properly.' He even sounded enthusiastic, and Sophie went downstairs more than pleased.

In the evenings while she sewed, sometimes repairing old but beautiful embroidery that she found about the place, George read the paper to extract all the political news. With Sir Roberts Peel's demise the Great Exhibition lost one of its firmest supporters, and *The Times* came out with a blistering attack on the whole concept. The proposed siting, in Hyde Park, came in for particular criticism to the despair of Prince Albert, and George said he considered it an even bet as to whether it went forward at all.

At the end of two weeks a missive came from Lady Louisa. She was sending them an experienced cook, Mrs Ackland, with the injunction not to be put off by her manner, which left something to be desired, for she was utterly reliable and could produce excellent menus, her soufflés, Lady Louisa knew from experience, being particularly delicious. She would arrive by the weekend and with her a Mr Street, who had been butler to the late Lord Uxbridge and was now looking for a post in the country. Lady Louisa thought him sufficiently experienced, and hoped her nephew and niece would approve, adding that she had a mind to spend Christmas at Plummers. Amabel and Henry would also love to come — what did dear Sophie think?

'Dear Sophie' said, 'Oh, heavens!' but thought it could be very enjoyable, filling the place with evergreens, dancing in the hall, and giving presents to everyone.

'It would be like old times,' George said. 'I'm sure we could persuade my father to come, or rather, you could.'

'I'll try,' she said.

Putting aside the disappointments and uncertainties of the honeymoon, burying her heartache deep, she philosophically accepted the fact that, having married the man she had wished to marry, even if it was not all she had expected, she now had to make his life as enjoyable as possible, her only source of hope lying therein. She wrote glowing accounts to her parents of the delight of poring over catalogues, arranging colour schemes, putting all the wedding gifts to use. On the mantelpiece in the new parlour she set out the candlesticks George had bought her in Delft and he agreed with her over the change of rooms.

'Though of course Aunt Louisa won't like it — she hates change!' Which made Sophie view the descent of that formidable lady with some misgiving.

George smiled at the look of consternation on her face. 'Don't worry, this is your house now.'

She saw very little of him before the evenings. He seemed to be in the saddle most days and his conversation was peppered with such remarks as, 'the cottages in Tinkers' Hollow are a disgrace, they'll have to be re-roofed,' or 'old Jackson owes six months' rent and I can't keep people on charity. They'll have to find the money or go. I can't think what Jardine has been about.' He approved of young Henry Box and prophesied good shooting next year. Absorbed in his horses, exercising his Arabs regularly, it seemed to her

119

that he lavished all his affection on them. Hadn't he said, when they first arrived, that his main concern had been for his horses? There was warmth in him, but not for her. Sometimes during dinner an unfortunate remark would lead to an exchange of words, often sarcastic on his part. She wished she could understand. Throwing herself into plans for the house seemed the best solution for at least there he supported her and approved of what she was doing.

She began to move about the village, to get to know the people, many of whom were employed in varying capacities on the estate. The Rector of the little village church was elderly and lived alone with only a village woman to cook and clean for him, and he was delighted at the advent of a new lady of the manor who took an interest in everything. He was no absentee parson, but an educated and perceptive man, and Sophie often brought him back for Sunday dinner, finding both his sermons and his conversation worth listening to. George approved of him and they talked of the capitals of Europe, for Mr Johnson had visited many in his youth. They were, Sophie thought, beginning to be part of the local life and she was enjoying it. Only one thing was missing and at night she lay by the unresponsive George and longed simply for love. Physical union, she began to see, was nothing if not done with love. Longing too for female company she asked George if she might invite Alethea for a week or two.

George shrugged. 'If you are ready for visitors.'

'I don't call my sister a visitor.'

'She will probably disagree with your colour schemes, having a taste for the vulgar, which thank God you have not.'

It was a small exchange, but it was typical, and in a sense the last words were a compliment, but she did not comment, only suggesting they might ask Maurice as well.

He cocked an eyebrow. 'You are determined to throw them together, aren't you?'

'I gather he has been visiting Clapham quite often while we've been away.'

'I grant you he seemed taken with Alethea's beauty, which was hardly surprising. I wonder if he has discovered the bird-brain that goes with it.'

'George! That was unkind.'

'Perhaps it was. The truth sometimes is. Anyway, Maurice said in his last letter that his ship will be ready in a couple of months so he will be off.'

One morning George insisted on taking Sophie to walk with him to the newly finished stables. Keeping her distance from the Arabs, she did say they seemed beautiful animals, white and proud and strong.

'Come,' he said, moving on and showing her a chestnut of a mere fourteen hands with a white star on her forehead. 'This is the little mare I picked out for you. I want you to name her.'

The mare stared at Sophie with soft eyes and pushed her head forward as if to nuzzle her. Involuntarily Sophie stepped back and George said, 'Good God, she can't hurt you with half the stall door shut. Let her smell you, get to know you.'

Having no desire to be sniffed at, Sophie said in a low voice, 'I do wish you would not try to insist on this, George. You know how I feel.'

'I mean to change that,' was his uncompromising answer as he opened another door to caress and talk to the Arab stallion, a horse of seventeen hands and, to Sophie, enormous.

'I've room for more beasts now,' he said, 'and I mean to start breeding on a large scale, though I'll only let Rojah here cover the Arab mares.'

Really, Sophie thought, when he was riding his hobby he could be very coarse. They walked back to the house together, and she was glad to get away from the smell of horseflesh and straw.

Invitations had been coming in from round the county, but one that George was particularly keen to accept came from his friends the Laytons, who had been abroad. He told Sophie to put on her prettiest gown, and she dressed with care, aware of a certain warmth that he at least wanted her to look nice. Phoebe had learned how to do her mistress's hair to perfection and the finished effect was telling, and the line of the primrose yellow dress was very elegant, the work of the London dressmaker who had made her entire trousseau. About her plain face, she thought wryly, nothing could be done, having no idea how much more attractive it became when she was animated, nor how her eyes lit up when she was interested in something.

Downstairs George nodded his approval and put her evening cloak about her shoulders. 'Very pretty,' was his comment and she murmured that she wanted to appear at her best for his friends.

The September evenings were growing chilly, but the night was clear, and wrapped in a warm shawl, with a rug over her knees, she enjoyed the drive. The Laytons lived in a small Georgian house, built some seventy years previously by a gentleman for his mother, and Sophie liked it at once, half wishing Plummers was as manageable. Monica Layton was a little woman, bright and bustling, with two young children in the nursery upstairs. She immediately gave Sophie a welcoming kiss.

'No ceremony here, my dear Mrs Randolph, or may I call you Sophie? George and Charlie have been friends since they were boys, and set half the county in alarms at their japes, I shouldn't wonder. Dear Maurice too − it was a delight to see him at the wedding. Is he coming down soon?'

She chattered on, making Sophie feel welcome. Charlie Layton was very different, a gentleman farmer, heavily built with a ruddy face and a rather raucous laugh. Good-natured and easy-going, he sat at the head of the table dispensing hospitality and pressing Sophie to more of everything. He drank a great deal and at the end of the meal when Mrs Layton rose and suggested that she and Sophie should leave them to their wine, he said, 'Let's take our port to the gun room, George. I want to show you a new purchase I've just made, perfect weight and balance, I think.'

'Incorrigible,' Mrs Layton said, smiling, and led Sophie into the drawing room, where coffee was brought to them.

In the gun room, after inspecting Charlie's new hunting gun, George pronounced it first-class and added that he would visit the particular gunsmith in Oxford to procure one for himself.

After that they settled down to finish the port, George in an old armchair he had occupied many a time, and Charlie with

122

his feet up on the table. 'It's the best thing in the world, to have you back,' he remarked, 'and settled at Plummers, too, with such a delightful wife. You stayed away too long.'

'Perhaps. The rift with my father went deep.'

'All mended now, as I saw at your wedding. No one will think of that wretched business. Long done for, eh? I read about poor Mrs Horton in the *Chronicle* − oh, a year or two back, I think.'

George set his glass down. 'The *Chronicle* was misinformed, Charlie, as my father was.'

Chapter Nine

In the carriage going home, George said abruptly, 'I'm going up to town tomorrow, just for a day or two — business with Warburton. You'll be alright, won't you, with an army of servants to take care of you?'

'I would be,' she agreed, 'but I think I'll come with you. It would be a chance to spend a little time with Papa and Mama.'

'I don't think so — not this time,' he interposed hastily. 'I mean to ride to Oxford and take the train. I shan't be above a day or two.'

'Why can't you take the carriage and then we can both go?' she broke in, but he repeated, 'Not this time. I'll settle my business and be back all the more speedily if I go alone.'

'But I would like to come. Why can't you spare a little more time and take me? Your father would love to see us, I'm sure, and I could go to Maples and look for a comfortable chair for my bedroom.' She gave him a quick smile, 'I sometimes think our forbears lived in acute discomfort.'

'My grandfather disapproved of anything that would encourage people to sprawl instead of sitting upright.' He gave her a propitiatory smile. 'Well, I'll arrange a visit for us later on, in October perhaps.'

'But why not now, as you are going anyway? Really, George — '

He was growing impatient. 'Really, Sophie! My dear, I have explained and I'd be obliged if you didn't go on about it.'

'I think it is extraordinary of you.' She was tired and growing a little annoyed at his refusal, not inclined to let the matter drop. 'I do so want to see Papa.'

'I'm sorry,' he said in a tone that indicated the opposite. 'I'm sure you have plenty to do here.'

'That is beside the point.' She was aware that she would be wiser to say no more, but she was not feeling particularly wise at the moment. If he wanted so much to go alone, surely it could only be because he wanted to get away from her for a while? 'However, if you have such distaste for my company, I shall find plenty to do. I never see you during the day anyway.'

'The answer to that is obvious enough. After the years of neglect − by the way, did I tell you, I've a mind to go into farming? There's some good land for sale beyond our north border. I must see to that as soon as possible.' He glanced at her but could only see her profile in the dark. 'I can't see why you are making such a fuss about this. You can be unexpectedly wilful at times.'

'Believe me, there are things about you that I did not expect.'

He was tempted to ask what specifically she meant, but he knew well enough and this caused him to withdraw into his corner and fold his arms. They drove the rest of the way in silence, Sophie feeling upset by their exchange. Sometimes he seemed to her quite beyond understanding.

In the morning he was gone before she came down for breakfast, not best pleased with himself as he set out. However, he refused to look the truth in the face. By God, he was her husband and he hoped he was not going to have arguments over every little thing. But escaping for a while to see Emily could hardly be called a little thing.

In Wilton Place Emily's maid said she was out but would be back shortly and would he care to wait? So he sat in her drawing room, the window open on what seemed a very noisy street after the quiet of Plummers. A pile of embroidery with a needle still stuck in it was discarded as if she had gone out in a hurry; several letters lay on the desk; a book was on the table by the armchair − all homely evidence of her daily life, in which he had no part, and he sat on the edge of his chair, his hands gripped together between his knees.

It seemed a long time before the door opened and he sprang

up. 'Emily!' he said eagerly reaching for her the moment she shut the door.

Letting him kiss her, she then freed herself, indicated his chair and sat down opposite him. 'I thought you might have learned a little wisdom, George. It would have been better for you to stay away,' was her opening remark, accompanied by a smile that turned his heart over.

'You aren't glad to see me?'

'I think perhaps I am not. You are a complication, George. But now that you are here, tell me how things are with you. Did you enjoy your trip abroad?'

'Enjoy it! My honeymoon?' he queried in a bitter tone. 'It was not what I think a honeymoon with you would have been. The whole thing is a disaster, Emily.'

'Oh?' She looked at him in swift consternation. 'Why? I don't want to be the reason for that. Or to spoil things for your wife.'

'It is I who've done that. I never should have married her. Even two days before I should have stopped it. The scandal would have been bad enough for everyone, but I'm used to causing such upsets, aren't I?' He gave a short, harsh laugh. 'And it gets forgotten in the end.'

'Does it? Perhaps. Yet I still sense, now that I am beginning to find a place in society once again, that some people remember, look oddly at me. And that poor girl. We did enough damage before, George. You would find yourself hard to live with if we became entangled again − and at the cost of her happiness.'

'Entangled! Is that what you call it? As for happiness, I wonder if anything can be worse than the life we now lead.'

'Is it as bad as that?'

'I don't know − yes, it is. We are like a pair of hedgehogs living together. At the least sign of a difference we each curl into a ball, all our prickles at the ready!'

Emily glanced at him in some amusement. 'I'm sure you are exaggerating. The first months of marriage, if one isn't in love, or even if one is, can be very difficult. Do you think she loves you?'

'Good God, no. We both accepted it as a marriage of

convenience. In any case, I've not made myself particularly likable since – ' he was about to say 'since we met again', but changed it to, ' – since the wedding.'

But Emily was not deceived. 'Then you are being very foolish, George. For good or ill you are married and had best stay away from me.'

'How can I stay away?' he asked in a goaded voice. 'It's you I love, Emily, it always has been. Surely we can't have met again, only to be torn apart once more? Say that I can come – at least sometimes.'

She had sat very still through these impassioned words, but when he got up to come to her, she said at once, 'For what? I cannot think sensibly if I am in your arms. And sensible is what we must be.'

'I don't feel sensible,' he groaned, laying one arm along the mantelshelf, where there were numerous invitations propped up. 'I only know that I love you and can't be parted from you. Let me come – now and again. For God's sake – '

'Certainly not for His sake,' she answered, and he remembered her strong adherence to her Church. 'I am probably damned already,' she went on, with a slightly crooked smile, 'but you – you have to go home and do the right thing by your wife.'

'She need never find out.'

Mrs Horton looked at him in some exasperation. 'That was the most naive remark. You should know only too well how people are "found out" sooner or later in any such deception. If you start visiting me, if some busybody tells your wife why her husband comes to London so often, I would pity your Sophie.'

Shaking his head helplessly, he began to feel it was all beyond his handling, and she went on, 'And I am not going to be any man's mistress on a permanent basis. That is certainly not part of my plans.'

'What plans?' he asked uneasily.

'Marriage,' was her forthright reply. 'Do you think I want to live alone in this little apartment for the rest of my life? We've been lovers, George, oh have we not? And when you found me again in June, that night was like recapturing the past, but it is not the future.'

127

He was out of his seat, pulling her into his arms. This time his mouth found hers, all the pent-up desire and frustration of the last weeks totally engulfing him. This was the woman he wanted, had always wanted — and whom cruel circumstances had denied him when he might have wed her.

At last he was forced to stop, both of them breathless, and she said faintly, 'Oh, don't you see? This will destroy us both — such passionate feelings, they don't, they can't last. We have little else in common. I certainly wouldn't want to bury myself in the country and that, I think, is where your heart is now. But it is not what I want.'

'You can say that, after the last few minutes? I can't live without you, Emily.'

Somehow she freed herself. 'That is foolish. We are not children, and experience has taught me that wild passion has small place in our lives. Oh yes, I want you in that way, it would be pointless to deny it, but I am certainly not, at this stage in my life, going to settle for being a mistress when I might be a wife.'

Aware of desperate hurt, he turned away and wandered to the window, staring out unseeingly.

After a moment she said, 'I think you had better go. In any case, I am going out tonight.'

'You are going out? Who with?'

She gave him a faint smile. 'My dear George, it is really none of your affair.'

Almost violently he retorted, 'Of course it is. Everything about you is my affair. But I know what you mean. I can't ever be your husband and I'm nothing to you now.'

'I wouldn't quite say that,' she murmured, 'but nevertheless it's true. I have my life here in London and yours is at Plummers. How does Sophie like the place?'

This almost seemed an irrelevance and he muttered, 'Very much, I think. Thank God there's enough money for us both to do what we want.'

'And that must be very satisfying, though I've never had experience of it.' She crossed over to the hearth, her hand on the bell. 'You must go, George.'

Reluctantly he said, 'I suppose I must, if you're engaged. With friends?'

She hesitated. 'With Major Bryce.'

'Bryce? *Bryce?* Good God, Emily, are you mad?'

'I don't think so. He was Lawrence's best friend.'

'But after what he did — '

'He will tell me about Lawrence's end. My conscience isn't at rest there.'

At the moment he could think of nothing so delicate as a conscience. 'All I want is to knock his teeth down his throat. If I saw him — '

'But you will not. Nothing would be served by venting your anger on the Major. He only did what a friend might be asked to do.'

He was astonished at her attitude. The truth was that, despite his overpowering desire for her, he did not understand her, or her complex make-up. Curiosity motivated her above everything else and he did not understand this either. Aware he was acting like a jealous lover, nevertheless he said, 'Send Bryce a note, cancel the arrangement.'

'Of course I am not going to do that. I have no reason to and it would be very discourteous.'

'No reason!' He controlled himself and added, 'Then I'll come tomorrow.'

'No, that's no good either. I'm being taken to the opera.'

'Not by Bryce, surely?'

'Certainly not. That would be the height of indiscretion and I am being very discreet these days. I am going with Sir James Kershaw and his sister. Do you know him?'

'No, I don't,' George said in a voice that indicated he wished Sir James in Hades.

'He is a barrister of some repute, with lodgings not far from here and a place in Surrey, near Guildford, I think. I met him through my friend, Mrs Laurie Saunders. He is a widower and lonely — as I am.'

George stirred, not caring for such details, but the last words riveted him. 'So you are sorry for the fellow. Emily, you must not let pity mislead you.'

She laughed at him. 'You really cannot take that proprietory tone. You are not my brother. Do you recall Gerald? He always thought he could tell me what to do.'

129

George consigned her brother to the same place as Sir James. 'I'm not dictating, but your warm heart − '

'Oh, rubbish!' she interrupted. 'You saw a side of me I revealed to no one else, George. Well, Laurence, perhaps, in the early days before his infidelities and his unstable conduct killed all that. Now − I only look to my own welfare. Believe me, I would not have accepted Sir James's invitation merely out of pity. He is charming, cultured, his conversation always entertaining and he makes me laugh. And he's wealthy.'

'My God!' George said with feeling, and she added sharply, 'I will not let my heart rule my head a second time, and nor should you.' She saw the look on his face and in a less stringent tone she added, 'My dear, I am sorry you feel as you do.'

'Don't tell me you didn't feel the same when I shared your bed last June.'

'Of course I did, but it seems to me you haven't been listening to a word I've said. You are mistaking what was between us for the kind of love that makes for a peaceful, contented life − which you must find with Sophie.'

In growing desperation, he said, 'You mean you think that would have been impossible between us?'

She shrugged. 'I rather suspect it would. Anyway, it is pointless to speculate. We really must agree to part.'

He came back from the window where he had been standing staring blindly down into the street, and though not attempting to take her in his arms, lifted one hand to his lips. 'You can't be so cruel.'

'Cruel to be kind − isn't that the saying? It is for the good of us both.'

'I don't believe that. We were born to be lovers.'

'Perhaps, and we were that summer, but fate has denied us twice. And I doubt if we can be just friends. It would be foolish to try.'

Something seemed to be dying inside him but he made one last, desperate effort. 'Emily, don't quite cut me off; let me see you sometimes, talk to you. No more, if you don't wish it.'

She gave him a faint smile. 'And how long would that resolution last? No, no, it is quite and absolutely futile. I won't be your mistress. Can't you see that would ruin my plans for my future?' She stepped back and he released her hand.

Despairingly he said, 'But I can't put you out of my mind, let alone my heart. Of course I want to see you, to know how things are with you, and yes — be your friend if I can be nothing else.'

She shook her head. 'If it became known you were visiting me, it would be assumed that it was not as a friend.'

'And you care for that?'

'Of course, and so should you. I have a new life now.'

'And I would be — what did you call me — a complication?'

'Very much so. People have long memories.' She opened the door. 'You have Plummers, Sophie, children soon, I hope. Be content with that — which is so much. More than you know, perhaps.'

Hardly hearing her, he said bitterly, 'You have changed, Emily.'

'Of course I have, and so have you,' she answered briskly. 'Goodbye, my dear, my once very dear George.'

'Not yet. Oh God, not yet. Let me come on Friday.'

'I thought you were going home tomorrow?'

'If I can't see you tonight, or tomorrow, I'll stay.'

She put his hat in his hand. 'Goodbye,' she said again. 'If Sir James makes me a proposal, which I think he will, I shall probably accept him.'

The door closed and he stood alone in the hall, gazing unseeingly as a nursemaid brought two children in from their walk.

In the Park labourers were at work on the site for the huge glass and iron building that was to house the Great Exhibition. Only one of Colonel Sibthorpe's elms had been saved, to be incorporated actually inside the structure. Over a thousand workmen were engaged, and George stood for a while, momentarily distracted into watching what seemed to be a vast undertaking. There were still prophets of doom who thought the whole thing crazy, but here it was taking shape, supposedly to be finished in the spring when the enormous structure would house crafts, inventions and artefacts of beauty from all round the world. He would have to bring

131

Sophie. And this thought brought him up short. Was he beginning to think like a husband? He must, of course, but how different it would have been if he had never seen Emily again! He could have done it then, grown fond of her perhaps, but now —

Turning away from this vast hive of activity, he headed for St James Street and his club, having no mind to go to Mount Street and be quizzed by his father. Maurice at least was away, staying with friends in Shropshire, according to his last letter, his leave having been extended for some reason best known to the Admiralty.

Settling in the smoking room of his club, George lit a cigar and picked up *The Times,* trying in a desultory way to absorb the latest news. There was a long account of young adventurers setting off for Australia to become rich in the latest 'gold rush'; Britain was buying up the Gold Coast from Denmark in an effort to stop slavery on the west coast of Africa; the Queen was to open the Exhibition on 1st May — but he read without absorbing a single word. At least the paper provided a screen so that no importunate acquaintance could annoy him.

He lingered in London for nearly a week, trying to keep away from Wilton Place, but walking there most days as if hardly of his own volition. Telling himself it interested him greatly, he haunted the building in the Park, watching with a great many spectators as giant girders were swung into place, marvelling at the almost visionary plan of Joseph Paxton. One afternoon he heard a workman say, 'Certainly, Mr Paxton,' and realizing that he was standing close by the actual architect, the Duke of Devonshire's head gardener and creator of the giant glasshouses at Chatsworth, he spoke to him.

Paxton was an alert man in middle age, brilliant in his own field, gardens and gardening his life, the design for this building born out of his lively mind. It had become his dream and he would talk to anyone interested. Always fascinated by the practical and mechanical, George responded, glad to be away from his own troubles for a while.

'The building is attracting more and more visitors, as you see,' Paxton said. 'The Prince himself rides over at times and insists on being kept informed of its progress, every day if you please.'

'I'd not realized it was going to be such a huge affair.' George gazed as an iron girder was lowered by sweating labourers into the pit dug for it, to rear high into the air.

'Yes indeed, the exhibitors – and we have had an enormous number of applicants – will need a great deal of space.'

'I saw the one in Paris a couple of years ago,' George told him, 'but this is much larger.'

'I believe so.' Paxton nodded. 'Have you read that *Punch* has nicknamed it the Crystal Palace?'

'No, I hadn't, but how appropriate.'

'I hope you will come when it is opened, and bring your wife.'

'I mean to,' George answered, and Paxton hurried off to speak to Charles Fox, of Fox and Henderson, in charge of the actual building work.

Yes, it was Sophie who would be on his arm when they came, and he wandered away to his club, bracing himself to go home, to put Emily out of his mind. He would, he must, but to put her out of his heart? That was another matter, yet under all the turmoil he knew that he could not live like this for the rest of his life, nor would it be tolerable if he tried to. He was to dine with her tonight, and he was filled with a deep sense of foreboding that it would be for the final time. So that the last thing he wanted, as he sank into his usual chair in the club, was to hear a familiar voice pronouncing his nickname.

'Randy! I had no idea you were in London. Is Sophie with you? Verity would love to see her. Why didn't you let us know you were coming?'

Glancing up to see Jack Fleming, his usual good-humoured smile on his face, George answered, 'How are you, Jack? Though I see there's no need to ask. No, Sophie is not with me. I came up to see Warburton last Friday.'

'And you're still here without calling on us?' Jack nodded to the waiter to bring him a brandy and soda and sat down beside his friend. 'Is your father well? I've not seen him for some weeks.'

133

'I believe so.'

Jack gave him a sharp look. 'Are you implying you are not staying in Mount Street?'

Fond as he was of Jack, George wished him, or himself, elsewhere. 'Not this time.'

Jack waited for the waiter to serve them and then, taking a sip, sat twisting the stem of his glass in his hand. 'I hope I am not right in my guess at your reason for being so secretive — but no, I can't believe that.' George shrugged and he went on, 'I wish you would tell me I am wrong, but have you been to see Mrs Horton?' And when there was no answer, he added, 'I see.'

Not looking at him, George said in a low voice, 'I suppose you think I am behaving like a lovesick boy.'

'Lovesick you may be, boy you are not,' Jack said with rare vehemence and set his glass down on the table between them. 'I hope you know that you are being an idiot?'

'Certainly!' George said caustically. Outside, the street was quiet, most people gone home, a few gentlemen walking along on their way to dine, carriages passing conveying folk to their evening's engagements. Making an effort, he asked Jack if Verity was at their Kensington home.

'No, she's gone on a visit to her mother — and don't change the subject. You can tell me to mind my own business, but I never have where you are concerned. And I'm not unsympathetic, dear old boy, but you really are courting trouble of the first water. Where do you expect this to lead?'

'God knows.' George lowered his gaze to the carpet, the pattern dulled by years of male feet.

'I'll tell you then — nowhere at all. If Sophie gets wind of why you have come to town, you will make her and yourself miserable. These things do get about, you know. And what about Mrs Horton? I can hardly imagine that, returned from the dead, so to speak, she would be happy to sit in her apartment on the off chance that you might turn up. You're a married man now, you know.' Beneath the lightheartedness of his nature there was a stern streak in Jack Fleming, and it was this combination that had brought George through his worst days. Jack believed in absolute

134

fidelity and had strong ideas on how a man should behave, having no time at all for philanderers; and seeing much good in his friend, it distressed him to see it ignored, buried deep, while the worst and obstinate side of him had the upper hand. He added, 'You haven't told me how Mrs Horton feels about all this. I'm sure she has other ideas for her future.'

George said nothing; Jack's words striking too near home. There was a long silence while they disposed of their brandies. At last he roused himself to say, 'She has said as much.'

'Has she indeed? Then you would be wise to end the whole thing here and now. It is folly to do otherwise. I know some men manage a wife and a mistress, but I don't think you are one of them. You have too much sense to try to live like that. Nor, from what you say, would it suit Mrs Horton. I never liked her, you know.'

Glancing sharply at his friend, George asked, 'Why not?'

'Because, to be quite frank, she's one of those people who is only interested in herself, her plans, her wishes. I pitied her for her unhappiness with Lawrence Horton, who was a pretty despicable fellow, but that's not the point. Can't you see that now, even if you couldn't then?'

George thought of his last conversation with her. 'Even if you were right, which I don't admit, what difference does it make? I love her, so other things are secondary.'

'I wonder if you *do* love her? Now don't bite my head off, but I wonder if it isn't just the residue of what happened all those years ago? I know you desire her, but that's quite a different matter and won't last.'

'That's what she said.'

'Then, for God's sake, let it go. There's nothing but misery and wreckage if you persist.'

Slumped in his chair, as if the life had gone out of him, George said, 'I suppose you are right − you must be right − except that −' he broke off. 'She wants to end things now. I'm dining with her tonight and then −'

Jack leaned forward and gave his knee a shake. 'Then do what's best, let your dining be the last time.'

'Yes − yes, only . . .'

Lightly Jack said, 'When you walk off in the teeth of a

135

gale, it's always the first step that's the worst, you know.'

With his sure touch he had said the right thing, for George smiled a little. 'You're thinking of that storm in St Petersburg and fighting our way back to the embassy through the snow, both of us somewhat in our cups.'

'And I fell into what seemed to be a hole but turned out to be a horse-trough filled with ice. My God, it was cold!'

They parted soon after on an easier note, and George made his way through the darkness to Wilton Place. It was a quiet dinner. Emily seemed to have little to say and he could only think that this might be the last time he sat at her table. He ate little and when the maid had cleared away and brought coffee with the port decanter for him, he said, 'I'm going home tomorrow.'

'Quite right, my dear George.'

'And you?'

'Oh, I shall be very busy. I've a great many invitations to dinners and parties and to the theatre. Sir James likes drama as well as the opera, and next week we are going to see a new young actor of great promise, or so I'm told.'

He did not want to hear any of this. Jealousy tore at him. 'I can't bear to think of you with other men, perhaps marrying again. This Kershaw fellow — '

'He proposed to me last night, during the third act of *The Marriage of Figaro*. Wasn't that appropriate!' George had caught her hand, crushing it, and she added, 'I haven't accepted him yet, but I may. Let me go, George. You are hurting me.'

Savagely he said, 'I want to hurt you when you tell me such things — damn the fellow! Will you accept him? Will you, Emily?'

'I have said I will consider it.' Throwing down her napkin she stood up. 'No, George, no more. You must go now, and this is goodbye. I mean it.'

'You are cruel, Emily. You have no thought of what you are doing to me.'

'I?' She gave him a pitying smile. 'You have your magnificent home, money, your wife, and you want to deny me any or all of that so that you may come to my bed now and again when it suits you. You are the selfish one, George.'

It was like a physical blow. In a daze he took a step towards

the door, where he stood, irresolute. 'I had hoped, but I see
— I wanted, once more —'

'No, indeed not. Much as I would like you to make love
to me, I won't have it. I shall probably marry Sir James and
there's an end of it. I won't let anything jeopardize that. It
was only out of pity I let you come tonight.'

'It is seen!' He put out his hand, touching her hair, pulling
at the pins so that it fell loosened about her shoulders.
Twisting his fingers in it, his mouth just above hers, he
said, 'I could make you — by God, I could!'

'I hope,' she said with a coldness in her voice that he
had never heard before, 'that you would not be so entirely
stupid.'

Letting her go, he made blindly for the door, seizing his
hat and gloves. Stupid! So that was what she thought of him,
that was what he was, and he took his rage and frustration
and misery out into the dark night.

Chapter Ten

Charlie Layton had given George a puppy, a golden setter whom he promptly named Brandy, and on his arrival home Brandy galloped into the hall, barking and leaping and expressing his joy on seeing his master home. Handing his greatcoat to the new footman, James, he was caressing the dog when Sophie came out of the parlour to find out what all the commotion was about.

She said cheerfully, 'Oh George, I'm glad you are back. I've so much to tell you. I've found the perfect material for the curtains and quilt for your father's room, the Laytons have been for tea, and the Rector, and Alethea arrives tomorrow. Papa and Mama are bringing her down.'

Brandy had eased a moment that might have been full of recriminations for his tardiness, but they did not come. He wished they had, for then he could have vented his miserable state of mind on his wife. Instead he bent to give her a perfunctory peck on the cheek. 'Shall we go into the library?'

'It's warmer in the parlour. James, send up a tray of coffee, the master will be chilly after his journey.' And in the smaller, cosier room, she added, 'I hope you have conducted all your business satisfactorily.'

He threw himself into the chair by the fire. 'Some of it.' But if Emily had yielded to him, what then? He thought he must be the biggest fool in Christendom. Rousing himself he asked, 'Did you say your parents will be here tomorrow?' And having seemingly a legitimate grievance he added, 'I thought we had agreed to postpone it until nearer Christmas?'

'Well, yes, but it will be November next week and I want Thea for a long visit.'

'As you please, but it would have been better to wait until you were certain I would be here. Your father would have thought it very odd if I was not on hand to receive them all.'

Busy pouring coffee, Sophie said calmly, 'Well, I thought you would be. Papa saw the chance to get away for a few days and as I'd written to invite Alethea it seemed to fit in very well. You said she would be welcome.'

'Of course.' Aware that he was being churlish over something that was largely his own fault, he gave his attention to his coffee, thankful that his wife could not see into his head nor guess that he had no wish to play host to his in-laws just at the moment, when he was still so sore after his parting with Emily. But he underrated his wife's perception.

From the moment he had come into the hall, she sensed he was not particularly glad to see her, nor to be home, and wondered what had upset him. Everything was going so well at Plummers. However, she was beginning to know him a little and an intrusion into his privacy with probing questions was the last thing he would tolerate. If there was something he wanted to tell her he would do it in his own good time, though confidences did not come naturally from him. Whether they ever would she didn't know and was wise enough to see such things could not be forced.

He put down his cup and asked if the Laytons had come for any particular reason.

'Oh yes, to tell me there is to be a balloon display at the end of next week near Oxford and they wondered if I would like to see it. I accepted, of course, and how Thea will enjoy it! You will come?'

'I doubt it. I've a great deal to see to having been absent for a week, and in the second place I've little interest in the things. I suppose they could be useful for scientific observation, but at the present time seem to be a mere side-show for the gullible.'

'My goodness, that puts us in our place!'

Uncomfortably George said, 'Oh well, go if you wish, but they are far from safe, you know. There was a bad accident after an ascent when I was in Paris and several people were killed, including the wife of the pilot.' Someone had mentioned balloons to him recently but he could not remember where or when.

'I hope there won't be an accident,' Sophie said, but she was undeterred. 'It will be quite thrilling to see one go up.'

He shrugged and asked if she could cope with the arrival of her parents.

She laughed across at him. 'Of course. It's not like having outside people. Family are easy. I shall put them in the blue room, which is finished, but Alethea will have to have one of the others not yet done. At least most of the work is completed downstairs and they won't be tripping over painters and paint-pots. Papa says he can only stay two nights; he has an assistant now, but I don't think he wants to leave him alone for long. How did you find your father?'

He should have expected the same question that Jack had asked, and answered casually, 'Well enough I believe,' which was only an implied lie.

'Do you think he will come for Christmas?'

'It's hard to say. I suppose it depends on how he is at the time.' Changing the subject, he remarked that no doubt Maurice would favour them with a visit when he returned from Shropshire, if the Navy didn't claim him.

'I do hope so. As for Alethea, she is so looking forward to staying here, especially to riding round the countryside.'

'I had forgotten she was so different from you. I'll try to find time to take her out, or she can go with Hedges, or Maurice when he comes. She can mount the mare I got for you, who needs exercise.'

'It was rather unnecessary to point that out.' Sophie kept her voice quiet and gathered up her writing materials, for she had been answering letters on the lap desk they had bought in The Hague. The new parlour was a greatly enhanced room, with new armchairs, fresh cream paint and paper with a Chinese motif that was, so the decorator said, all the rage at the moment. She spent her time in here now, only occasionally visiting the darker music room in the evenings to play the piano. George, who was not very musical, told her she played very well, which made her laugh.

He glanced at her now and then had the grace to say, 'I beg your pardon, Sophie. As you imply, I am a clumsy oaf.'

'I didn't say that, but you seem to have come home in a very disgruntled mood,' she answered lightly.

'I'm only tired. I think I'll have an early night.'

He went out, Brandy trotting at his heels, and she sat on by the fire. Having wondered why he had stayed away so long and watching for him every day, any hope that he would be pleased to see her and to be back at Plummers had faded the moment he walked through the door. Nothing was as she had wished it to be, but at least she was growing to love this house, the village and its people, the friends she was making — more than she knew, for her visits to the sick, and her generosity to those in need were earning her respect and liking. Mrs Box gave it as her opinion that the new mistress of Plummers was a 'right 'un', while her brother wished he could have stayed on in Mr George's service.

There was so much to occupy her that Sophie had early made up her mind to find her fulfilment in the life here. From living in a doctor's house she was well aware of hunger and poverty in the world, and even in this pleasant spot there were the wastrels, the men who drank their wages instead of providing for their wives and children, and it was these thin little creatures, often without shoes or proper clothing, that drew out her sympathy. There was much to do here, people to help, if only —

She braced herself and went up to bed. There she found George apparently already asleep, and she stood for a while looking down at him. It was impossible not to see that for some reason he was far from happy. Why was she so sure that she alone could remedy that? She had no reason to think so, but she was quite certain that only he could give the core, the heart, to the life she had chosen. But he would not unbend, nor admit her to his inner self. A great wave of love and longing swept over her and leaning down she touched his forehead with her lips.

It was the merest whisper of a kiss, but George was not asleep. Feigning it because he did not want any more conversation that night, he lay with closed eyes, but was sufficiently wide awake to be astonished. Long after Sophie had undressed and come to bed, warring emotions were tearing at him. Emily had called him stupid and Sophie had kissed him! It was all too much, and he had a desire to go down to the cold yard and put his head under the pump.

The Sterlings arrived in due course. Mrs Sterling was quite overwhelmed, as her daughter had been, by the size of Plummers. 'My dear,' she said when Sophie had taken her up the sweeping staircase to her bedroom, 'you can make this the show-place of the county.'

'I mean to make it a home,' Sophie said quietly. 'I hope you'll be comfortable Mama?'

'How could I not? Everything of the most tasteful. Dear child, I am so glad for you. Tell me, have you met many people? Do you have satisfactory servants? To walk into such a place – '

Sophie permitted herself a smile. 'It was not quite like this when I came. We have had weeks of noise and workmen everywhere and there's still more to be done, though the worst is over. But yes, thanks to Lady Louisa – I must try to remember to call her Aunt Louisa now – we have an excellent, rather fearsome cook, and a butler who couldn't be bettered. And yes again, we have met a great many people, all very welcoming.' She could not resist the mischievous impulse to add, 'We have even dined at Blenheim Palace with the Duke and Duchess of Marlborough.'

This was beyond even Mrs Sterling's wildest ambitions. 'My dear! Oh, this is splendid. What may you not be able to do for your sister?'

Sophie laughed, but did not comment, wondering what her mother made of Maurice Randolph's visits. 'Dear Mama, it's so good to have you and Papa here.'

Her sister was even more enthusiastic. 'I can hardly believe all this.' She waved an encompassing hand as they went down to dinner together. 'To own this house, to be Lady Randolph one day – oh, Sophie, it's all so grand.'

Sophie laughed, tucking her hand into Alethea's arm. 'It may seem so, but really it's a house to be run like any other, albeit on a larger scale.'

'You must be so happy, and how you must bless Great-Aunt

Adela. Maurice said the other day that she had quite revived the family fortunes, because in a way we all share in it, don't we?'

Sophie gave her a sharp look. 'He's back from Shropshire?'

'Oh yes, more than a week ago. He means to be here by Saturday. Didn't you know?'

'No,' Sophie said. 'That piece of information hadn't reached me.'

'Well, I am surprised. He must have told George when he saw him. You did say George had been in London? But never mind that. Shan't we have an enjoyable time together?'

'Very,' Sophie said quietly.

The dinner was excellent – turtle soup, salmon, jugged hare and saddle of mutton, followed by numerous desserts – and Mrs Sterling, who had a healthy appetite, remarked that Sophie had a treasure for a cook. Thinking of Mrs Ackland, Sophie hid a smile, however she could not fault the dinners she sent up. There was a great deal of news to exchange, Alethea bright and lively as usual, George making a genuine effort to play the host and liking the doctor well enough for it to be no burden. Afterwards, while the two men sat over their port, the ladies chattered in the parlour and Sophie showed them the pieces they had brought back from Holland. She had no chance of a private talk with her father. Nor would it be as it had once been, for now she had anxieties and feelings that must be hidden. Later, when she took Alethea to her room, Sophie closed the door and reverted to the conversation on the stairs. 'You seem to have been seeing a great deal of Maurice since the wedding.'

'Yes, indeed.' A warm colour enhanced Alethea's lovely complexion. 'We have been riding together, and taking drives, usually with Daisy or someone, all quite proper, you know, though Maurice laughs at Mama's propriety, saying we are brother and sister now. He dines with us every so often and he does enliven the table with his naval tales.'

'Are you in love with him, Thea?' And seeing her sister's blush, Sophie laughed. 'Well, there's my answer. Obviously you don't think of him as a brother. Has he spoken to Papa?'

143

'Not yet. But I'm sure he will.' Alethea was curled up on the bed. 'What a pretty coverlet. I used to think how exciting it would be if he became an admiral, only of course now I think, if we do marry, he would have to resign from the Navy. He couldn't go away for two or three-year voyages and leave me alone all that time. I'm sure he wouldn't want that.'

Sophie was aghast. 'Have you discussed this?'

'Oh no,' Alethea said naively, adding, 'but he will want to be with me, won't he? Not the other side of the world?'

Remembering what George had said of Maurice's ambition and single-mindedness, her sister could not for one moment envisage this. 'You know,' she said at last, 'if one loves a man, one has to accept his work, his career, whatever it is.'

'George gave up the diplomatic service.'

'Not for me, for his father's sake and for Plummers, before he even met me.'

Alethea was pouting a little. A lovely child, Sophie thought, but still so immature. She added, 'I think you must not set your hopes too high. You might be asking too much of him.'

Recovering a little, Alethea said airily, 'I don't think so. He loves me − he would do anything for me.'

'Are you quite sure? Aren't you perhaps mistaking a natural gallantry, a pleasure in having a sister, for something deeper?'

'How could I be so deceived? Don't be a spoilsport, Sophie,' Alethea retorted, so that Sophie said quickly, 'I don't mean to be, Thea darling, but −' It was of no use to say any more, she could see that.

'Wait until he comes,' Alethea went on. 'You will see. But don't say anything to George, will you? Not yet. Let Maurice tell him.'

'Not if you don't want me to.' If George could have secrets, so could she, but there was one that she couldn't let pass.

When he eventually came to bed she was still at her dressing table, and her sister was no longer uppermost in her mind. It would be wiser perhaps not to broach the subject tonight, but this would not keep. Dismissing Phoebe, she said, 'I'm surprised you didn't tell me that Maurice was at home and planning to come down almost at once.'

George got into bed and lay staring at the ceiling. Lying always entrapped one. At last he said, 'I wasn't at Mount Street, I stayed at my club.'

'And omitted to tell me? Why, George?'

'I didn't think it mattered either way.'

'Oh? You went for two days and stayed a week – at your club, obviously without going home to your father, and you didn't think to tell me?'

'I'm sorry,' he turned restlessly. 'I suppose I should have done.' Except that, deep in his own troubles he had not considered she might be anxious. 'Come to bed. It's late.'

'Did you see your father at all?' She got up and laid aside her dressing gown.

'No.' To such a direct question he could not lie.

'But you inferred to me that you did.'

'Not directly.'

Taking the remaining candle to the little table by her side of the bed, she said, 'You don't think an inferred lie as bad as a straight-out one?'

He did, in fact, and to his annoyance felt the colour rise in his face. The whole wretched episode was a disaster, but he couldn't explain that. In a hard voice, born out of his own unhappiness, he said, 'It won't occur again. I had my reasons for wanting a little privacy in London, but I don't wish to discuss them. As I had to remind you before, we should, in Maurice's parlance, allow each other a certain leeway.'

'Very well.' She blew out the candle and lay down, with cold sheet between them. 'But I can't help wondering what was so private that you couldn't stay in Mount Street.'

'Oh, for God's sake,' he said irritably, 'let it rest, Sophie. One of your great faults is your inability to let a matter rest. I've told you it won't occur again. Goodnight.' And then, aware of his unpardonable unkindness to the innocent party in this wretched triangle, he leaned on one elbow and in quick remorse kissed her lightly. 'I hope I am forgiven?'

Tears stung her eyes, and hardly able to respond she murmured, 'Oh pray let's forget it,' before turning on her side away from him, her eyes fast shut on the insistent moisture. It was all very well to ask to be forgiven, but for what? What had he been doing in London that was so private? Whatever it was, he was not going to tell her — could it have been because he was seeing another woman? Such a thought had never occurred to her before, but now it presented itself as a possible explanation. At least the lady concerned in that court case was dead, but how did she know if there was not someone else? Had he found love, which he never professed to feel for her, with another woman? The thought totally horrified her, and for a few moments she stared at it and the pictures it conjured up. But this was surely nonsense. In any case she must not let it upset her — as Alethea said, she had so much. But she would have sacrificed Plummers, lived in a small house, anything, if she could have had even affection from George. Not for the first time, she thought of that drive back to Clapham with him, just before their wedding, when he had kissed her hand, smiled at her and told her they would do very well together — how could he have changed so much? It was the money — it must be that that was all he wanted. If he had a mistress she would probably never know. And with her intuitive perception she was sure that he was not a man who would find any joy in such deception. And on her side of the bed, cold away from his warm body, she turned her face into the pillow, her unhappiness equalling his.

In the morning everything looked much better as they entertained their guests, and the two days of the visit passed very pleasantly. George took the doctor and Alethea riding round the estate, while Sophie consulted her mother over patterns of materials and plans for the rest of the house. In the afternoon, however, she secured her father for a walk in the garden while her mother rested and Alethea was in the saddle again. Autumn had come and the gardener's boy was sweeping up the piles of bronzed leaves.

'I have so many ideas,' she said. 'Mr Jardine secured us an excellent gardener, and he and I are planning for next summer. I want a rose garden there, and a mass of bulbs by the terrace wall, with more down by the lake. There's a walled kitchen garden that has been badly neglected, but Chivers has it in hand now and we are going to build a glasshouse for growing peaches and nectarines and perhaps grapes, and he can bring on all sorts of delicious flowers for our conservatory.'

Dr Sterling smiled across at her. 'You are happy, my darling?'

'Oh yes,' she said, but turned her eyes away, looking at the view of the lake. 'How could I not be with such a – ' a moment's hesitation ' – such a beautiful home.'

But the omission of a husband from this reply did not escape the doctor. Over the rest of the visit he watched them closely, and being a man well used to understanding people, saw that beneath the obviously genuine pleasure at playing host and hostess, there was an odd politeness between them that denied any sort of real intimacy. There were no little private jokes, nor exchanged smiles, intimations of things shared. He said no more but he went home a troubled man.

A few days later Maurice arrived like a fresh breeze off the sea, and he and Alethea enlivened the house with their laughter and their fun.

'I'm surprised you have not sailed yet,' George said when his brother arrived. 'It's been an inordinately long leave.'

'Ah, this is my piece of news. Instead of having the sloop I was first ordered to, I'm to command a frigate at present being built at Chatham. How's that for preferment?'

The girls exclaimed, Alethea less exuberantly than usual. 'I'm so glad,' was Sophie's response. 'They must think very highly of you at the Admiralty,' while George said, 'Well done, old fellow. When do you expect to take command?'

'Not for a month or two yet. I might even manage Christmas here. She's a fine ship, George. I've been down several times to see her – she's to be named the *Orion,* a good name, don't you think? How would you feel about riding down with me? There's an excellent tavern where we can sleep the night.' George seemed pleased at the idea and Maurice went on, 'I must admit I'm anxious to get aboard and assess her capabilities, wherever their lordships decide to send us.'

'Won't you have a short cruise first to try her out?' his brother asked.

'We might, of course, hard to say. But there's talk of the China station.'

'The other side of the world!' Sophie exclaimed and he laughed.

'Only what sailors expect. I've sailed there before, and found Shanghai fascinating. I'll bring home some exotic Chinese fallals for your parlour.'

For the rest of the meal Alethea drooped, unusually quiet, but Maurice teased her into better spirits, saying he had made enquiries for Frank's ship and learned it could be in home waters for Christmas, which cheered that young middy's sisters. He also said rather mysteriously, 'I have plans for Frank,' but refused to add to that statement.

At the end of the week Charlie Layton escorted his wife and Maurice shepherded Sophie and Alethea to the balloon show. George had reluctantly agreed to come, but in the end Mr Jardine came in with a crisis concerning the purchase of the new land, and he sent them off without him. However, he heard a graphic account of it over dinner.

'There were two balloons,' Maurice explained. 'One took a flight and the other went up as a captive with anchoring ropes.'

'It was so very interesting,' Sophie put in. 'Charlie talked to the young man in charge, a Mr Fox, who is a nephew of Charles Fox, of Fox and Henderson who are building the Exhibition in London.'

George's attention was caught. 'Do you say so? I visited the site several times when I was in town and actually talked with Mr Paxton. A very knowledgeable man. So young Fox has turned to ballooning? Was he in charge of the affair?'

'No, only the captive one. Mr Layton knew his brother at school apparently, so he explained it all to us, how everything worked — valves and things,' Thea added vaguely.

Maurice laughed. 'I think the finer points escaped you, Thea. You see, George, there's a valve at the top that is closed for flight and opened to release gas when a descent is wanted. There's also a grapnel for anchoring the balloon, and sandbags for ballast which can be released at will. A

148

fascinating process, and I'm determined to take a flight sometime. The car was already fully booked when I applied. But the girls went up in the captive balloon, which I promise you was quite safe as it wasn't released, and they only rose about a hundred feet.'

'The view was wonderful,' Alethea broke in. 'To go up so silently and gracefully, and see the fields and the trees all laid out, and cows and sheep looking smaller and smaller, was quite breath taking.'

'You went up with Monica?' George was amazed. 'Charlie too? He must have weighed down the basket.'

'Car,' Maurice corrected him. 'Charlie was dead keen and he went off with the fellow in charge of the show. The flight cost him twenty guineas − I think his wife wonders what he will do next − but they came down just south of Woodstock and a farm cart brought them back, balloon and all. Mrs Layton is well plucked and didn't turn a hair when Charlie went floating off! She wouldn't go up, of course, because of her interesting condition.'

'So she stayed with Sophie? I thought you said −'

'No such thing,' his brother interrupted vigorously. 'Mrs Layton was with Mrs Fox, so I took the two girls up.'

George stared at his wife. 'Do you mean to say that you − *you* went up? Why, you won't even −' Encountering a speaking look, he finished lamely, 'I thought you didn't care for heights.'

She gave a little shrug. 'Oh, it is not heights I dislike, and this was too intriguing to miss. There were people clamouring to go up and it was only due to Charlie that we got the chance in the captive balloon, which made several ascents until there was no more gas sufficient for it.'

'It comes in cylinders,' Maurice explained. 'Unless, of course, they are near enough to a gas station to fill up from the main supplies.'

The balloon topic lasted quite a while, Alethea laughingly describing the releasing of some of the sand on to the heads of the people below. 'There were a great many spectators and a number of carriages,' she finished. 'The owner must have made a great deal of money. Such a spectacle!'

For the rest of dinner George sat almost silent, but at

149

last he said, 'I'm glad you all had such a good day. Well, Maurice, now that the flat season has started, would you care to go to the Newbury races? I thought tomorrow?'

In their bedroom that night, Sophie said, 'I suppose I should thank you for not making the obvious remark. There is a difference between horses and balloons, for me, anyway.'

Stiffly, George answered, 'I can see you are determined not to forget what I said in Holland.'

'I will own I want to make you take back that word you used.'

'Timid? Well, it was ill-chosen and I beg your pardon for it, for I see it caught you on the raw. Only I wouldn't have thought you one to harbour grudges.'

She put down her hairbrush. Was she doing that? Perhaps, but there was a streak of determination in her that was engaged in a strange battle and she couldn't let go.

Standing warming himself in his nightshirt by the fire and with his back to her, George went on, 'I must admit to being amazed that you stepped into a balloon, even a captive one.'

Sophie was looking at his back and thinking of a book of advice to young females that her mother had given her; it had advised that no woman should make any overtures to her husband until at least the first year had passed, or after the birth of their first child, but throwing caution out of the window she turned towards him. Accustomed now to 'gentlemen's needs', she was acute enough to see that Verity was happy with Jack in a way she was not with George. Maybe only a child would win her way into his heart.

'If I had had Monica's reason for not going up,' she murmured, 'I suppose you would not have thought that timidity. I am sorry I have not.'

'Good God!' He swung round. 'We've only been married for a few months. I shall be glad when it happens, but it's early days and I would never — what a poor opinion of my character you must have! As for that word, I wish you would forget it. I'm sorry I ever used it, but for the life of me I can't see why you won't mount a horse, but are brave enough to go up in a balloon. Most women wouldn't.'

'There have been lady balloonists,' Sophie murmured. 'Charlie told us about a Mrs Green for one. But never mind that. Are you angry with me for going?'

'Angry? No, just amazed, though I don't think Maurice should have let you go up without my permission.'

'Oh, George, don't be pompous.' She saw the annoyance in his face and added hastily, 'It just seemed so exciting. Anyway, I couldn't let Thea go up alone with Maurice.' She gave him a little smile. 'The balloon was not alive and wilful like a horse. Mr Fox seemed to control it very well. By the way, I brought one of the showbills home for you to see. There, on the table.'

Picking it up, he saw in large letters 'BRYCE'S BAL-LOONS, a great spectacle, flights arranged.' But he read no further. Of course! It was Emily who had spoken of them and of Major Bryce, and now the man was intruding into his life once again. Rather hoarsely he said, 'I don't want you to go up ever again — do you understand?'

'Of course I do,' she answered lightly, bewildered by this vehemence. Could it possibly be that he cared? 'There was really no danger,' she added, 'and Maurice wouldn't have —'

'Maurice would do anything scatter-brained. Anyway, it's not that —' He stopped abruptly. 'Just remember what I said.'

It was impossible to understand him, she thought, and it couldn't be because of the ballooning that he was standing there looking suddenly so dejected. Going to him, she ignored the advice in that tiresome book and slipping her hand through his arm laid her head against his shoulder. 'I am sorry if it has displeased you. If you had been there it would have been different. Are you very tired, George?'

'I suppose I am. Shall we go to bed?'

Not exactly freeing himself he leaned forward to blow out the candles and Sophie let him go. Why didn't he take her in his arms, be pleased, admire her for what she had done, give just the smallest reason for her to believe he cared? Instead he was simply cross and she had no idea why. In bed she thought he was not going to come to her tonight, but after a while when it seemed he must have fallen asleep he said in a goaded voice, 'I suppose you think I've been a bear to you?'

'A little grizzly at times.' She gave a low laugh. 'We don't seem to find it easy to live together, do we?'

'No,' he muttered, 'and none of it's your fault.'

'Oh, I can be prickly,' she admitted. 'Mama always said so. It's only because I speak my mind.'

'I'm glad you do. I couldn't stand a "yes, George – no, George" wife.' Moving over he leaned above her, but thought with shame that it was physical need and frustration that drove him, and for the first time wished that he could love her.

After a few weeks Alethea was fetched home in the Sterling carriage, reluctantly because Maurice was staying on for a while. He was enjoying himself, frequenting the races with his brother, looking up old friends and making new ones. Beginning to prepare for Christmas, Sophie put the quarrel and the horrid suspicions over George's London visit to the back of her mind.

In the middle of December they went up to town together. London was dank and grey, the trees in the Park gaunt. As they drove past the building rising against the skyline, Sophie said, 'I'd no idea it would be so large. We will visit it, won't we? I see they're beginning to put the glass in.'

'I suppose it is what everyone will do. It is well named as the Crystal Palace, don't you think?'

At Mount Street, after the first greetings, Sophie drew a stool beside her father-in-law's chair and said, 'We've come to take you back to Plummers for Christmas. We've asked Aunt Louisa; Amabel and Henry are coming with the children as well as my family, even Frank, we think. Do say you will come. We have a lovely room ready for you, the one on the south-west corner, the warmest there is.'

Lord Randolph looked at her. Six months of marriage had given her an added poise, country life putting colour in her cheeks, and he had heard from Warburton, who had it from Mr Jardine, of the vast and tasteful improvements in the house as well as the mark she was making in the village and among the surrounding gentry. Touching her cheek, he nevertheless said, 'I never leave London in the bad weather.'

'But we are in such a mild spell just now,' she pointed out, 'and we have plenty of rugs and hot bricks in the carriage. Do come, dear sir. I want you to see what we have done at Plummers.'

'I've heard a great deal about that, but – '

'Oh, no buts,' she begged. 'We do want you with us. We'll have such a Christmas, you'll see, such as Plummers hasn't known for years. You'll bring Harper, of course, and between us he and I will look after you.'

As George came in then, his father glanced up at him and could not keep back a smile as he said, 'Well, my son, this little witch of yours is persuading me to go back to Oxfordshire with you, against my will, but not, I promise you, against my inclination.'

Sophie kissed his cheek. 'Dearest father, we shall enjoy ourselves so much. When would you like to go – would Thursday be too soon?'

Dismayed that their visit was to be so short, George could do nothing but agree. Then, announcing that he was dining with friends at his club, he left them together and went off through the winter darkness to Wilton Place. There the maid answered the door.

'I'm afraid Mrs Horton is not here, sir. She's gone abroad to one of them watering places.'

'Alone?' The question he should not have asked slipped out.

'No, sir, with Sir James Kershaw and his sister. She told me they expect to be away about two months.'

He left and walked to his club where he ordered a solitary dinner. So it was over. At last he must accept the fact. His life would never run with hers, nor would he go to Wilton Place again. Sure she had decided to marry Kershaw, he wondered if she would return with the thing done. He must forget as she had so obviously done. But how could he? Emily had everything, beauty, wit, charm, intelligence – and passion. Was she going to give all that to this wretched lawyer? It was unthinkable, intolerable. But also inevitable that if it were not Sir James, there would be someone else who would be the recipient of what he jealously termed his own. Abandoning his half-eaten dinner, he emptied a bottle

153

of brandy before going home, long after he knew Sophie would have retired, to the empty bed in his dressing room, worn out by emotions he was beginning to hate. A great longing for peace of mind, for contentment began to rise in him — if only he could find it.

Chapter Eleven

Christmas was a tremendous success. Under George's guidance the outside staff brought in great streamers of ivy and branches of holly while Sophie superintended the preparation of the bedrooms for their numerous guests. George spent considerable time with Mr Street, choosing the wines, the menus being Sophie's province. By now she knew just how to handle Mrs Ackland and prefaced her wishes with such remarks as, 'Of course, Mrs Ackland, you will be familiar with this dish and if you could serve it among others on Christmas Eve − it is his lordship's favourite,' or 'Your pastry is so deliciously light, perhaps you would see if Mr Roberts can send us over some venison for a pie.' The stillroom and the stock cupboard were filled and Mrs Ackland was satisfied that the stuffed goose for Christmas day would be at the peak of perfection.

Lord Randolph found the journey tiring and was glad to reach his room, but the new hangings about the old-fashioned bed and the comfortable chair by the fire earned his approval and he murmured to Sophie, 'Just to my taste. I think I'll go to bed now, if you would be kind enough to send my dinner up.'

She left him to Harper's care, and in the morning, much refreshed, he walked with her about the house, inspecting everything. At the end of the tour, back in the library where he liked to sit, he said warmly, 'You have brought fresh life back into this house, my child. When my beloved Margaret died, the place died too. It was too full of memories for me, but now −'

'I hope I have not changed too much?'

She looked tentatively at him, and he chuckled, 'Not for me, but wait until my sister gets here!'

After luncheon George showed him the new stables and his comment was that he had seldom seen better horseflesh, a remark which pleased his son.

In the evening George wanted to put his father at the head of the dinner table, but Lord Randolph refused. 'No, no, my boy. This is your house now. I should like to sit on Sophie's right — if I may, my love?'

Mrs Bodiley, on a Sunday afternoon visit to the retired butler, informed him that he would be amazed at the change in his lordship. 'I've not seen him so lively since her ladyship died, and he dotes on Madam. He even spoke to me this morning of driving over to see you tomorrow.'

'Well, I never,' Mrs Box exclaimed in a flutter. 'I shall have to set a fire in the parlour,' while her brother blinked and added, 'That's mighty good of his lordship. I never expected — though I did hope to see him at Christmas, Mr George wanting me to help in the dining room. You'll have to put an iron over my best coat, Sarah.'

Lady Louisa arrived with a great deal of luggage and her aged retainer, Delia, and on being ushered into the parlour gazed round her with considerable surprise. 'I can see there have been a few changes. Good heavens, this was the music room!'

Rather dreading her arrival, Sophie explained and asked if she did not think it made a much better parlour.

Her ladyship, conceded majestically that perhaps it did, nevertheless regretted the loss of light for the piano, adding that she did not much care for the fad for all things Chinese. However, she had to admit the whole made a bright, pleasant room.

'If that is the worst she has to say,' George murmured in Sophie's ear, 'we can be thankful!'

The house began to fill. Jack and Verity Fleming arrived to a warm welcome from both George and Sophie, Verity whispering that she was now in an interesting condition and she hoped her darling Sophie would soon enjoy the same felicity.

'Not yet, I'm afraid,' Sophie said, but it was a great pleasure to have her closest friend here and she looked forward to a long intimate chat later.

Jack, meeting George on the landing, said, 'Well done, old fellow, I can see that you've pulled about,' at which George gave him a wintry smile and said, 'At least I can make it seem so.'

The Sterlings arrived on Christmas Eve, and on hearing the carriage, Sophie was at the door when a young gentleman bounded out and up the steps to sweep her into his arms.

'Frank! Oh, you have come. Let me look at you, I do believe you've grown.' She laughed up into her brother's face, delighted at the glowing look of health. 'It's been a whole year.'

'And now you're a married lady! Mr Randolph, how do you do, sir,' as George appeared, 'Only I suppose I should say George now that you are my brother.'

He pumped George's hand, then gazed round the hall, for a moment bereft of speech, giving Sophie a chance to greet their parents and sister. Frank's meeting with Maurice struck her as comic. As they went into the drawing room, the senior sailor emerged from the library and Sophie said, 'This is my younger brother Maurice. Frank, here is Captain Randolph.'

His exuberance instantly tamed, Frank stood stiffly erect and said, 'Your servant, sir. Sophie told me – I have been looking forward to making your acqaintance,' all the while at attention.

Maurice laughed. 'At ease, Mr Sterling. We are not on the quarterdeck now. We are brothers too, so I shall just say I'm glad to meet you, Frank,' thus setting the young man so much as ease that he contrived to follow Maurice around and sit beside him if possible, though still with considerable deference. Thereafter he became Maurice's devoted attendant, passing his cup of coffee, his glass of wine, all with the greatest respect, which tickled his sister. However, he was soon equally happy dashing about the house with the train of excited children who thought him a hero at seventeen.

Amabel and her husband had brought their brood – John

who was four, Louisa Jane, three, and the new baby George Henry with attendant nurse and nursemaid. They filled the house with their noise and fun and John's first antic was to take a tumble down the magnificent staircase from trying to imitate his cousin George's habit of going up or down at least two steps at a time. However, he was not unduly hurt and welcomed the arrival of the Layton children, who inaugurated a game of hide and seek. Louisa Jane, on being thought too young to join in, indulged in a screaming tantrum and had to be removed upstairs. In all this mayhem Sophie was only aware of a deep longing for the day when her own children would romp in this house.

Maurice organized the dancing, George having hired musicians from Oxford for the Christmas days; these might be indifferent in performance but, well fed and with George's punch flowing liberally, the dancers enjoyed themselves too much to care for that. Brandy went wild with excitement and had to be shut in George's study. Charlie Layton, red-faced and hot, but beaming with delight, insisted that they performed some of the old country dances, including the Sir Roger de Coverley, and Lady Louisa actually took the floor with her nephew. Sophie watched them thinking meanwhile how well George looked in evening clothes. Halfway through the evening the Waits came from the village to sing carols and Christmas songs and be regaled with punch and mince pies, while Lady Louisa remarked that they had improved since her day, adding with satisfaction as they went up to bed, 'I don't know when I've eaten better. Sophie, my dear, the cook I sent you seems to be a treasure.'

'A treasure,' Sophie agreed, 'but a law unto herself. You should see her kneading bread. It's a quite terrifying experience!'

The next morning the meet was held at Plummers for the first time in many years, and George confided to his father that he hoped, when Sir Joshua Maxwell retired, that he might be elected Master. Mr Street brought out the stirrup cup while Sophie and Verity stood on the steps to see them go. Verity remarked on how well Alethea sat her mare, in black riding habit with a yellow feather in her hat, her profuse fair hair confined in a net. She had edged her horse near to Maurice's and they were drinking their hot wine and laughing together.

In the evening the party was augmented by more local guests and the dancing went on until past midnight, so that it was nearly one o'clock when Sophie crawled into bed.

'You must be very tired,' George said, 'but I hope you feel it was all worth it. I must congratulate you. We've not had a Christmas like this since I was a boy. You could see how my father and Aunt Louisa enjoyed it all.' He gave a great yawn. 'Thank God it only comes once a year. I really couldn't stand all this uproar more often.'

'But you did like it?'

'I did, oddly enough. When I was abroad all I had were Embassy balls and such, not a family affair like this. Well done, Sophie.' He bent over, and touched her cheek with his lips, and she drifted happily into sleep.

With the exception of Dr Sterling, who felt two days away from his patients were enough, everyone remained to enjoy the fun on New Year's eve. The whole party walked over to the church for the watchnight service and brought the Rector home to drink a toast to the arrival of 1851.

'The year of the Exhibition,' George said. 'May it prosper.'

In the morning Lady Louisa and the Flemings departed. Amabel and Henry with their offspring were to pay a visit to his parents, who lived near Aylesbury, and everything was packed and carried away by James and the under-footman in a flurry of children and nurses. Amabel and Sophie remained alone for a few minutes in the deserted bedroom.

'I must say just this,' Amabel was tying her bonnet strings. 'I've not had so much fun for years. Really, Maurice does make a party, doesn't he? And all the children enjoying themselves were a sight to see. We've not all been together, not at Plummers, oh, for years, not since Aunt Margaret died, and after that — ' She broke off. 'Well, I'm sure you know about that awful court case. I was only sixteen at the time but I remember reading about it in the papers, to the horror of my governess! Papa was alive at the time and we took in several papers — I'm sure Mama never knew I'd sneaked one or two away to the schoolroom. All the family

159

were mortified, but I never thought it was George's fault. It was all that scheming woman's. I think I was a little in love with him then, for all he's my cousin.'

Sophie smiled a little and said, 'I'm not surprised. I've seen that portrait at Mount Street, the one painted for his twenty-first birthday – he was so handsome, and still is.'

'Most people think Maurice outshines him in that department, but George has always been my favourite. I'm so glad you are so happy together.' Amabel had no reason to think otherwise and gave Sophie a hug. 'No one remembers that horrid business any more, but I'm rather sorry Mrs Horton is back in town and still so very beautiful. I saw her at a reception, though naturally I didn't speak to her.'

Sophie stood very still. 'What did you say? Who is back in town?'

'Emily Horton, the lady in the case. Didn't you know?'

'But – George said she had died.'

'Oh, that was a mistaken report in the paper.' Amabel looked suddenly uncomfortable. 'My dear, I'm so sorry. I never thought you might not know. Well, I suppose George thought it all best forgotten and saw no need to tell you. I don't think he knew before he came home last year – neither did I, and I've never liked to mention it to him. He can be very forbidding when he wants.'

'He – nobody told me.'

Amabel caught her hand. 'Don't look like that. It doesn't matter. No one cares for any of that now – nor for her.'

'I hope not,' Sophie said in a low voice. 'Now, have you got everything?'

A maid knocked and came in, saying the children were safely packed into the carriage and Lord Storrington would be obliged if his wife would come down.

Sophie and George saw them off, and then, saying she must see Mrs Bodiley, Sophie hurried away. But instead of seeing the housekeeper she fled to the sewing room, where no one would be at this time of day. It was a small room facing west, with a window seat from where one could see the sun set on clear days. In the distance were meadows, the largest, known as Big Field, grazing some sheep, George's latest project. On

160

the table rows of sewing thread of every colour were laid out in boxes, with needles, pin cushions and scissors ranging from small to large. The linen was mended here, sheets were repaired and sent up for use in the servants' quarters; table napkins were cut out and hemmed by a sewing woman from the village who came in twice a week, an institution set up by Sophie.

She came here sometimes in the early evening to watch the sky, but this morning it was overcast and dreary, with rain beginning to turn to sleet, and it suited her mood better that the fiery beauty of a winter sunset.

It was an unbelievable shock. The woman with whom George had been so violently in love was alive and back in London − and he had not told her. But the reason seemed obvious. Everything was falling into place − his visits to London, his staying at his club instead of in Mount Street, his strange moods. Sitting with both hands to her burning face, and jumping to even more conclusions than there were, she tried to assimilate all that Amabel had said. He had known, since the summer, apparently, perhaps even before their wedding, and had not seen fit to tell her. Having admitted to lying about where he was staying in town, he must have had still more to hide. Telling her about the court case just before their wedding, he had made as little as he could of it, wanting her to think the whole thing in the past, his mistress dead. But that woman, whom she saw only as a misty figure, was apparently far from being in the past and it seemed obvious that it was she whom George went to London to see − though she remembered that he had once said, in the windmill on Brixton Hill, 'not that I would go down that road again.' So he couldn't have known when he made that remark. Or had he? When had he found out that Mrs Horton was alive after all? It must be she who drew George to London, made him lie. Sophie recoiled at the thought. Oh no, no! How could he? Were they still in love after seven years? Lovers even?

Sitting stiffly erect, her hands knotted together, she thought − I'm not going to cry, I'm not − but the tears were close. It was his deceit that was almost the worst blow. Yet honesty on her part made her realise at once how hard it would have

161

been for him to come to her with the truth. Even if he could bring himself to say that the report of Mrs Horton's death was a mistake, was he likely to say 'I am her lover again'? Of course not. He would be discreet so as not to hurt her, but it did hurt – so much. Amabel said Mrs Horton was beautiful – did she then have George enslaved once more? But he was *her* husband and couldn't have married Emily Horton. Had he wanted to? When did she return? Before or after the wedding? Surely it must have been just before, and that would account for the change in him on their wedding day.

Tormented by these thoughts, two tears trickled down her cheeks, but impatiently she brushed them away. She loved him even more than when she had married him, had been nurturing the certainty that one day he would return that love. But now it seemed a forlorn hope. If only that woman had not come back! It had changed everything for George, and she began to see that he too must have been in his turn tormented by what had happened. She began to feel pity for him, and an unreasoning hatred for the woman who had caused all this sorrow. Well, she was not going to give up. The will to fight rose in her – George was hers and she was not going to relinquish her hope for their happiness, one day.

Bracing herself, she stood up, pressing things to hand, and she must face the day. Downstairs at the depleted luncheon table, her mother said, 'You look pale, my love. No wonder you are tired after such a house party.'

'Not really.' Sophie forced herself to be cheerful. 'I suppose it's just the result of so many late nights. George and I usually keep country hours.'

They were still sitting over dessert when a letter was brought in for Captain Randolph.

'Ah,' Maurice was suddenly alert, 'from the Admiralty. My orders, I expect.' He opened the letter and after a quick perusal he said, 'Yes, at last. I'm to board on Saturday, probably sail on Monday. A short cruise to Jersey to straighten out any difficulties and then, as I thought, the China station.' Glancing round, he saw the varying responses, his father looking grave, his brother nodding

162

as if it was only what he had been prepared for, Alethea with a swift flush she could not control, until his gaze rested on Frank.

'Well, Mr Midshipman Sterling, will you care to sail under my command?'

Frank's jaw dropped. 'Sir! *Sir!* Oh, wouldn't I just? But Captain Gilbert − '

'He has released you and will take another lad when he sails again. The Admiralty has arranged it.' Maurice was smiling at the boy's unabashed delight. Turning to Mrs Sterling, he added, 'You were to go tomorrow anyway, weren't you, ma'am? Could you see Frank packed and ready to join me on Friday? I'll take him with me to Chatham.'

'It's very good of you.' Mrs Sterling foresaw a great career for her son under the captain's influence. 'It's a long voyage and we'll all miss him, but he's a sailor now and my husband will agree we couldn't give him into better hands.'

'Thank you,' Maurice said lightly. 'I'll try not to sink the ship!' He chattered on, describing his last visit to China when he was not much older than Frank, and when the meal was finished, said, 'George, if you can spare me a few minutes in the study − '

Mrs Sterling went upstairs to oversee the packing. Frank, still in a daze, was to see to his own, but before he disappeared he gave Sophie a hug. 'Isn't this just splendid? It couldn't be better. He − he's such a capital fellow, isn't he? I mean, fun as a brother at Christmas, but I can imagine what a captain he'll be, though of course once on board I shan't dare to speak to him unless I'm spoken to.'

'Won't you?' Sophie was amused.

'Oh no, it wouldn't be the thing at all. I'm only a middy, you know, but I'll work hard for my promotion.'

Sophie blessed Maurice for his interest in the boy and went away to the parlour with Alethea. 'Come,' she said, 'don't show that woebegone face to the world. You must not wear your heart on your sleeve.

'But he knows, Alethea lapsed into tears, 'he must know what it will mean to me. Sophie!' − as a thought struck her − 'Do you think he's talking to George now − about us?'

'It would be more correct for him to speak to Papa.'

'But Papa isn't here. I can't bear it, this voyage — so far, so long. I hoped — '

Sophie comforted her as best she could, but that evening, changing for dinner, she said casually to George, 'What did Maurice want with you after luncheon?'

'Only to discuss some money matters that he wishes me to put in Warburton's hands.'

'He didn't mention Thea?'

'No. Did you think he would?' He came to stand by her dressing table. 'I hope that foolish girl hasn't read too much into his nonsense. It's all been just his fun, you know.'

'I know, I know — and I have tried to warn her. But you must see, George, how likely he is to turn any girl's head. You don't think he is seriously taken with her?'

'Seriously? I doubt it. But I might be wrong. Only I can't see Thea as a Navy wife. She needs someone who will be there to pet her and care for her, but keep her firmly in hand, and an absent husband could hardly do that.'

'Then he has led her on, let her think — '

'He has just been himself,' was George's dry comment.

He was right, of course, but dinner that night was a subdued affair. Maurice's thoughts were turned totally to his new command, though he did say it was the best leave he had ever enjoyed with two new sisters to enliven it, a remark hardly likely to please Alethea. 'As for Plummers,' he finished, 'the transformation and you two here means that I shall think of it as the place to make for on my next leave.'

Only Frank was scarcely able to contain his excitement. Sophie wished for her father to confide in, having seldom been on really intimate terms with her mother. However after dinner, when they all dispersed about their own affairs, she decided to confide her anxieties in her mother, and followed her to her bedroom.

'Mama,' she began tentatively, 'did you not notice Thea seems a little upset? I really am afraid that she may have hoped too much for an understanding with Maurice, which I don't think will come.'

'Well, my dear, I'm not saying it wouldn't be nice in some

164

ways, but far too lonely a life for her, even if she came to you or us when he was at sea. I hope for better things for her.'

Sophie was obliged to leave it at that as her mother began to talk of the invitation from Lady Louisa for Alethea to spend some of the coming London season with her.

Guessing George and Maurice to be talking guns in the gun room, Sophie went back downstairs for a word with Mrs Ackland about an early breakfast, refraining from ringing for her, for the poor woman had done enough this last fortnight without being summoned to climb the stairs at ten o'clock at night. On her return, seeing the candles still burning in the large drawing room, she went in to see if anyone was there. Surprisingly, the door to the conservatory was open and she had started across to close it when she heard voices.

Alethea's, unmistakeable, was low and intense. 'But I didn't know, at least I never thought − I don't want to wait and wait −'

'Thea, I've never suggested that. We have had a great deal of enjoyment together these last few months, but I consider that Navy wives have a lonely time of it and that's not for you − even if we think we are suited, which perhaps we might be if the situation were different. You are very young and −'

'I'm not,' she retorted in a rising voice that Sophie knew of old to be indicative of tears. 'I'm eighteen, you know I am, and lots of girls are married at eighteen. Oh, Maurice, I can't bear for you to go.'

'Try to understand,' he said gently.' It's not for you, not now at any rate. I'm fond of you, Thea, but −'

'Don't say as a sister!' Her voice rose in wail. 'I can't bear that either, and it isn't true, it isn't. You don't think of me like that − I know you don't.'

'Perhaps not entirely. When I come back − we'll see.'

'When − it's so far and so long.'

'That's the way in the Navy.'

'Couldn't you give it up? We'd be so happy.'

'Good God, no! It's my life, which you should have realised by now. And I won't ask you to wait for me − not dance with other young men, not have a good time at parties because you are promised to me. That is certainly not for you. When I

165

come home I'll take my chances on whether you remember me, or,' his tone was light, 'whether you are married with a brace of children. Now Thea, don't cry.'

Aware she should not be listening, Sophie slipped quietly away. It was all just as she had feared. Poor Thea, she would think her heart broken, and she waited quietly by her bedroom door for her sister to come up. When Alethea did, it was to hurry past, sobs wracking her, and into her own room. Sophie heard the key turn and for the first time felt angry with Maurice.

'He must be quite heartless,' she said to George when he joined her. 'He has led her on, you know he has.'

'She may have seen it that way, but I'll wager she made more of it than he intended.'

'You are as bad.' Illogically, Sophie rounded on him. 'You should have spoken to Maurice.'

'I? I wouldn't think of interfering. I'd get no thanks for it. Maurice has an iron streak under the surface, which perhaps you have never seen, though I've no doubt the men under his command have.' George got into bed and lay with his hands behind his head. 'I warned you a long time ago that Thea had best not set her hopes on him.'

'Poor, poor Thea. She's so upset and it's all his fault.'

'Rubbish. He said quite plainly he enjoyed having the sisters we never had.'

'Well, I think his behaviour is reprehensible.' Sophie got into bed, blowing out the candle.

In the darkness, broken only by the last glow of the fire, he retorted, 'And I think your sister is a born flirt. She enjoys it. And I'm sure you will be surprised how quickly she gets over this, once Maurice has gone.'

Neither spoke again, George thinking it a storm in a teacup and Sophie seeing him tarred with the same brush as his casual brother.

In the morning the Sterlings took Maurice with them in their carriage to London, which Sophie privately thought unfortunate in view of last night's exchange in the conservatory. Alethea was pale and red-eyed, Maurice quieter than usual, and Sophie wondered if he regretted his 'fun' going too far. But she could see he had no intention of changing their relationship.

The weather had turned colder and there was a hard frost whitening the grass as farewells were said on the steps. Lord Randolph had risen early to see his son go and Sophie insisted on putting a warm cloak about his shoulders. George, hating more than he would admit to see his brother go, tramped off to his refuge, the stables, but the old man stood watching the carriage until it had quite disappeard. Two tears trickled slowly down his face.

'A long business,' he muttered, 'two, maybe three years. I shan't see him again, you know.'

'Who is to say?' Sophie tried to speak in a rallying tone. 'We all hope you have years yet.'

'I doubt it. I feel I am living on time I should not have had, though I thank God for it.' He paused and added, 'When you have your children, my love, don't make a favourite – it is a bad mistake.'

'You mean Maurice?'

'Yes,' he answered in a low voice. There were no further tears but the moisture lay on his wrinkled cheeks. 'He always was, but perhaps it was partly because he is so like his dear mother. And he was such an easy, happy child, always biddable, whereas George – I never got to the bottom of him. A dark, sullen boy who kept his own counsel, never confided in me, though I believe he felt the loss of his mother deeply.'

Sophie thought of the young George, lonely and grief-stricken, shut in on himself, brooding over his mother's death, and finding no place of meeting with his father. Were he and Maurice close then? She didn't know, and at thirteen Maurice had gone to sea. Glancing at the ice-encrusted lake, seeing two small boys playing there, the dark and the fair, she remembered the words she and George had exchanged last night and wondered if he had said anything to Maurice this morning. Yet she doubted it. Becoming aware then that her father-in-law was shivering, she said quickly, 'Come in, pray come in at once. This wind is bitter.'

In the library she sat him down by the fire, ordered fresh coffee, and made him drink a little. He thanked her but

167

seemed disinclined to talk. Desperately sorry for him, she was sure that the future must seem long and bleak before Maurice returned, and longed for something to take his mind from the voyage. Knowing what would fill the gap, she felt an inclination to weep too, but she suppressed it — if only, oh if only a child would come.

They sat in silence for a while, and she thought he was dozing, but suddenly he opened his eyes, sat up and said, 'I mustn't be a pessimistic old fool. I am much blessed in you, the daughter I always wanted, and as for George — well, you are making something of him at last.'

'I'm glad,' she said simply. 'I can't tell you what it means to both of us to have you here.' For whatever difficulties she and George had, they were private, and she enjoyed knowing that father and son were finding new pleasure in being together, George consulted the old man on many things concerning Plummers, Lord Randolph responding with a great deal of interest.

But very early the next morning, before either Sophie or George was awake, there was a knock on the door, and in answer to George's summons, Harper, in his dressing gown, came a yard into the room.

'I'm sorry to disturb you, sir — madam — but I've just looked in on his lordship. If you would come — I think he is very ill.'

Chapter Twelve

Without waiting for his dressing gown, George hurried along the corridor, Sophie following with only a wrap about her shoulders. Lord Randolph was indeed ill, flushed and feverish, his breathing short, and he seemed restless, his eyes closed.

George leaned over him. 'Father — can you hear me?'

The sick man opened his eyes. 'Maurice? No, he's gone — Oh, it's you, George. I — I think I may have taken a chill.'

'You have indeed,' George said quietly and Sophie glanced at him, wondering briefly how much it had hurt him always to come second to a younger brother.

'If only Papa were still here,' she exclaimed while George, sending Harper to summon the local doctor, went away to dress. Sophie sat by the bed, holding one of the hot dry hands. She had come to love this old man and could only wait here, praying he would not be taken from them.

In the briefest time Harper reappeared, miraculously clothed, and announcing the doctor had been sent for. 'His lordship had this fever and attack on the lungs before, ma'am, when Mr George was called home,' he said in a kindly tone. 'Please God he'll come through this one.'

'Amen,' Sophie echoed. 'How long have you been with him, Harper?'

'Near on thirty years, ma'am. I've got to know his ways and what he likes. You can be sure I'll do what's best.'

'I'm sure you will,' Sophie said with a faint smile, 'but I'm a doctor's daughter, you know, and not unused to medical

169

matters.' She went away to dress, to be ready when the doctor came.

Half an hour later, Dr Gradely arrived. He had been out all night with a very sick old lady and had been about to snatch an hour or two's rest when Hedges came for him. But, after a quick examination of Lord Randolph, he said, 'You were quite right to send for me.' He suggested several remedies, adding that with careful nursing the patient might pull through.

'Tell me what to do,' Sophie said simply.

For the next few days she scarcely left the room, Harper sharing the nursing and doing what she could not do. He became her devoted slave, confident, after the first doubt, that his master was as safe in her hands as his own. Only when George insisted that she should eat some dinner, or snatch some sleep, did she reluctantly leave her post. He too sat by the bed for long hours, slipping away now and again if he was needed downstairs.

Once, when consciousness returned, Lord Randolph opened his eyes and seeing his son, said, 'George – dear boy – you will see to everything. I know I can count on you.'

A slow flush mounted to George's face and Sophie thought suddenly that perhaps the 'dark, sullen boy' was finally disappearing into the man he was now. She caressed the hand she held on the other side of the bed and said, 'You aren't going to leave us, not yet, dear sir. I won't let you. We need you too much.'

He smiled a little. 'A useless old man? But I would like to stay until . . .' His voice faded into a mumble and Sophie could not raise her eyes to George's. They both knew well enough what he meant.

The days passed. Dr Gradely was in and out, waiting for the fever to break, while the watchers sat on by the bed, in deep anxiety. On the fourth night, Sophie relieved George at midnight, telling him to get some rest. She also sent the valet to his bed, saying, 'You are too valuable to me in the daytime, Harper, for you to do without sleep now.'

'But you will call me if you need me, Madam – if his lordship – '

'Of course. I know how anxious you are.' She gave him a quick smile.

The dark hours passed slowly. Once or twice she held a glass of cordial to the sick man's lips, or turned his pillow to the cool side. The candle guttered and she lit a fresh one, but, exhausted herself with long hours of watching and worrying, towards dawn her head slipped forward on to the coverlet and she slept.

It was daylight, the curtains partially open, when a hand on her shoulder roused her. It was George, and she sat up abruptly, pushing back her untidied hair.

'It's all right,' he said in a low voice. 'The fever's broken. Dr Gradely's here.'

She sprang to her feet as Harper brought the doctor in, but she didn't need telling, seeing at once the change in her father-in-law. His colour was normal and he was sleeping peacefully.

The doctor put his hand on the sick man's pulse. 'I think he'll do now, Mrs Randolph.'

'Oh, thank God!' Sophie burst into unstoppable tears.

'There.' The doctor patted her shoulder. 'You are worn out with watching over him and I don't wonder. You needn't worry any more. His lordship should recover, but it may be slow. He will have to take life very quietly – damage to the lungs, you know. Mr Randolph, take your wife away and see that she has a long rest. I'll sit here until the valet comes back.'

George drew Sophie's hand through his arm and, trying to repress the last of her sobs, she walked shakily with him down the corridor to her room. There he put his hands on her shoulders and looked down into her face. No beauty here, only a pale face, eyes shadowed with watching and reddened by weeping, but this morning he saw things he had not looked for before – unselfish compassion and a genuine love for his father. And for himself? With one finger he wiped the last tears away and said, 'Your care of my father these few days is something for which none of us can ever thank you enough. Now you must at least lie down on the bed and rest. I'll send Phoebe up with some tea, then you must try to sleep.'

Bending he kissed her mouth with a new lingering warmth

171

and then went away, while she sank down on the edge of the bed in a daze of muddled relief and joy.

Lord Randolph mended slowly. The dark winter days were short, and Sophie spent much of her time with him, reading from the *Morning Chronicle* or the *Gentleman's Magazine* which George had sent from London. The paper was full of the coming Exhibition, furious letters declaiming against the potential danger from the thousands who would be flocking to London to visit it, even the Duke of Wellington warning that soldiers would be needed to control the crowds that could so easily be roused to public disorder. As one writer put it, 'Complete idiocy has seized our great men.' Prince Albert was in despair, nearly dead from overwork and infuriated by all the prophets of doom. Lord Randolph predicted a great deal of inconvenience for those who lived nearby, including himself.

'You had best spend the summer here then,' George suggested, to which the old man contrarily replied, 'What, and miss all the excitement?' He became quite animated about it and called Colonel Sibthorpe, who was still protesting in the House of Commons, a witless fool. There were arguments about what amount should be charged for admission, and when Joseph Paxton suggested it should be free, Lord Randolph remarked that all his success had gone to 'the gardener's head and how did he think the country was going to pay for this great palace of glass?

When he was downstairs again he and Sophie played cards; he was very fond of Bezique and Piquet, his thin hands holding the cards carefully, though once when he dropped them he said, 'We must begin again now you know my secrets.'

He revealed other secrets to her — his love for his wife, the enormity of his grief when she died, the feelings he had had that any contemplation of a second marriage, even to give his boys another mother, was totally abhorrent. Abandoning Plummers, he had lived a more and more stultifying and lonely life in Mount Street. Later, with Maurice at sea and George banished, his companions, apart from his sister and her family, had been his political friends and members of his club.

'Cold comfort,' he told Sophie. 'Pride kept me from calling George home − a terrible thing, pride. It can kill as surely as a bullet, and there were times when I felt like recoursing to that.'

So Plummers had lain neglected and forgotten, with corridors and rooms that had known laughter and the fun of boys silent and deserted. He had pushed all thought of it, and the once happy years, to the back of his mind, and apart from instructing Warburton to pay the least number of servants necessary to maintain the place, never spoke of it.

Now, however, he smiled at Sophie and said, 'You have restored this house in a way I never dreamed of. If there is a heaven from which to look down and observe us, my Margaret must be pleased.'

His words warmed her, all the more when he added, 'And George is a different man. I'd no idea he would come to care so much for the life here, but it's obvious that he does, and you have had a hand in that too, I shouldn't wonder. When he is a father the metamorphosis will be complete. Why, my dear child, what's the matter? Have I said something to upset you?'

'No, no.' She blinked back the threat of tears. 'I'm only tired and a little stupid this afternoon.'

'You are worn out with caring for an old nuisance,' he said, stroking her hand, and she was thankful that he did not attribute her mood to anything else. But it was true that George had taken to country pursuits. He hunted twice a week in the season, was always in the saddle inspecting the estate, especially his newly acquired farmland, and had taken to having long consultations with his farm manager. He talked pigs and geese and sheep with Charlie Layton until Monica and Sophie declared they were becoming a pair of bores. He came in at night, often muddy and tired but with a healthy look of satisfaction, and with two of his Arabs in foal was looking forward to their arrival. Sophie thought he was more relaxed, less touchy, his father's illness having brought a new understanding between them, but the hope Lord Randolph had spoken of still seemed as far away as ever.

173

Seeing the old man's concern, at once she began to talk of her plans for a village school. The nearest one at Woodstock was a long way off, and the younger ones arrived home exhausted, sometimes crying with tiredness, and she was determined to put an end to that.

At the end of February his lordship decided that he was well enough to go home. George and Sophie both pressed him to stay but he shook his head.

'You are a kind pair, but I am beginning to miss London and my club, and it's time I went back to my own house.'

'This is as much your house,' George said.

'Not now. I abandoned it for too long, nearly ruining it into the bargain, obstinate old fool that I was. Now it is yours, my dear boy, and a fine job you are making of it. I shall come again in the summer. No doubt the Exhibition will drive me out of London – crowds and carriages milling everywhere, and a great deal of nuisance even in Mount Street, I shouldn't wonder. Would you both care to go to the opening? This morning's post brought me an offer of tickets.'

Sophie was instantly enthusiastic, George slightly less so, saying he would get away if he could. 'If Leah has foaled, and Jassy too, by the end of April,' was his proviso.

'But that's no reason why Sophie should not come and stay with me,' Lord Randolph said firmly.

He departed a few days later and life settled down to the normal routine. Sophie became absorbed in the plans for building and endowing the village school and even George studied them in the evening and, setting aside a piece of land for the project, went with Sophie to Oxford to talk to a recommended builder. He seemed to her gentler since his father's illness and in consequence she was happier, but the longing to become pregnant grew. Keeping busy she tried not to think of it too much, though the vision of children playing by the lake would not leave her. George never mentioned the subject but she knew how much an heir would please him.

However, the days went pleasantly by, and they shared companionable evenings.

One morning George came into her painting room with a letter in his hand. 'I've been looking for you. I suppose I

174

might have guessed you'd be at your damned painting.'

Sophie put down her brush. 'And I don't have to guess that you've probably been with your damned horses!'

'*Sophie!*'

'Well,' she conceded, unable to keep back a smile. 'I know I shouldn't swear, but you asked for that.' There was a smudge of green paint on her hand which she inadvertently transferred to her cheek.

George flung himself down in a chair and gave way to unusual laughter, drawing a responsive giggle from his wife. 'I'll say this for you,' he said when his mirth had abated a little, 'I never know what you're going to say next. You've quite restored my temper.'

She gave him a quick smile. 'What did you want me for?'

'Well, it's this matter of old Jacob Watts. Since his wife died, that rascally son of his has moved in with his thoroughly disagreeable wife, and apart from making the old man's life hell, they're behind with the rent. Jacob never was, and now I'm sure the son takes the rent money and spends it at the Green Man. I could throw them all out of course, but – '

'I know them,' she said. 'I used to visit Mrs Watts before she died and take her something occasionally, but when I last went to take Jacob a piece of venison pie, young Mrs Watts was insolent and wouldn't let me in, though she took the pie. She said the old man was asleep.'

'They've got to go,' George said firmly. 'I'm not a charitable institution. However, I don't want to turn Jacob out with them. He's served the estate for too many years.'

'Can he manage the rent on his own?'

'Not really. I suppose his wife taking in sewing helped, but without that – '

'She did several household things for me.'

'I know, and as you are about the village so much I wondered if you had any ideas. Jacob doesn't seem to have any relatives and since his wife died there's no one to care for him but that wretched son. Quite apart from that, if young Watts isn't going to pull his weight, which he isn't, I must have the cottage for a farm worker who will. It's a tied cottage, so he's no right to stay there doing nothing.

175

It's only Jacob I'm concerned about.'

Sophie thought for a moment. The she said, 'What about Henry Frant and his wife? They've room enough in that farmhouse now that their son has joined the Army and their daughter is in service. They already have Mrs Frant's old father with them and he and Jacob could keep each other company. I'm sure Mrs Frant would agree, she is such an amiable woman.'

His brow cleared. 'Now I would never have thought of that, but what if the two old fellows can't agree?'

'They already play cribbage together now and then,' Sophie told him.

He got up. 'I'll go and see them at once. Thank you, my dear.' He gave her a sudden grin. 'Now you can go on with your damned painting.' And with that he left her laughing over her canvas.

She thought she had seldom seen him in so good a mood. He had turned to her for advice and she had been able to suggest a solution for his problem. A warmth crept over her. Surely, now, he was putting the past, and Emily Horton, behind him, immersed in all his new responsibilities. It was impossible not to hope so.

As the spring approached and the weather grew warmer Sophie spent more time in the garden, and she was there one afternoon in March, watching the planting of the new rose bushes, when a balloon and Major Edgar Bryce came floating down to take a disastrous hand in their affairs.

She saw the balloon some way off and both she and Chivers watched in fascination as it came gently towards them, a large ball of bright red and blue and gold, she thinking it looked like the one she had seen at the ascent last autumn.

Chivers said, 'There's a queer thing, ma'am. Why folks want to go up in that basket affair, I can't guess. Looks mighty dangerous to me.'

'It's not really.' Sophie smiled at his incredulous gaze. 'I went up in one last year but it was quite safe as it was still tethered to the ground.'

He looked at her with respect. 'Did you now, ma'am? That were brave of you, even if it was tied up.'

'An interesting sensation,' she told him. 'Look, it seems to be coming down. It can't land here.'

The balloon skimmed over the roof of the house and over their heads so that they could clearly see the two men in the car, one holding the rope controlling the valve, while the other was untying the grapnel. One of them shouted down to her, but she could not make out what he said, and with the grapnel hanging loose the balloon cleared the lake and the trees of a small copse beyond, descending out of their sight.

'Well, I never,' the gardener said. 'It must've come down in Big Field. Whatever next?'

'Oh dear.' Sophie tried to see what was happening by mounting the terrace steps, but the balloon was invisible. 'We had better go and see if it has landed safely. I hope no one is hurt.'

The car appeared to have come down without mishap, the grapnel having caught in a ragged alder bush, and the great balloon now deflating rapidly, almost on its side and flapping like an uncontrollable monster amid a muddle of ropes. The two men were busy expelling the last of the hot air, taking care the covers were not torn.

'Are you hurt?' Sophie called and she and Chivers hurried through the wicket gate into the field. 'Did you mean to come down here?'

The elder of the two men straightened and came towards her. 'Ma'am, how kind of you. Thank you, no, neither we nor the balloon are damaged. We were about out of hot air, and seeing this large field we made for it just in time. I must apologize for trespassing on what is presumably the property of that large house?' She became aware of her gardening apron, the floppy straw hat tied under her chin with a scarf, and wondered if he thought her one of the staff. 'Yes, it's our field,' she told him, 'but the important thing is that you landed safely. It must be hard to guide something so obviously independent.'

He smiled at her, certainly not now mistaking her for a servant. 'It's not always easy, but I've had a great deal of experience. Allow me to introduce myself — Major Edgar Bryce, at your service.'

'Oh.' She took his profferred hand. 'I came to a ballooning

display last autumn near Oxford. Was that yours?' Having had time now to observe him she saw a man of perhaps forty, of average height, sturdy and well made; he had thickly curling dark brown hair, a neat moustache and small beard, and his brown eyes were sharply alert. Flashily dressed in a light green coat decorated with a velvet collar, check trousers and waistcoat, and his shirt frilled and tucked, he was not a man one would fail to notice, and she remembered now having seen him in the distance on that day, taking up the free balloon with several excited passengers, including Charlie Layton.

He bowed slightly, saying, 'I'm delighted, ma'am. Did you come up? I don't recall — '

'Only in the tethered balloon, but I enjoyed that. One day perhaps — '

His companion, having assured himself that the balloon was safely flattened, joined them and was introduced to her as Stephen Fox. Shaking the hand of this fresh-faced young man, Sophie said, 'I do remember you, sir, from last autumn. I am Mrs Randolph, and that is our house back there. You sailed so gracefully over our roof, though at one point I thought you might land on it.'

'I try never to do that,' the major retorted with a laugh. 'I've been ballooning a good few years now and though there are accidents, I've never yet, thank God, ended up sitting on someone's roof.'

Laughing, she said, 'Now it's come back to me — Bryce's Balloons, I saw the sign. What do you do with it now?'

'We have to get hold of a cart, or young Stephen here could hire a horse somewhere and ride back to my place near Henley to bring our own — with your permission, ma'am?'

'Of course,' she said at once. 'You are welcome to use one of our farm carts. My husband is out today, but I'm sure he would have no objection.'

'And he is?'

'George Randolph, sir, the eldest son of Lord Randolph who really owns Plummers and this land.'

A flicker of recognition in his eyes, instantly suppressed, caused her to ask, 'You know him, sir?'

'I know of Lord Randolph,' her unexpected visitor answered, 'though I've not had the pleasure of making

178

his acquaintance. I've only lived in Oxfordshire a few years, but I did hear that his lordship lived in London, and that this place had fallen into disrepair.'

'So it had, until we came last summer.' It did not occur to her to ask him if he knew George, for surely he would have told her that he did. Yet at the mention of George's name an odd expression had crossed his face, which if she had known him better, she might have recognized as presaging pure mischief – a gleam of devilment that had got him into trouble on more than one occasion. But she saw only that he was a good-looking man with a pleasant manner.

Sending Chivers off to see about a cart she had no hesitation in adding, 'Now, while your balloon is being packed up, may I not give you some tea?'

He accepted smoothly, and leaving his assistant to supervise the folding and loading of the balloon, he followed her into the house. Hastily removing her apron and the ungainly hat, she rang for tea. When it came, he sat in George's chair by the fire, drank his tea, and answered her questions about ballooning.

'If I ascend from my land at home,' he explained, 'there is no gas main to which I can attach a pipeline, so I have to use hydrogen in cannisters, which is more expensive, though more efficient. Coal gas is unreliable and varies in quality, but I don't expect such technicalities to interest a lady.'

'Oh, but they do. After I had visited your display I read an account of the Montgolfier brothers – they started it all, didn't they? I found it a quite fascinating story, such ingenuity and courage.'

He was relaxed, leaning back in his chair, amusement in his dark eyes. 'You must let me offer you a flight one day, ma'am, in return for your hospitality. I have permission to make an ascent from Hyde Park during the Exhibition. Might you be in London for that?'

She answered that she and George would be staying in Mount Street for the opening, and he begged her to attend his ascent. Smilingly she agreed that if it were possible she and her husband would come, which for some reason seemed to amuse him.

Looking round the large drawing room, taking in the

179

present air of prosperity, he remarked on the fine pictures and the beautiful porcelain displayed in a cabinet. Quite at her ease, she told him how they had found Plummers last summer and the army of workmen they had had to bring in.

'There is still a great deal we want to do, of course. My husband's interests lie very much with horses, particularly some Arabs he brought home from Morocco over a year ago, so the stable block was the first thing he wanted to repair. My concern, with the summer coming, is the garden and new glass houses — perhaps I need Mr Paxton to build one for me!'

He laughed and said, 'You have not been married long, I think?'

'No.' Sophie was sure she was blushing a little. 'Since last summer. My father is a doctor in Clapham and although we have a comfortable house, coming here was a great change for me.'

'It must have been a prospect to daunt any lady, but may I say this room shows your excellent taste.'

She acknowledged the compliment, asking in turn if his almost equally recent move had pleased him.

'An uncle left me his house — nothing like this, of course — small but comfortable and with quite a sizeable amount of land, so much better for my purpose. A large mansion with little land would be no good to me; my balloons need space.'

Everything about him spoke of success and self-confidence, and she thought perhaps he had inherited 'quite a sizeable' income with which to indulge his hobby, though his next words disabused her of the idea that ballooning was a mere sideline for him.

Explaining the possibilities of ballooning — their practical use of balloons for military observation, as well as for pleasure trips — he remarked that people always seemed willing to watch, or take an active part in a spectacle, and that he had had an enthusiastic reception in America.

Mr Fox came in to say that he was going with the cart, and somewhat to Sophie's surprise, the major said, 'Yes, do so by all means,' and made no move to accompany him.

As they sat on together she began to wonder if he was

waiting for George to return, wanting to meet him perhaps, though she had no idea why, unless it was to thank them both for their hospitality. Beginning to wish he would go, though wondering if she should ask him to stay for dinner, she was thankful to hear George come in.

'My husband is back,' she said rather unnecessarily, as they heard his voice in the hall. 'He will be pleased to make your acquaintance, Major Bryce.'

'Will he indeed, ma'am?' he queried, which she thought an odd reply. She was not kept in ignorance of his meaning for long.

The door opened and George came in, prepared to be courteous to an unexpected visitor, whose name Mr Street did not know. But he stopped dead on the threshold, a sudden rush of blood to his face.

'Good God!'

'As you so rightly say.' Bryce got to his feet. 'Well, this is a strange thing, Randolph. I'll not offer you my hand as rejection is not something I would care for.'

'You're damned right,' George retorted. 'What the devil do you think you are doing, drinking tea in my house? The sooner you're out of it the better.'

Sophie had listened to this exchange in growing amazement. 'George! What can you mean? The major is here by my invitation.'

'But not by mine.' George had not moved from the door where he remained with one hand on the knob.

Looking from one to the other, she said, 'It is quite obvious that you and Major Bryce are aquainted, though until this moment I was ignorant of it. Sir,' she turned to Bryce, 'you didn't say − '

'You didn't ask,' was his amused reply and she wondered why he appeared to find the whole encounter something to bring that odd smile to his face. He added, 'When I landed this afternoon, I had no idea whose property this was but I must admit that when you told me I was tempted to take your husband unawares, to see what seven years had done to him. A great deal, it seems, with this place and,' he inclined his head gracefully, 'a charming wife.'

'Well,' she said, not quite mollified by this, 'I consider

181

that somewhat underhanded of you. George, the major is our guest. At least come and sit down.'

He broke in to say roughly, 'The last thing I want is to sit down anywhere with him. You know nothing about this, so I suggest you leave us.'

Bryce leapt on the blunder. 'So she knows nothing, eh? How deceitful of you, Randolph, though only what I would expect from you. You are good at deceit, aren't you? And you have not told your lady of your past?' The major was beginning to enjoy himself – there was nothing he liked better than an affray of any sort.

Realising the door was still open to curious ears, George closed it and came further into the room. 'What I did or didn't tell my wife is none of your business. But you are a damned liar in saying I'm a deceiver. Of course she knows the bare outline, which was all that I considered necessary,' he added pointedly.

Edgar Bryce leaned one arm along the mantelshelf and laughed. 'Half-truths, eh? Well, you always were a dishonourable cur, and apparently still the same. I consider you in part responsible for my friend's suicide.'

Sophie gave a stunned 'Oh!' and glanced at George, whose face was dark with anger as he crossed the room.

'How dare you? And in my own house?' Becoming aware of his wife, standing rigid in disbelief at what she was hearing, George said sharply, 'Sophie, I have asked you to leave us, while I knock his damned teeth down his throat.'

She did not move, but stayed, aghast at the sight of the two men, one cynical and amused, the other seething with emotions that amazed her. Nevertheless she said sensibly, 'Certainly not. While I am here, at least you will not, I hope, behave like a schoolboy. What is all this about?'

'Let it alone.' George's voice shook. 'You will obey me, if you please.'

'I don't think I will until you are calmer. Major Bryce, perhaps it would be better if you were the one to leave.'

'Willingly,' he agreed in a sardonic tone. 'I think perhaps I've achieved enough for one afternoon!'

'Did you plan it?' George demanded. 'Did you bring that

abominable contraption down on my land on purpose? But for *what* purpose, eh?'

The major shrugged. 'That at least was accidental. I'd no idea you were playing the squire at Plummers, though I'd been told your father owned it. Fortuitous, don't you think? Enabling us to air past grievances perhaps?' He glanced at Sophie. 'It is obvious your husband has been less than honest with you, ma'am, for I don't believe you know what lies between us.'

George strode across the room, sending the small gate-legged table flying and the tea things with it. Above the sound of smashing crockery there was that of a stinging slap as George hit Bryce in the face. Sophie gasped, even more stunned when the major without hesitation slapped him back.

'Stop it!' she exclaimed. 'Stop it, both of you − what can you be thinking of? I'll not have this in my drawing room!' But neither of the men paid the least attention.

'There!' Bryce taunted her husband. 'Now what do you want? A duel on your lawn outside? Rather out of date, duelling, don't you think?'

'Get out!' George hurled the words at him. 'Get out or I won't be responsible. God! I'd like to kill you, here and now.'

'I think Mrs Randolph might not care to have my blood added to the mess on her carpet.' Stepping over the broken crockery, Major Bryce sauntered to the door as if he dared George to lay lands on him. 'Well, do you want to try? I assure you it wouldn't be easy. The boot might end on the other foot − though *I* have no mind to end in court!'

'Go to hell,' George exploded. 'Get out of my house and don't come back, you evil-minded devil. When I think of the anguish you caused − '

'I? I was merely a spoke in the wheel of your wicked dealings − though I may still have a surprise in store for you. The other party concerned no longer bears me any ill-will, you know.'

George turned his head twice, as if trying to assimilate this, his voice unsteady as he retorted, 'I don't believe you − liar!' Sophie laid a hand on his arm but he shook her off. 'Go,' he

183

repeated, 'or a horsewhip is what you'll get.'

'Oh, I'm going,' — the unwelcome visitor's smile was even more mocking — 'but I am not the liar.' It was so very satisfactory to have caused so much friction. At the door he paused. 'Mrs Randolph, thank you for your hospitality, forced on you, I know. Now I believe you should ask your husband some questions, some very pertinent questions about his behaviour seven years ago. He'll not come well out of it, I assure you.'

'If you don't shut your mouth, by God I'll shut it for you,' George swore. 'And don't come near me, or my wife, ever again.'

Bryce glanced at Sophie. 'Oh, I don't think I can promise that. I found your wife's company most pleasant. Calm yourself, Randolph, I'm going, I'm going.'

George, repressing further angry words, flung open the door, and seizing Bryce's beautiful coat by the lapels, almost threw him out.

In the hall James hastily found the visitor's hat. The major took it, elaborately straightening his coat, and brushing it where George had laid hands on him.

'I suppose it's no good asking you for a horse to carry me home? I'd return it, of course. No,' — seeing the expression on the face of his unwilling host — 'I suppose not. Well, no doubt I can find one at the inn in the village.' He went out without hurrying appreciably. He hadn't enjoyed himself so much for a long time. But he was sorry for the poor girl that the heir to Plummers had married, and he wondered if she had the character to stand up to him. Somehow he thought she had.

Chapter Thirteen

In the drawing room George closed the door and set his back to it, his arms folded as if he would contain the feelings he could not, at this moment, control. Still shaking with the force of them, he exclaimed, 'Well? What the devil do you mean by bringing that man in here? How could you do anything so idiotic?'

Sophie looked in amazement. 'I cannot think why you should say such a thing to me. It seemed the hospitable thing to do and I had no notion it would upset you so much. I still have no idea why, though it is obvious there is some quarrel between you.'

'Some quarrel! By God, there was! And to see that damned wretch sitting here with you, drinking tea — '

Before this onslaught, directed at her innocent head, Sophie sat down rather suddenly, trembling a little now that the scene was over. 'How could I know, how could I guess that you even knew Major Bryce? You gave no inkling when we told you of his balloon show.'

'No one, as I recall, mentioned that name.'

'No? Well, even when I told him your name, though he did look surprised, I'd no reason to think your meeting would have been like this. Your behaviour was quite extraordinary. In fact I've never seen you so angry.'

He began to walk up and down, to the window and back, kicking some smashed china aside. 'I had cause,' he muttered. The whole wretched incident had transported him back to that gloomy courtroom and he saw again the implacable faces of lawyers to whom it was just another case. Even Emily, beautiful and telling in black, had had no effect on them, and he remembered looking with loathing at the husband who had brought this on her, who had put his own injury above any consideration for her. He thought he had put it all behind him, was free of it, but he was not. At last he said, 'To find him here, cursed liar that he was – ' and then stopped abruptly. At the trial Edgar Bryce had spoken no more than the truth – damn him, damn him! He could see the fellow now, standing there, elegant, assured, like the poseur he was.

'Had you not better tell me what all this is about?' Sophie suggested. 'I think it must be something to do with that trouble you were in all those years ago. You didn't tell me much, but Amabel – '

'Oh, so she's been gossiping has she? The stupid girl never had much sense.' George had the sensation of having his back to the wall.

'Amabel is not in the least stupid and she only briefly mentioned what she thought I knew. Only I didn't, because you never trusted me enough to tell me.'

Under this reproof, he swallowed hard before forcing out an answer. 'I see that perhaps I should have done, but it seemed irrelevant to acquaint you with the details of a sordid court case six years in the past when I met you. I did tell you, you know I did, the bare bones of what happened.'

'You did, but you led me to think it was a brief affair soon over, though of course I should have realised that it could not have been if it drove you away for all those years. I suppose I didn't want to think ill of you. You certainly didn't put any blame on yourself as far as I recall.'

Ignoring this cut he went on doggedly. 'I told you all that I thought necessary, and if I gave that impression it was by the way.'

'Oh, do sit down,' Sophie said. 'We must talk about this, and I can't if you will prowl up and down.'

He obeyed, flinging himself into the chair so lately vacated by their visitor. 'What do you want to know?'

'All of it,' she said. 'I think I must if I am ever to trust you again. Why do you hate Major Bryce so much? And why did he seem to despise you?'

186

George reached for the decanter on the table by his chair and poured a brandy which he drank at one gulp. Then, without looking at her, he said, 'When I was barely twenty I fell in love with a married woman – you know that much. She hated her husband who treated her badly, and she returned my love. We had a few blissful months. Then Bryce took a hand. He was her husband's friend, and when he saw me – ' hesitantly, 'by the worst ill-luck, leaving her house at three in the morning, he told her husband, who was away at the time. Then Horton, damn him, put a private detective to watch us. So it all came out. I told you about the court case her husband brought. Bryce and the detective both gave evidence, and damning it was, destroying us both. She left London, her husband went to America and I was banished abroad by my father, who had to pay the considerable damages. He said he didn't wish to set eyes on me for a very long time – which he didn't.'

Absorbing this shattering tale, imagining its effect on the young George, she felt an instant pity for him, caught in a situation beyond his handling. 'Go on,' she said, but in some dread, 'let me have the rest.'

'There is no "rest",' was his short answer.

She felt a chill settle on her despite the fire. He was not going to tell her that Emily Horton was alive. Oh please tell me, was her silent plea, please tell me – be honest – no more deception. To hide her desperate longing, she knelt on the floor to pick up the pieces of broken china.

But he did not tell her. All he said was, 'When I came home over a year ago, as you know, my father and I patched things up. Leave that, for God's sake. Let one of the servants clear it up.'

'Such a pity,' Sophie said abstractedly out of her misery, 'it was part of Amabel and Henry's wedding present to us.'

In some exasperation he went on, 'But you knew about my return only a short while before we met; I know I told you something about why I'd lived abroad.'

'I see now that it was as little as possible. And Aunt Adela had died.' She added dully, 'Would you say that was fortunate for us both?'

'Of course it was. It's foolish to think otherwise. Don't

you think.' he added more calmly, 'that motives can be forgotten in the life we now have here?'

'I suppose so. What happened to the husband in the case?'

'For heaven's sake, we don't have to talk about him. Anyway, he's dead, died last winter, I think.'

'And you told me she had died too.'

'Yes.' The little word hung on the air. George was now more miserable than angry. Forced into a corner where he must lie to his wife or confess to the resurgence of that old affair, it was the lie that came out.

Sophie knelt, looking at a piece of broken teacup in her hand — fragile, smashed, like all her hopes. Everything seemed to be falling into place. Obviously Mrs Horton had been free when George met her again — it must have been before their wedding. Did he have a tussle to decide between his old love and Aunt Adela's money? It seemed to Sophie that she herself was the last to be considered in this wretched turn of fate.

Seeing the tension in her face, George said in a toneless voice, 'Be careful, you'll cut yourself,' and remembered once knocking over Emily's table with his cup and saucer on it — if only such trifling memories would leave one alone!

Taking hold of her hand he helped her to her feet, but almost immediately let go of it. 'The intrusion of that fellow has upset me, I admit it, but I don't think any purpose to be served by discussing it further. I see it wasn't in the least your fault.' Pausing, he added, 'I doubt if he'll show his face here again, but I shall give Street instructions that if he does he is not to be admitted. And should you see him anywhere, please don't speak to him.'

'I always try to obey your wishes, George,' she said calmly, 'but if I should meet the major, though I won't seek to speak to him, I will certainly not refuse to answer if he addresses me. I've no reason to. He was extremely polite to me, and it would be the height of discourtesy to cut him.'

'I won't have you speak to him.' For a moment he raised his hand and she wondered in sudden amazement if he was about to strike her. But he lowered it at once, merely saying stubbornly, 'Do you hear me?'

'Yes, I hear,' she said, 'and so I imagine can anyone who is in the hall. Don't shout at me, George. This whole thing seems to have been blown up — like one of the major's balloons — and it is all so long in the past. There is no present for what happened, is there?'

Again there was the briefest hesitation, while thoughts chased desperately through his head. But he could not bring himself to speak of Emily's return, seemingly from the dead. There was that one night, never to be forgotten, buried deep but alive. Only never to be spoken of. He could have said the report of her death was a mistake, that he had seen her a few times, but he dared not trust himself. There was no need, he told himself, and at last murmured, 'No, none.'

She rang the bell and when James came, said, 'There has been an accident. Pray have this mess cleaned up,' and went out, passing George without a glance.

There seemed no place to hide her misery except the sewing room. Throwing herself down on the window seat, she gazed out at the twilight sky, seeing no beauty this evening, only aware of a sense of betrayal and an awful hurt. It was as if the last chance for love had gone. He had been seeing Emily Horton since last summer, she was quite sure of that. He had been lying and deceiving her, not knowing that she knew, thinking himself safe, no doubt, and she rocked herself to and fro as if the agony of it was almost more than she could bear. He had not been to London since before Christmas, but perhaps he had met Mrs Horton closer to home, perhaps on those long days when he was out? There she stopped herself. Even if he had not had any sort of assignation, that hardly mitigated what he had done before. Finding Mrs Horton again after so long, he had believed it was she whom he loved, not his bride, yet he had still gone through with the wedding for the sake of the money. It was despicable, horrible, and she felt sick at the thought of it. And what did Major Bryce mean by saying that the third party in the case no longer bore him ill will? He could only be referring to Mrs Horton and was taunting George in as malicious a way as possible. But she was less concerned with that, than that the woman from the past was still capable of causing such trouble. Curiosity made Sophie wonder what she was like,

189

if she was very beautiful. Certainly someone with the looks and personality that Sophie could not hope to compete with. How to bear this thought? How to keep silent? The night sky, the peace of the stars, the still moonlight, offered no answer.

The gong sounded for dinner and she realized she had not changed. Doubting if she could eat a morsel, she nevertheless forced herself to go down — she must face him sooner or later — but there seemed to be nothing to talk about.

The next few weeks were painful for both of them, each trying to preserve some sort of normality, both nursing secrets. Mr Street, from his position in the dining room, said privately to Mrs Bodiley that he thought there was something very wrong above stairs.

'Oh, they're very polite,' he told her, 'but the talk is only of trivial matters, if they talk at all. Ever since that balloon man came I've known something was wrong — all that shouting in the drawing room, which I couldn't help but hear, and then that broken china. Of course you know the family better than I do, but — '

'Mr George was never an easy boy, and he doesn't seem to have changed overmuch,' the housekeeper said uneasily, 'though he was never one to throw things about. And I've thought Madam pale and a little distracted since then. I wonder if — ' She shut her lips firmly. Street knew nothing of the old troubles and she was not going to enlighten him. Not that she knew if the unexpected visitor had anything to do with it, but she could hardly help putting two and two together, and her heart ached for the young mistress who had done so much for Plummers.

George was out everyday for even longer hours than usual, and when he came in he was silent, preoccupied. Sophie calmly went on with her own occupations, only able to hope and pray that he would recover from the disastrous intrusion of Major Bryce and that the past would eventually bury itself again. He had not made love to her since that day, now more than two weeks ago, and this too made her miserable. It was as if he had said he no longer cared even for the serious business of producing an heir. It seemed as if their life together was kept by a thread, too fragile to stand any strain, that at any moment it might snap into outright estrangement. Longing for someone to confide in, to be able to unburden herself, there seemed to be no one. Monica, as the wife of George's oldest friend, was not a suitable confidante of such revelations, and only Verity would serve that purpose. At least when she and George went to London for the Exhibition, she could spend a day with Verity, though she thought sadly that things had come to a wretched state for her to wish to leave Plummers. Now, a few weeks in town, with the interest of the Exhibition and the season just beginning, would be a godsend.

A letter came from her father-in-law suggesting they should go up during the last week of April. He added that Alethea would be staying with Lady Louisa for the whole of May to be taken about in the hopes that the London balls and parties would take her out of herself, but for Sophie, at this moment, Alethea's sorrows paled into insignificance beside her own. However, the prospect of seeing her sister and the rest of the family was a cheering one and no doubt the Exhibition would be a great entertainment. She did wonder if Major Bryce would have his balloons in the Park, as he had said he would. If the chance came, would she take the flight he had offered? George would undoubtedly forbid it, but, unhappy and wretchedly disillusioned, she thought perhaps an act of defiance might show him what he had done to her.

At dinner one evening she mentioned Lord Randolph's letter and George, his wine glass in his hand, merely said, 'I don't know if I shall be able to go.'

'What can you mean?' she asked in suprise.

He did not look up. 'Well, I can't be away when the mares foal, nor will they be so obliging as to produce at exactly the same time.'

'But your father – he's expecting us and he would be so disappointed –'

'Then you will have to go and explain.'

Not knowing what to say to this, Sophie ate a mouthful of her fish before somewhat injudiciously remarking, 'You were always off to London at one time.'

He gave her a swift glance, but the only answer she got

was, 'So I was.' There was a pause as Mr Street appeared to serve a sirloin of beef with roast potatoes. Then, at a glance from his master, he withdrew.

It was Sophie who broke the silence. 'Do I dare to hope that Plummers is now more important than what drew you to London in the autumn?'

'What an odd remark,' was his comment. 'You must be aware that in the early days here, there was still a great deal of paperwork for Warburton to engage in.'

'Oh − it was Warburton you went to see?'

'You knew that,' he said sharply, his dark eyes fixed on her face now, as if he sensed she was trying to imply something he had been convinced she knew nothing of. But it led him to think of those days, of the lodgings in Wilton Place and all the torment of longing to hold Emily in his arms, until suddenly he felt he could no longer sit here eating beef. Thrusting his plate away, he refused Mrs Ackland's apple pie, of which he was normally very fond, and spent the rest of the meal emptying the decanter of port.

For her part Sophie wished she hadn't been so pointed in her remarks, presently going up to bed alone, and wondering where all this subterfuge would end. Happiness she had ceased to think of. She had not long blown out her candle when she heard George in his dressing room. A few minutes later he came in and climbed into bed beside her. For one instant she thought it meant he was sorry for his behaviour of the last weeks, but it was the briefest hope.

He threw himself over her, his hands hard, not gentle, his mouth on hers demanding. He was breathing fast, deep in some emotion which she knew was far from love for her, taking her in a manner that horrified her. When he rolled away she felt bruised, miserable, and was thankful when without a word he got out of bed and returned to his dressing room. It was Emily Horton who had been in his head, driving him in his desire, she was certain of that, and she pressed her face into the pillow that he might not hear her rending sobs.

In the morning she sent for her breakfast to be brought up to her, and later lunched alone. At dinner George behaved as though nothing untoward had happened, making conversation about a shoot being organized by the Duke of Marlborough to which they would be invited.

'I don't like seeing birds shot,' she said pettishly, and he merely shrugged his shoulders, but he did not look directly at her.

'No doubt the ladies will be offered some other occupation. You know you like visiting Blenheim.'

So life slipped back to normal. He came to her bed as usual, without any of the extraordinary emotion of that tempestuous night, but they were as far apart as ever. George could not have explained himself. But neither could he blind himself to the knowledge that he had behaved abominably to Sophie, used her as the means of assuaging his desire for another woman. Put baldly like that, he was disgusted with himself while pride kept him from anything remotely resembling an apology. A man of strong passions, he had never yet had to subdue them for the sake of another, and now, totally unable to speak of such intimacies, he did not know how to make amends. In consequence he was more withdrawn than ever, and the effort to appear his usual self, to talk of everyday things, could not but be obvious. Sophie began to long for the end of the month and the visit to Mount Street.

And then there occurred what she ever after thought of as the night of the foal.

Spending the day with Monica, both unabashedly worshipping the latest addition to the Layton family, all of three weeks old, she had tried to hide her feelings, but Monica, assuming her downcast spirits were only because of her empty nursery, tried to cheer her by saying, 'I'd been married nearly two years when John arrived, you know, and now I seem to be in the family way with great regularity.'

Sophie managed a smile. How could Monica have any inkling of the situation between her and George? 'You are a comfort,' she managed to say. 'My father-in-law can barely hide his longing for a grandchild.'

It was not lost on Monica that Sophie did not mention George, but she merely said cheerfully, 'Try to be patient, my love. Don't worry about it, and I'm sure nature will surprise you soon. Do you like the names we've chosen – Victoria Sophia? And we want you to stand godmother.'

Touched, Sophie accepted readily and as she went home in the carriage she thought at least it would be something to talk about this evening. The house was quiet. James took her cloak and bonnet and she went into the library. The door to the study was half open and George was sitting at his desk, a newspaper spread before him. There was something about his attitude that made her go in. One look and she asked 'Is something the matter? Is there bad news in the paper?'

He jerked upright, folding the sheets together. 'Nothing of any moment.' Making an effort, he asked, 'Have you had a pleasant day?'

'The baby is quite delightful,' she said lightly, 'but too young to be of any interest to a mere male. All Charlie would say was that he hoped she would soon look less like a prune!'

He managed a half smile, but his attention was not on what she was saying. Throwing the paper into the waste basket, he said 'Shall we go to the fire? You must be chilled after your drive.' But Sophie was not deceived. Something had happened.

It was towards the end of an even more silent dinner than usual, served to them in the parlour instead of the large, chilly dining room, when James came in to say that Hedges would be grateful for a word with the master, 'He says it's urgent, sir.'

'Leah!' George sprang up, abandoning his cheese. To Sophie he said, 'It's too soon. Hedges must be anxious to call me at this time. If I'm a while don't wait up.'

'I hope the mare is all right,' she murmured. 'I know how much –' but he was gone.

There was an April wind blowing that seemed to defy the hope of spring in the garden outside and it found every cranny in the house, whistling in the gallery above. She sat on by the parlour fire, gusts of wind occasionally billowing out so that she made a mental note to order the chimney to be swept. Hoping the jackdaws were not nesting again, she took up the book she had on hand, but after reading for an hour put it down. George had been gone all evening. Staring into

194

the fire and musing, dwelling sadly on the strained relations since Major Bryce's visit, the evening passed slowly. James came in to see if she wanted anything, and ask whether the fire should be made up at this late hour.

'Yes, another log,' she said. 'I don't know how long the master will be, but I will wait up. You may go to bed, James. And be so kind as to tell Pheobe to do the same.'

The long case clock in the hall struck midnight. Restlessly, not knowing quite why she was staying up, except that this birth meant so much to George, she wandered about the room, into the library and thence to his study. The paper still lay in the basket and picking it up she laid it open on the desk, wondering what had so riveted George this afternoon. From his attitude then, not good news, and she turned the sheets, scanning them, seeing nothing of interest until she came to the announcements of births, betrothals, marriages and deaths. Something here perhaps. And then she saw it.

The engagement is announced of Major Edgar William Bryce to Mrs Emily Rosamund Horton, relict of the late Captain Laurence Horton. The marriage will take place quietly in London.

So that was it! No wonder George was upset! She stared down at the letters until they jumped and then carefully put the paper back into the basket exactly as she found it. Were they never to be free of this woman, of her influence on their lives? Though not knowing the complete story, she still had an inkling of what it would mean to George that the passion of his youth was to marry the man he loathed. Obviously Mrs Horton did not share that feeling, and perhaps that was the worst part of it. Did it not show how deep his love for Emily Horton went that he could not bear the thought of her marriage to anyone, let alone to Major Bryce? No wonder there was none to spare for her! The lying would go on and she didn't know how to bear it.

Straightening up, she braced herself. That had to stop, somehow, sometime. In no way could she endure to live with it for the rest of her life – nor, she thought perceptively, could George, not the real George she glimpsed now and again, a man of straightforward dealings and capable of

195

great feeling. This was destroying him and she had to stop it, but how? Back by the parlour fire she sank down in her chair, her brain teeming with unanswered questions. She should go to bed, of course, sleep on all this − Papa always told her to sleep on any important decision − but she could not. The matter must be resolved and, uncharacteristically, she decided it could not wait.

Wrapping herself in a cloak, she slipped out of the side door into the stable yard. It was a clear moonlit night, bright enough for her to see her way. Lights burned in the far stable, where only the Arabs were kept, and she went in through the half-open door. George and Hedges were in one stall, both in shirtsleeves, George holding up the mare's tail, Hedges with his forearm deep inside her.

Sophie stood rigid. It was a little more earthy than she had imagined and she remained rooted to the spot, until George suddenly became aware of her and swung round.

'What the devil are you doing here?' was his ungracious demand.

'I thought −' she began, 'you were so long. I came to see −' Hedges, glancing first at his master and then at his lady, hastily withdrew his arm.

'Go back to the house,' George ordered sharply. 'This is no place for you.'

Not moving, she said, 'I am not so poor-spirited as you think. Can I be of any use, hold the lantern? It doesn't give much light hanging from that hook.' And without waiting for an answer she took it down and held it so that it lit the stall, the mare and the two men. In the box on one side Jassy was restless, heavy with foal herself, while on the other the author of all this night-time activity moved about, throwing his head up now and again and shaking it, as if he sensed something unusual was happening in the middle of the normally quiet dark hours.

Hedges had turned back to the labouring mare. 'Look, sir − a breach, as we thought.'

'Put that lantern back and go,' George almost threw the words at his wife. 'Go, for God's sake, and leave us to it.'

The fury and resentment in his voice staggered her,

stemming seemingly from far more than her intrusion into his world of horses. Her hand shaking, she turned to put the lantern back, but at the same moment Jassy, aware of all the unrest, suddenly kicked at her half door. The latch gave way and she backed out. In sudden terror as the mare's rump pushed against her, Sophie retreated hastily, dropping the lantern. It rolled on its side, oil escaping, and a snake of flame caught at the straw, spreading across the floor. Hedges sprang out of the stall, hardly aware that the straw was beginning to burn, to catch hold of Jassy by the mane and push her back, closing the door more firmly. Leah, terrified, momentarily pinned George against the wall. With his shoulder he shoved her away, at the same time yelling, 'What are you doing, Sophie? Get back – get back! Hedges, the bucket –'

But before either he or the groom could reach the fire, Sophie had righted the lantern and with great presence of mind seized a horse blanket hanging on a rail and flung it over the creeping flames, stamping on it until the fire was out, only the blanket giving off a few wisps of smoke. In a few seconds the danger was past and she hung up the lantern, to lean against a post, shaken and breathless, but triumphant.

'Oh well done, ma'am,' Hedges said with rare impulsiveness. 'The stables might a'gone up in no time.'

George seemed to be fighting with himself, his face red with more than exertion. His back to Sophie, he said, 'It's coming, Hedges. There's a hoof.'

'We'll need the rope,' Hedges seized a length from a hook. 'Here, sir.'

They set about delivering the foal. Sophie felt a little sick, incapable of movement, her gaze riveted on the panting mare. Fastening the rope about the two small hooves, both men dragged at it. A few moments later as the calf slithered free, Hedges said, 'Oh Gawd, sir, it's dead.'

George swore in language Sophie had never heard before. For his first Arab foal to be stillborn was a tragedy for him, and with tears running down her face, she fled back to the house. If she could only have comforted him! But he did not want her, had never wanted her, and she wept for George,

197

for herself, for the pathetic little corpse. Her right hand was throbbing, stinging so fiercely that she realized now how badly it had been burned, and hurried across the yard to the dark kitchen. There she lit a candle and reaching into the large, gloomy larder found some butter to smear on it. The pain was very bad but she shut her mouth firmly to control any sound, wrapping a cloth round the burns before going to her room.

Finding it impossible to undress by herself, she crawled under the coverlet where the pain kept her wakeful for long hours. But it was nothing to the agony of mind that tormented her through that dark night.

Chapter Fourteen

Heavy-eyed and pale, Sophie waited next morning for George to join her at the breakfast table. Her hand was very painful; even with some of the lotion from the medical box her father had fitted out for her, it was very sore and stinging and she had covered it with a piece of lint. She had no appetite and neither apparently had George, for he did not come, but presently she heard him in his study. Instinct told her to leave him alone. Instead she went to the parlour, where she tried to answer letters. The whole affair seemed like a nightmare – the dimly lit stables, full of queer shadows, Leah in labour and the two men sweating over her, George so angry that she should be there. His reaction had been unbelievably harsh and it was impossible not to think it the result of that newspaper announcement. Then the moment of sheer terror, Jassy backing into her, the fire catching hold; at least if that was her fault it was she who had scotched it.

Unable to concentrate and finding it uncomfortable to hold the pen in her scorched hand, she left her desk and wandered over to the cushioned window-seat, an innovation of her own, and she was sitting there, staring out, when George came in. He was dressed for riding as usual and he too looked haggard.

A little unsteadily she began, 'George, I'm sorry. I can see I should not have – '

'No, you shouldn't,' he interrupted, 'but for my part I had no right to speak to you as I did, especially in front of Hedges, and I beg your pardon for that.'

Blinking, she said, 'I was stupid to go out there, only I

wanted to understand. It's part of your life I don't share, and I thought — '

He made a rather impatient gesture. 'Oh my dear, not that again, if you please.'

'No — very well. But I'm sorry about the foal.'

'So am I,' he agreed grimly. 'It represented a great deal of money.'

'I was thinking of the mare and the poor little foal. Does everything have to come down to money?'

He stared at her. 'Is that what you think of me? Heartless, greedy? Well, you are probably right.'

'No, no,' she broke in, but he went on, 'You know what I think about my Arabs, and running a stud is a business, like any other.'

'I'm sorry. I didn't mean — oh dear, I have made so many mistakes, said too much.'

'On several occasions! As for last night, please try to accept there are some things not fit for you.'

'I know that now. It was awful. And I nearly burnt down the stables.'

For the first time the grim look relaxed and he tried to smile. 'My beautiful stables! But your quickness undoubtedly saved them.'

'Well, that is something.' She hid her burned hand under a fold of her dress. 'I shall keep well away next time.'

'You would be wise,' was his firm reply. 'Now I'm going to London. I'll be back tomorrow evening, or Thursday morning at the latest.'

'To London?' She was momentarily startled. 'For such a short time? Why?'

'Business. I can't be away too long. Jassy — '

Colour flooded her face, and for the first time real anger gripped her. Plunging into dangerous waters, despite sleeping on the wretched business, only certain the moment had come to let go of any restraint, she sat erect, her eyes fixed somewhere around his middle waistcoat button. 'Do you think I don't know that I come second to your horses? And to the very much alive Mrs Horton?'

Now she had really shaken him, and his indrawn breath

hissed. 'What the devil — My God, you know! Since when may I ask?'

'Christmas,' Sophie whispered.

'Ah, my loquacious cousin again, no doubt. She used her stay in my house to regale you with scandal.'

'It had to come out!' And then she cried, 'You have lied, lied and cheated me from the beginning. I know now why you changed at the time of our wedding. *She* came back just before it, didn't she?' With a derisive laugh she added, 'That must have been hard for you — a choice between Mrs Horton and Aunt Adela's money. I see that I had no place in it at all.'

'Stop! Stop, for God's sake. You make it sound — despicable.'

'And so it was.' She raised her eyes to his face at last, saw it flooded with dark colour. 'I understand it all so clearly now. You have lied to me, haven't you? All those visits to London when we first came here. I suppose you were — still are perhaps — lovers again. So you had her and the money. How very fortunate, except that you had to have me as part of the bargain.' Anger and bitter hurt kept her far from tears this morning, while George, in the face of this onslaught, sat down suddenly on the window seat.

At last he said, 'I can't deny that she did come back — two days before our wedding. Before, I swear to you, I believed her dead. It was — it was an unbelievable shock. And then it was too late. After the wedding she — ' He broke off. To talk of this with Sophie was a sort of agony — Emily's rejection of him too sore a wound to expose, even now.

'Oh?' she queried. 'Did she have a few finer feelings left? Did the two of you consider that it might be cruel to break it all off so near the wedding? Very considerate. But of course the money was your biggest consideration.'

'Don't,' he said, 'don't, Sophie, for pity's sake. You can't know what I went through in that forty-eight hours. It was torment. And I had come to like you, to think we could share a reasonably good life together — which we have been doing. At least I thought so. Since Christmas and my father's illness — '

'It might have been possible once,' her voice went cold.

'But since I've known the truth it has been like a canker lying between us, eating away what little we had. I've had to look at you differently, knowing you were not the man I thought you that day we went to the windmill.'

'Sophie! How can you say that?'

'Oh, very easily!' She threw the words back at him. 'You have always thought me timid and amenable, easy to manipulate, but I'm not, and I won't have that woman ruining our lives any more.'

'She won't — I told you the truth when I said it was all over.'

'But it isn't. You have lied to me ever since we married. You never told me she was alive, never trusted me. There were chances — oh, yes, there were, but you said nothing. Didn't it occur to you that the truth might come out?'

Stricken, he said hoarsely, 'I don't know — I thought — I hoped —'

'That I'd never find out. Oh, George,' her voice began to break, 'how could you have played so dangerous a game, tricked me, lied to me? How can I ever trust you again?'

'I don't know.' Through linked hands he was staring at the floor. 'I seem to have ruined everything. It all went wrong. How could I know she would come back? You've no idea what hell those two days were.'

'But Aunt Adela's money!'

'Oh, damn the money,' he exploded. 'Of course I wanted it. In our situation my father and I would have been less than human if we hadn't seen it as a life-saver. And,' — at last he raised his eyes to her — 'you haven't behaved all that well, hiding from me since Christmas that you knew Em — Mrs Horton — was alive.'

'I wanted you to tell me,' she said in a low voice. 'I wanted you to be honest with me.'

'Like waiting for a schoolboy to own up to stealing sugar plums?' George was stung. 'Good God, I'd have preferred that you confronted me with it instead of letting me go on thinking you didn't know. You performed your part surprisingly well!'

'Perhaps I should have spoken after Christmas,' she murmured, 'but with your father so ill —'

'A good excuse to postpone a monumental confrontation! Perhaps you shrank from that! At any rate, one could say *you* have lived a lie these last three months.'

'It only matched your own lie.' Caught on the raw, she added recklessly, 'How you must hate me for coming between you and her. Do you lie in bed with me, make love to me, wishing I was her? The other night – '

He sprang to his feet, his face crimson, 'This conversation has gone far enough. I'm going to town now – perhaps you will be more rational when I get back.'

'Are you going to her wedding to Edgar Bryce? Oh yes, I saw the paper last night. Or to stop the marriage, I wonder? George, how can you be so foolish?'

'I see that you can't understand.'

'I understand that you love her, not me – but if you go, George, it is the end of any kind – I'll not say love, for we never had that – but companionship between us. I can't and I won't endure such humiliation – or scenes like the one when Edgar Bryce came here. George, don't go.' She was not pleading, but facing him with a vital decision.

He was halfway to the door. 'I must,' he said painfully, 'don't you see? I owe it to her, at least to try to make her see what a mistake it would be, after what he did to us.'

'It doesn't seem to me that he did more than tell her husband he was being cuckolded.'

'Sophie!'

'Well? Isn't that the truth?'

He put both hands on the table in the centre of the room and stood leaning on them, drawing a deep, shaken breath. 'I never thought you could think, let alone speak, so harshly. I see that I have misjudged you.'

'Yes,' she answered, 'I think you have. I must have more of my mother in me than I thought.'

For a moment, daunted by her words, he seemed unable to speak. Then, hesitantly, he said, 'But I have to go – please try to understand – if only to find out why, how she can even consider it.'

Dully she said, 'It is your decision. I shall not expect you tomorrow, remembering last time when you went for two days and stayed a week, lying about everything when you got back. I suppose you were lovers then?'

He straightened, came back to her. 'My God, if you only knew how unjust that is. No − if we're being honest this morning, I have to say I wished it and she would not. There − now you know how low I've sunk.'

Gazing at him, at the familiar brown coat, the fresh white shirt, the hand bearing his signet ring, she said steadily, 'If it is true that you were not lovers in fact then, were you before − before our wedding?'

He turned his head to look out at the view towards the lake, the silvery green leaves on the willows. 'That is a question you should not have asked. But yes − once.'

The little word lay between them. An odd sort of relief swept over her, but only for a moment. 'If that is all in fact, do you still want to be her lover? I don't want to believe that, George, but I think I must.'

'I don't know.' His voice was so low she could barely hear it, close as he was. 'I no longer know anything any more. If she marries Bryce − God, what a betrayal! I've got to try to stop it.'

'It doesn't seem to me that it is any of your business.'

'Not my −' He broke off. 'But it is. At least I've got to try to stop such a disaster.'

'How do you know,' she asked practically, 'that it would be a disaster? Major Bryce seemed a very personable man.'

Struggling for words, George muttered, 'It seems the worst nightmare − Bryce with her. I can't make you understand, but it is worse than anything I could have imagined.'

Sophie had not known she could be so cold, so hostile. 'Let her go, George, to the major, anyone. She doesn't belong here, between us. But only you can send her finally out of your heart.'

He stood there, grappling with this thought, staring out at the sunlit garden. At last he said, 'You are not mincing your words this morning, are you? Try to understand that I have to go. When I come back we can talk about it again − and I won't lie, Sophie, I swear to you I'll never lie again.'

'But if I ask you not to go?'

'Don't ask it of me, I beg you. Try to understand that I have to do this.' A new thought, crystallizing into certainty, was forming in his mind – that it was the coming back that would be important. 'It will be the last time – I promise you.'

But she was telling him coldly that if he must then he had better go at once. 'I don't think I care any more. I am your wife, George, and must make the best I can of it, but – but I doubt if talking, even the truth, will mend any of it now.'

'Tomorrow,' he said, 'I'll see you tomorrow.'

'It's hardly worth your coming back. Have you forgotten we are to arrive at Mount Street on Saturday? Hedges can drive me up.'

'He can't leave Jassy,' George straightened. 'Nor can I for longer than I can help until the foal is born.'

'Oh,' she said with a sarcasm he had never heard from her before, 'I am perfectly well aware who comes first in our establishment.'

The words stung him. Hardly knowing what he did, he went to the table, poured a glass of sherry and then left it there, untouched.

'Wellings can take me up,' she said firmly. 'I mean to be in Mount Street for the opening of the Exhibition, as your father has gone to such trouble to arrange it for us.'

'I *had* forgotten about Saturday.'

'I'm not surprised – what with your mares and Mrs Horton!'

'Sophie!' He seized her burned hand and gripped it. 'Stop, for pity's sake.' Hardly aware she had winced he squeezed it harder. 'I can't bear this – I can't!'

The pain was fierce but she kept back the tears. 'I shouldn't have said that, though it's true enough. Go, if you must, but I mean to be in London by Saturday. I won't disappoint your father. There will be so much to see, I'm sure he will want several visits and so shall I.' She knew her voice sounded brittle.

George released her poor hand, unaware of the lint, thinking it a handkerchief. 'Damn the Exhibition,' he said and walked out of the room.

Emily Horton was well satisfied with her choice of a second

husband and the last thing she wanted was George on her doorstep. But much of the fight had gone out of him. On the train journey from Oxford he had had time to think. All the accusations Sophie had thrown at him were now like sledgehammers in his brain. How could he have compared her hiding since Christmas her knowledge of Emily's reappearance to his own catastrophic lying? He had deceived her, behaved abominably. Because he was so wretched and frustrated himself, he had made her life miserable, and by the time he reached Paddington his main desire was to turn round and go home by the next train. Hating loss of dignity above all else, he felt diminished by the scene with his wife. Nevertheless he was determined to do what he had come to do, and instead of going home he bought himself a cup of coffee. Of course he must see Emily, find out why, how she could have brought herself to accept Edgar Bryce – it seemed a loose end to be tied up. And he had to know how he would feel when he saw her again, even if it was playing with fire. From Paddington he took a hansom cab to Wilton Place, and mounted once more the steps where a little less than a year ago he had been so astonished to see her alive and still so beautiful.

The same maid answered the door. Mrs Horton was visiting her brother, she told him, and would be back by tomorrow afternoon. He went out again into the street. This had happened before, he thought. Only this time he was not going to skulk in his club.

On the way to Mount Street he paused to look at the huge, gleaming Crystal Palace. Wooden panels protected the ground floor but above the clear glass was alight as the exhibitors worked late to put the finishing touches to their stands, from fine porcelain and English furniture to eastern carpets and Indian silver, from exquisite jewellery to large machines – everything that man could design. He stood for a few minutes, more overwhelmed than he had expected to be by the sheer size of it. Sophie was right, it was a historic affair, something that must be seen, but whether he would stroll the aisles and galleries with her on his arm was another matter.

He walked home, found a tolerable explanation for his

hasty visit, and promised his father he would bring Sophie to town in a day or two.

Lord Randolph eyed him. 'It must be something very important to bring you up so precipitately.'

'Yes, very, someone I have to see. You look well, Father.'

'I never expect to be in prime health again, but for an old man I keep reasonably so. And how is that dear Sophie?'

'Well too, busy packing when I left,' George answered with a slight distortion of the truth which he hoped would be the end of lying.

Lord Randolph, who did not study certain columns in the paper, merely said, 'I consider it very odd that you should come up, go back and come up again all within the space of a few days.'

His son shrugged. 'Needs must. Have you heard from Maurice?'

His father gave him a sharp look, but followed his lead. 'The last letter caught a ship returning from Lisbon, a week or two ago. I doubt whether we shall hear any more for a long time.'

'What did he have to say?'

'Only that he is pleased with his ship, that he has a tolerable crew of cut-throats, and that Frank Sterling is doing very well.'

'I'm glad to hear that. Did he mention Alethea?'

'Not specifically, though he sent his best wishes to all of them. Did you think he would, or should?'

'Not really. The silly girl had her head turned, but no doubt a season with my Aunt Louisa will set it the right way round again.'

'Perceptive of you.' Lord Randolph gave him a faint smile. 'Your brother no doubt behaved in his usual reprehensible manner, but when David Sterling brought her to town a couple of weeks ago he called here before delivering her to South Street. She seemed remarkably cheerful for one whose heart was broken three months ago.'

'I'll lay odds she will have snared a suitable husband by the end of the summer.' George remarked, glad the talk was turned away from his affairs.

But almost at once his father said, 'I wish you had brought Sophie today. It would have been much better.'

Briefly George explained about the stillborn foal and his need to wait for Jassy's delivery. 'No doubt she'll be here by Saturday,' he finished, earning a penetrating glance.

'You mean that you may not? How is she to see the opening of the Exhibition if you are not here to escort her? I'm too old for all that excitement. And why my sister wants to rattle around being pushed and shoved by all and sundry I really don't know.'

'But you said you had seats?'

'So I have,' the old man said contentiously. 'Your aunt proposes to go with "Puss" Granville and his party, and take Alethea with her, to hobnob with all the great names of society, no doubt, but it will still be a vast crush. I have four seats for you and Sophie, Amabel and Henry.'

George stirred uneasily. 'If I can't get back, surely somebody in the family could escort her?'

'It would be better if you were here,' his father said, betraying some annoyance. 'I went to a great deal of trouble to get the seats. However, I suppose if you must skulk in your stables, Henry's young brother, Nigel, could take your place. He's all agog to be there and has put off going back to Oxford for that purpose. And then there's the Granvilles' ball which you are supposed to be attending − but I suppose Nigel can stand in for you there. I presume you wouldn't object?'

'Of course not, though he's still rather wet behind the ears. Sophie will put up with him, and Henry can take charge of the party. But I am not skulking, as you put it. I need to be there.'

Lord Randolph said nothing for a moment, beyond suggesting that, it being near dinner time, George might pour them some sherry. After a few sips, however, he remarked, 'You always were secretive. Do you really expect me to believe that a mare dropping its foal must keep you away? I presume that groom of yours − what's his name − knows his business?'

'Hedges. Yes, he does, but after losing the first one, it's important to me to be there.'

'More important than your wife's pleasure?'

'She understands,' George said sharply.

'Does she indeed? How accommodating of her. Well, I at least will be pleased to see her as soon as she can come and to make her stay as pleasant as possible.'

Goaded, George said, 'I'm not abandoning her — a few days —'

'Yet you had to come up today?' They seemed to be back to the old days of indulging in verbal fencing. However, after a moment Lord Randolph made a deprecatory gesture. 'It's your affair, I suppose. But I sometimes wonder if you know what a treasure you have in your hand?'

Startled, George sat sipping his sherry, but at last all he said was that he would look forward to taking his wife to the Exhibition when he was free to do so. Hoping to distract his father he asked him whether he had seen the outside.

'A huge vulgarity, *The Times* called it,' his lordship remarked, not in the least deceived, and only hoping his son was not playing fast and loose with the girl he looked on now as a daughter. 'Well, I expect I shall go when all the excitement has died down. It's there until October.'

After these exchanges they managed to dine together amicably enough, talking of uncontentious matters, but George could not rid his head of his father's words — Sophie a treasure? His mind was in a wild state, trying to grapple with this statement, with Emily's forthcoming marriage, and finding no peace anywhere.

A restless night had George heavy-eyed as he spent the morning taking advantage of Warburton's presence, at luncheon he was entertained by the lawyer's hopes that the Exhibition would provide opportunities for good investments. No one, George thought, seemed to be giving their attention to anything other than the monstrosity in Hyde Park.

At about three o'clock he went to Wilton Place once more and there found Emily coming down the stairs as he was about to go up. In a blue gown, with the prettiest spring bonnet on her head, she made a charming picture and he stood gazing up at her, but her reaction was hardly welcoming.

'Oh dear, so you've seen the papers? Well, George, it is no good looking at me like that.'

'I must talk to you,' he said desperately.

'If you think to change my mind, you are wasting my time and yours.'

She would have gone on down, but he blocked her path. 'Please, Emily — a little of that time.'

'Well,' she said again, 'if you must. You may accompany me to my dressmaker and then take me to tea at Gunters. Such a civilized place for exchanging unnecessary talk. I have a hackney waiting.'

He stood aside and they went out together to where the cab was standing, the sorry-looking horse reluctant to move. Conscious only of her closeness in the confines of the cab, he could think of nothing to say, his questions too probing for the short journey.

Outside a smart establishment in Berners Street, the driver halted. 'Half an hour,' Emily said, 'no more.'

George got out and walked up and down. He had never seen London so busy, nor such a motley crowd. There seemed to be every nationality on the streets, snatches of French conversation or German, dark-skinned men, black-bearded fellows from far south, some wearing turbans or African dress, Chinese in black silk caps. If there's not trouble, he thought, it will be a miracle. But there seemed to be extra police on patrol, several groups of soldiers marching towards the Park. He waited impatiently, and promptly in thirty minutes Emily reappeared.

Gunters, as might have been expected of so famous a tearoom, was crowded, but after a few moments, they were ushered to a vacated table in a corner, where George ordered tea and a plate of Gunters' renowned and delectable cakes.

Mrs Horton gave him a teasing smile. 'No doubt you have come to tell me I am off my head and should be in an asylum?'

'Of course I have,' he burst out and then lowered his voice. 'I thought you were going to marry that lawyer you told me of.'

A waitress came to their table to serve them and inspecting the silver salver of cream cakes, Emily chose a pink confection, which the waitress set on her plate. George waved the girl away and Mrs Horton poured their tea before she answered.

'I did consider it, but I soon discovered he was quite dominated by that sister of his, who was determined to continue to live in his house after we married. I could not see myself sharing a house, and a man, with Josephine Kershaw.'

'Was there no one else then but Edgar Bryce?'

'Don't sneer, George, it doesn't suit you. Of course there have been others these last months, but none that could compare to Edgar for looks and manners. He always was an entertaining creature.'

'He entertained a court room, as I remember. I beg your pardon – I suppose I am sneering again!' George was aware he sounded like a sulky boy.

'I wish we could have this conversation without recriminations, she said. 'I don't wish to look back seven years. Edgar really only stood up for Lawrence, and I've long forgiven that. After all, it was I who needed to be forgiven, wasn't it? I hope I have learned enough wisdom with the years to keep myself from getting into such a situation again.'

'For pity's sake!' He glanced round the elegant, busy room, the pretty cloths and china, the glittering chandeliers, glad their table was in a secluded corner. 'The past leaves its scars. How can you forgive, let alone forget, any more than I can?'

'If that is your attitude,' she murmured, 'then I am sorry for your wife. I have put it behind me, as any sensible person would do, and so must you. It is really too foolish to let that sorry affair spoil your life today.'

'Sorry affair? Is that what you think it?'

'Well, so it was. I'm not denying what we felt for each other, but we are both seven years older, and from this distance, that is how I see it. Edgar has come into sufficient money, and I am quite fascinated by ballooning. I have already been up – it's exciting and dashing and tells me I'm not too old for adventure.'

Restlessly, he remembered that last autumn Sophie had gone up in a captive balloon and called it a wonderful experience. How unkind he had been to her!

211

On the other side of the table Emily finished her pink cake and went on, 'We shall travel a great deal, of course, but our home will be at his house near Henley,' adding with a provocative smile, 'so we shall be near neighbours, shan't we? I hope that if the four of us meet you will behave like a civilized member of society?'

He thought of the scene in his own drawing room, Bryce taunting him, the smashed china, and how Bryce had said the third member of the past affair was not averse to him. He knew now what the major meant. And remembering his own ungovernable fury of that day, it suddenly seemed incredibly childish. He had always relied on his sharp, sarcastic tongue to deal with those he disliked, but somehow Edgar Bryce had caught him on the raw, unleashed something in him that he would have preferred to have had under control. Nothing was worse than being made to look a fool.

Making one last effort he said, 'It is obvious you are set on this, I can only say — don't, Emily.'

She laughed. 'You ought to congratulate me on my good fortune in securing such a personable, ambitious and charming husband. If ever a man was likely to end up with a title, he is.'

'A mountebank!'

She glanced at him and sighed. 'Jealousy doesn't become you either, George. Really, you ought to be over it by now. I am over you, I promise you. Another cup of tea?'

He threw down his napkin. 'I see I have wasted my time coming up. Marry him then, and I hope we don't meet again.'

'It is quite immaterial now whether we do or not.' She rose, and there was nothing for him to do but pay the bill. Outside he put her into a cab and she held out her hand.

'Goodbye, George. I didn't mean to sound so hard. Of course we will never quite forget each other, but I don't mean to spend the rest of my life mourning that we didn't marry. Edgar will be a husband much more to my taste, as things are now.'

He had taken her hand, but let it go. It was the final unkind jibe.

At Paddington he caught the last train to Oxford. When

he got there the livery stable was closed for the night and
he was forced to stay at the hotel which shared his name.
And there he lay wakeful for a second night, his thoughts
tormenting him. Through all the trauma of his own misery
and confusion, he had made Sophie suffer in many ways,
not only physically — shame came at the memory of that
night two weeks ago — but mentally too, none of which
she deserved, and now if her hard and truthful words had
hurt him he only had himself to blame. Had he, at last,
tried her too far? Oh God, he must see her, tell her — but
was that last quarrel beyond mending? Too much said? He
didn't know — only that he must get home to her.

The next day he was delayed at the livery, fuming with
impatience, and it was consequently nearly midday before
he rode up the long drive to Plummers.

In the yard a groom ran out to take his horse, and followed
by the delighted Brandy, he entered the house. Encountering
Mr Street, he asked where his wife was.

'Why, gone, sir. I thought you would know. She left
yesterday for London.'

For two, three interminable days George waited. Jassy
regarded him with soft, devoted eyes but showed no
disposition to produce her foal.

'Can't be long, sir,' was Hedges' opinion. 'I'll call you
the moment she starts.'

He roamed about the house, followed by the faithful but
puzzled Brandy, the park being the better place for a walk.
To George the house seemed empty, far emptier than when
it had been abandoned and forgotten. He hadn't realized
how Sophie had imbued it with her presence, her taste, her
ideas and enthusiasm. Her workbox and the little Dutch
writing desk lay unopened, her chair vacated, their shared
bed empty, and he sat down on it, fingering the fringe of
the coverlet. She was only gone for a short while, he told
himself, to the confounded Exhibition, and he would follow
her as soon as possible, then bring her back. But after such
a quarrel how could they patch it up, wipe out the memory
of things they had said? Let alone be happy! He had wrecked
everything, ruined any chance of happiness. There was no

sign of a child yet, but would even that mend their broken lives? It was all his fault. She was right in saying he put even his horses before her — and was doing it again.

Should he abandon Jassy, go to London at once, beg her pardon, tell her Emily was nothing to him now? And was this true? Drawing in a deep breath, he knew that it was. He tried to envisage Emily at Plummers, and could not. If Sophie complained there were things he did not share with her, he saw for the first time that there was far more he could never have shared with Emily. There was something beneath the beauty, the smile, the charm, that was cool, dismissive, calculating. How was it that Jack had seen it all those years ago and he had not? He was the three times fool Maurice had called him. But he had loved her — once. Or was it only a stormy desire, a physical passion that had burned itself out? Now, miraculously, it seemed as if Emily's final repudiation of the past had shown him where his heart lay. Even his father had seen in Sophie what he had not and he wondered in amazement how he could have been so blind.

He sprang from the bed, startling Brandy into action, and ran down the stairs shouting for Morgan. 'I'm going to London at once,' he said when his valet appeared. 'Pack a night valise for me. I'll be ready to go in fifteen minutes. You can pack the rest of what I'll need for a week or so and follow me on a later train.'

Out in the stables Jassy stood patiently while Hedges groomed her. 'Nothing yet, sir, but — '

'Never mind Jassy,' George interrupted. 'You will have to manage. I'm leaving for town at once. Saddle Emerald for me.'

'Are you sure, sir?' the startled groom asked. 'She's still new to us and I don't call her properly broke yet. Too frisky by half.'

'It's her speed I want,' George said, and with his minions scurrying about on his behalf, was gone in under fifteen minutes. Heading down the drive, Emerald more than frisky, he thought Hedges was probably right. Jerking on the reins, he swore at the mare, but she went galloping headlong between the lime trees.

Watching from the stable entrance, Hedges muttered,

'Nought to choose between you for wildness. What's got into the master, I wonder?' He was about to turn away when he saw a grey-brown shape, at this distance maybe a fox or a rabbit, speeding across the drive, almost under Emerald's hooves. The mare shied, rearing high. For a second George struggled with her, but she unseated him, pitching him off her back. He landed on the grass and rolled over, cracking his head against the trunk of a lime.

Hedges yelled for the stable lad and seizing a blanket pelted down the drive. Their master was unconscious. Lifting him carefully on to the blanket, with some difficulty they carried him back to the house. Emerald, apparently satisfied with her morning's work, trotted back to the stables.

Dr Gradely was sent for and when George opened his eyes an hour or so later it was to find himself lying on his own bed with the doctor bending over him.

'What the devil ...' he was beginning, struggling to rise, when a firm hand restrained him.

'Lie still, Mr Randolph. You've had a nasty tumble from your horse.'

'Good God! I remember now, a damned rabbit. But I have to go to London.'

'Not today. You must rest. I don't think you've broken any bones, but –'

George sat up, putting a hand to his head and bringing it away with blood on his fingers.

'You see? There's a cut on your scalp,' Dr Gradely said, as though satisfied to be right. 'You must not think of going anywhere for a day or two.'

George lay back. His head ached abominably, and while his wound was dressed he submitted, fuming. It really was infuriating that now, when at last he knew what he must do, he had been thrown by a fractious horse and a rabbit. But tomorrow – whatever the doctor said – he would go to London.

The morning dragged by. He slept for most of the afternoon, ate a tolerable dinner, and was undressed and getting into bed when there was a knock on the door. It was James to say that Hedges would like a word. A few seconds later his groom appeared, but George was already out of bed and seizing his shirt.

'What is it? Has Jassy started? I'll be dressed in a moment.'

'No need, sir. She's dropped a fine little filly, healthy as you like.'

'Then why the devil didn't you call me? I wanted to be there. Are you sure everything's all right?'

'You know you can trust me, sir,' Hedges sounded slightly hurt, 'but as for calling you, the doctor said you was to rest, and coming down to a mare in labour ain't what I'd call restful. At least you can sleep easy now.'

He went out, and alone once more, George sank back against the pillows. It was great relief, a moment he had anticipated with such hope − the first Arab filly added to his stable. But a groan escaped him. At what cost? Oh God, at what cost?

Chapter Fifteen

'How very plesant it is to have you here again.' Lord Randolph surveyed his daughter-in-law with deep satisfaction. 'But you are looking a trifle peaky, without the roses you usually have in your cheeks.'

Sophie smiled across at him. 'I suppose I'm just a little tired. I have been so busy with all my plans for the visitors we hope for this summer, and then there's the school. Did I write to you about that?'

'I believe you did.'

'Well, the village does so need a school of its own. George has given a piece of land – that field by the end of the churchyard – and we had plans drawn up by an Oxford builder. The walls are three feet high already, and the rector can hardly contain himself! He has found a lady, in her thirties, I think, who he says will make an excellent school mistress and who would like to live nearby. George has promised her a cottage and we shall endow the school, of course.'

Hoping she sounded bright and cheerful, as if everything was going well, she had determined in the carriage on the way here to reveal nothing to anyone of the dreadful quarrel. Everything had gone so disastrously wrong, far more than she could have believed possible when she began her married life with such high hopes. Having discovered in George a man with secrets from the past and an entanglement from which he seemed unable to extricate himself, she had to face the fact that she counted for little in his life. Plummers had been giving them a joint purpose but could that now be enough, or was their relationship shattered beyond repair?

If Mrs Horton had not come back into his life, she was sure all would have been well in time. As it was he was clearly devastated by the news in the paper. Feeling an emotional sympathy for him, at the same time her anger simmered, directed less at George than at the woman who was still creating such havoc in his life. Only, recalling the things she had said to him two days ago, intended to shock him into seeing what he was doing, it seemed possible that she had alienated him for good. Did she still love him? Oh, did she not! Far more than at the beginning, though she could hardly have said why. And, deep in her own distress, she had not taken in his few words that showed a changing heart.

So one more effort must be made, one last fight for him, for herself, for Plummers. But how? What should she do? Even the secret she nursed, if it really was true, could hardly be used for this — it smacked too much of blackmail. Unable to see any answer to the whole unhappy situation, she could only hope and pray that when they met it would somehow be resolved. And with Mrs Horton marrying again and choosing George's old enemy, surely this must close the final chapter of that unhappy affair.

Wondering what had happened when he saw her, whether he had set off for home again, her only enlightenment was Lord Randolph's remark that George seemed to have taken leave of his senses, dashing up to town one day and back again to the country the next. Grumbling that it was annoyingly uncertain for everyone, he added, 'He is being very tiresome, not that that is anything new, but doubtless you will not mind going to the opening with Amabel and Henry and Henry's young brother, Nigel. A silly lad, but he's at that age, and there doesn't seem to be any harm in him.'

'Of course I don't mind,' she murmured, 'though I hope George will be back in time. If — if the mare has foaled — '

His lordship snorted. 'Those wretched horses!'

There was no sign of his errant son the next day and after luncheon, when he was taking a rest, Sophie had herself driven to Verity's house in Kensington. Fortunately her friend was at home and delighted to see her.

Settling in an upstairs sitting room, Verity said, 'The rooms at the back are the only quiet ones these days. Really, the noise and traffic the Exhibition is causing goes on from dawn to dusk, and once it is opened it will be even worse. I can't go, of course, not in this state, but Jack has promised to take me before it closes in the autumn. He of course wants to be there as soon as the public are admitted after the grand opening. I suppose you are lucky enough to be going to that?'

'Lord Randolph got tickets for us.' For a moment Sophie studied her friend, happily in her sixth month of pregnancy. 'It's good to see you looking so well.'

'I feel it, though a little unwieldy,' Verity said, smiling. 'And Jack is quite absurdly excited. He wants a boy, of course, but I don't mind. I wish you − '

'Don't,' Sophie broke in. 'Oh, don't − I might be, I'm not sure − but it couldn't be at a worse moment.'

Verity saw her distress and came to sit beside her on the sofa, putting her arm round her. 'Darling Sophie, what an odd thing to say. I'm happy for you, so will Jack be, for you both. Why should it be a wrong moment?'

Sophie seized her hands. 'Don't tell anyone, not yet. I'm hardly certain.'

'I won't if you don't want me to. But surely you have told George?'

'No − not yet − '

'Well, you will have to soon. Do bring him to dinner, tonight perhaps?'

Sophie looked down at her hands, still clasping Verity's. 'He − he isn't here.'

'Oh? I had assumed you would have travelled up together. My dear, I can tell something is very wrong. What is it?'

Despite her resolution, Sophie was not proof against Verity's affectionate concern, and she threw herself into those comforting arms, wracking sobs shaking her.

Verity let her weep, waiting until it had subsided and Sophie lay exhausted against her ample figure. 'Now,' she said gently, 'hadn't you better tell me what all this is about?'

Sophie gave one last shuddering sob, and then it all came out, the whole sad story – from her honeymoon to the last disastrous scene in the drawing room at Plummers. 'I thought – I thought at Christmas when you were all with us, that the past was really buried, that there was hope, that George was really – but then there was that bit in the paper – '

She became incoherent and Verity straightened, her eyes bright with anger. 'I am more horrified than I can say. It is quite dreadful. I must say I thought at Christmas, and so did Jack, that you were settling so well together. You'd done so much to Plummers and seemed to be happy with it.'

'I thought so too. And I used to think it needed only a baby to complete it all.'

'You poor darling. How could he behave like this? I didn't see the announcement in the paper, but Jack did. He said he was sure it wouldn't matter either way now.'

Sophie shuddered. 'I'm afraid it matters only too much to George. Oh Verity, what am I going to do?'

'Jack must talk to him, make him see sense.'

'Oh no, no,' Sophie cried out in great distress. 'Verity, no, he must not. If George knew I'd told you any of this he would be so angry. Please, please promise me that you'll not speak to anyone at all about it. Please – '

'Hush,' Verity soothed her. 'Don't upset yourself any more. If you don't want me to, I won't. But when I look at your poor hand – '

'That was my own fault.'

'That's as maybe. But you are probably right. Jack cares so much for both of you, and it might send him off to do something headstrong that wouldn't achieve any good at all. He says he never liked Mrs Horton, and to hear of her causing trouble all over again is really too much. One can hardly blame the woman for remarrying, but I suppose it was her choice of husband that caused George so much distress.'

Sophie gave a long sigh. 'Perhaps when they are married that will put an end to it. I'm glad I told you.'

'I should think so!' Verity kissed her cheek. 'We've never had any secrets, have we? And if you really are expanding, that must make all the difference. You'll see.'

'But I can't tell George — not yet.'

'Why not? Surely that would put everything right?'

'Oh, don't you see? He will think I'm using it to make him sorry, and if I'm wrong he'll think it even more of a cheat. I've got to wait at least until we have come to some sort of understanding.'

'Well!' Verity exclaimed. 'Of all the contrary logic!'

'Perhaps, but I can't use it as a weapon. You do understand that, don't you? And when George comes — I wish I knew what to say, what to do.'

'Let him make the first move; be guided by his attitude when he gets here. I think maybe you are right. You want a happier moment to tell him the good news.'

'*If* I'm right.'

'It sounds as if you are, darling. I hope so. And I also hope,' Verity added severely, 'that George has been quite as unhappy as he made you, only more so, which is what he deserves.'

'Oh dear, poor George.'

'Poor you. You never were very good at thinking of yourself, but try for once. It is he who has treated you abominably. But it is possible, you know, that such a quarrel may have let out all the misunderstanding and unhappiness, like opening a poisoned wound.'

Sophie went back to Mount Street, much comforted both by the release of sharing it all and by Verity's sturdy common sense.

The great day of the opening arrived with no sign of George. The Storringtons collected Sophie, bringing Henry's young brother. Nigel was eighteen, as dandified as he could be, and took umbrage when his brother said, 'I wish you would not always make such a peacock of yourself.'

Taking the peacock's arm, Sophie said, 'I think he looks very smart and I'm proud to be escorted by him,' which quite restored the youth and he blushed with pleasure. Henry took charge of the party, and a little after nine o'clock they joined the crowds converging on the Crystal Palace. It was a day, it seemed, for which the whole world had been waiting. The

221

sky was blue, the sun shining to make a perfect May Day. Thousands of spectators, without tickets, lined the route of the royal procession, for the day had been declared a public holiday – a recipe for disaster, the pessimists said, but the crowds were in a cheerful, amiable mood, and the sellers of hot pies, baked potatoes and toffee apples were doing a fast trade.

Lord Storrington shepherded his little group through the main south entrance where they stood for a moment, quite breathless with amazement at what they saw. The high central hall, the Transept, was surrounded by galleries and with aisles spreading out from it. The crystal fountain spewed water high into the air, catching shafts of sunlight, like myriad diamonds. At the far end was one of Colonel Sibthorpe's elms, a sop to the poor man, filled with twittering sparrows who were constantly flying in and out of the leaves and up into the girders, where no doubt they thought to escape, seeing the sky above, but finding only glass.

'Something will have to be done about them,' Nigel exclaimed in horror. 'Look at my coat, dammit.'

Amabel laughed. 'How unfortunate! Never mind, my dear. Jenks can sponge it when we get home.'

He had taken out his handkerchief and was doing the best he could, disposing of the dirtied square of linen in the nearest waste bin. 'You ladies had best watch your bonnets,' he advised gloomily, to which Sophie replied that she did not see how she could watch the top of her bonnet.

They were in festive mood as Henry conducted them up an iron staircase to their seats at the front of a gallery. There was some dismay as clouds rolled up and the sunshine briefly disappeared, but after a few spots of rain, it cleared and the day stayed fine.

Inside it seemed an interminable wait. Amabel was leaning over the balustrade, looking at the favoured élite below. 'There's Mama. See, Sophie, she's between Lord Granville and Colonel Reid, and there's Lady Granville with one of the young Devonshires. Oh look, your sister is with an escort. I wonder who? Oh, it's Lord Bentley. He's quite ancient – must be forty, I should think – but fabulously rich.'

Sophie peered over, saw Alethea laughing archly up at her

222

companion, sighed and said, 'Here we go again! I wonder how many admirers she will collect this season? Your mother really is being so kind to her.'

'She's so beautiful,' Amabel said enviously, 'and in that pink gown – ' and when Henry leaned towards her, remarking gallantly, 'My love, you in your own sweet way – ' she interrupted to say resignedly, 'Don't tell me I'm as beautiful as Alethea because I know I'm not.'

'I'd rather have you,' her husband said, in such a forthright manner that the others laughed.

Looking over the gallery at the rows of ladies' bonnets below, the tall hats of the men, many in uniform, to while away the time Henry pointed out the celebrities. 'That's Wellington in the front there – well he deserves the ovation he got just now. I'm glad he's in uniform, dear old boy. Over eighty now, you know. And beside him is Lord Seaton – who did something spectacular at Waterloo, I think – with Lady Seaton and their eldest daughter; she's sitting next to Lord Anglesey. That's Mr Fox, head of the building firm who did it all, and Mr Paxton, the architect, that fellow with the curling side whiskers. After this there'll be knighthoods for them, I shouldn't wonder. And see that man in a black cloak with the odd floppy hat? That's Tennyson.'

Sophie, who had read *In Memoriam* when it was published last year, stared at its author, remarking that he looked more pirate than poet! Listening and looking, it seemed as if everyone who was anyone was here, even the denigrators to see the disaster they had prophesied.

But nothing at all went wrong. The building did not fall down, no one was trampled to death in the crush, nor did the galleries, which had been tested by the military pushing heavy baskets of shot along them, collapse. The organ, crashing out, failed to shake the foundations as someone had gloomily foretold. Sophie joined in the chatter and laughter, all the while thinking how different it would be if George was sitting beside her, instead of this excitable youth. But she must try not to think of him, only enjoy today – yet how could she, with this dreadful chasm between them? A chasm seemingly made worse because of the secret

223

she must hide, at least for the moment.

Staring at the lines of magnificent statues – some classical, some scriptural, some equestrian – making a path to the royal dais under a great canopy of crimson cloth, fringed in gold, Sophie mused that it seemed the place was filled with colour. There were flowers everywhere, palm trees, shrubs, evergreens, and the aisles were filled with trophies and artifacts of every sort, stretching away and waiting to reveal, she thought, even more magnificence.

At last the Gentlemen-at-Arms arrived, Beefeaters with their scarlet tunics embroidered with the royal insignia, and state trumpeters in gold coats and black velvet jockey caps. The scene was so glittering, so brilliant, that Sophie thought she would not have missed it for anything.

Just before midday an enormous wave of cheering reached them from outside, telling the waiting audience that the royal party was approaching. There was a fanfare from the trumpeters as the procession formed, and then by craning their necks Sophie and Amabel saw the Queen, a diminutive figure in pink watered silk and holding the young Prince of Wales by the hand. She entered accompanied by the Prince Consort, who held the hand of their little princess, and the cheering inside rose to a crescendo, almost drowning the music. Sophie tried to memorise everything so that she could recount it to her father-in-law, and perhaps to George, if they were still on speaking terms, but it all passed in a haze of excitement.

Only the Queen's words etched themselves on her mind. 'God bless my dearest Albert, God bless my dearest country which has shown itself so great today!' And Sophie was among many who could not keep back a few tears of love and loyalty and patriotism.

The Archbishop of Canterbury invoked God's blessing on this World Fair, from which so much new life and new trade was expected, and then the Hallelujah chorus, sung by massed choirs, filled the building. After that the royal party took nearly an hour to tour the Transept and one or two of the aisles.

'There's so much to see,' Sophie said to Amabel, 'I'm sure we shall have to come several times.'

Leaning over from his wife's far side, Henry said, 'Some wag has worked it out that if one spent three minutes looking at every object, it would take thirty-six years to see the whole!' This reduced the others to laughter while Sophie struggled to say that they only had until October.

The procession passed on, the old Duke offering his arm to Lord Anglesey, who had lost a leg at Waterloo. The line of worthies seemed to go on and on: foreign royalty, leading statesmen, the military in splendid uniforms, Turkish representatives in startling clothes, the Chinese equally so in their long, vivid silks, and Sophie was quite surprised to see by the great electric clock over the south entrance that it was nearly two o'clock.

People began to move around now and Henry conducted his family down to the ground floor, where they joined the squash in the Fountain Court before moving into one of the aisles.

'I can understand why it will take so long to see it all,' Sophie said. 'Oh, I like this Canadian exhibit.'

The emphasis here was on timber. A log cabin and the life-size figure of a woodsman were arresting, and there was some attractive furniture made from fine Canadian wood. Amabel exclaimed on a tête-à-tête double chair. 'Perfect for Alethea to conduct her love affairs,' she added, making Sophie laugh and say she wondered where her sister had got to.

The two men wanted to see some of the machinery — steam engines, printing presses, machines for making envelopes and another for the new steel pens. They were all amazed by the great wheel that turned majestically, producing steam.

'A terrifying thing,' was Amabel's comment. 'Sophie, do let's move on to see the Nottingham lace. I like these designs for sleeve endings.'

They spent a considerable time at the Minton porcelain stand, where Henry Minton and his nephew had arranged an eye-catching display. 'Oh,' Sophie sighed, 'it is all so beautiful. Do let's walk through the medieval hall. Look at that statue of a knight, and what exquisite tapestries!'

There was a great press of people wanting to see the Koh-i-Noor diamond under its protecting dome. Police and soldiers were in evidence in case of trouble, but to Sophie's mind the great jewel was outshone by the Hope diamond, seemingly even more brilliant and better displayed. It was here they encountered Lady Louisa and Alethea.

'What a crush,' her ladyship remarked. 'I am quite dazed by it all. Sophie, my dear, have you seen the Paisley shawls? You must not miss them – pure Cashmere and quite lovely. I shall have to put in an order.'

'One hardly knows where to start,' Sophie said. 'I must see the Indian silver.'

'And the Chinese carpets,' Amabel put in. 'Ever since I saw yours in your drawing room, Sophie, I've wanted one, but they are so expensive.' She glanced at Henry, who groaned.

'I can see this exhibition is going to empty my pockets, and a great many others', I shouldn't wonder!'

Alethea clung to her sister's arm, in transports over the whole glorious affair and full of chatter about all the engagements Lady Louisa had arranged for her.

'If I'm not dead by the end of the season, I shall be quite surprised,' her ladyship said, but in fact she was enjoying herself enormously, and considered a week with more than one empty day very poor. However, after a while she said she thought that, considering the months the exhibition was to stay in the Park, she would go home, but on seeing Alethea's crestfallen face, she added, 'My dear child, I won't drag you away. Stay with your sister and come back to me later.'

Henry found a buffet where he procured coffee and sandwiches for them all, before they tackled the Eastern Gallery, home of the Indian exhibits. The Palace finally closed for the night at six o'clock and Sophie admitted to being very tired when she was delivered back to Mount Street.

'But it was all worth it,' she told Lord Randolph. 'There can never before have been such an array of the world's art and invention and industry!'

'Could you face another visit tomorrow?' he asked. 'I've a mind to go before the prices come down for the general public.'

'Are you sure, sir? Lady Louisa found it quite exhausting

and went home long before the rest of us.'

He smiled fondly at her. 'What, did it defeat even my indefatigable sister? Well, I realize I am too old to do a great deal, but perhaps I can choose one or two stands from your catalogue, if you will study it with me after dinner?'

It was decided they would see the most recent English inventions, improvements to lamps, telescopes and clocks, as well as the French stand with its fine bronzes and statues, including an equestrian one of Napoleon that Lord Randolph particularly wished to see.

'I remember all the trouble he caused,' he added. 'I lost a brother at Waterloo. Did George tell you?'

'I saw his portrait at Plummers. He was very handsome, and I thought it was so sad that he was killed.'

'A fine fellow, only twenty-two. So many young lives wasted, but Napoleon had to be stopped. Did you not think Maurice like him?'

He seemed very lively tonight and full of anecdotes, but Sophie was glad to escape to bed. She had enjoyed it all, but nothing really seemed of any moment until George came, even if she had no idea what would happen when he did.

In the morning Lord Randolph appeared quite boyishly to be looking forward to his outing, announcing that he felt very well and prepared to walk about and see the exhibits. 'I've ordered the chaise to take us and fetch us home in two hours. Not long, of course, but − '

'Quite enough for you,' Sophie finished. 'Several short visits will be best, don't you think?'

They were just finishing breakfast when a note was brought in. It was very brief.

Dear Sophie,

I have had a tiresome fall from my horse. No bones broken but a bang on the head. Dr G. wants me to take a short rest. There is no need for you to return. I plan to be in London in a day or two. G.J.R.

She would not have expected more, given the situation between them, but when she read it to George's father, the old man raised an eyebrow.

'Very brief. Tells us nothing, but presumably if he's seen

Gradely and for once is doing what he is told, there seems to be no cause for concern.' Glancing at her, and not blind to the trouble in her face, though he had no idea there was another source of it, he added, 'Do you want to go home? Though if he plans to come in a few days' time — '

'No,' she said and slipped the note into her pocket. 'He says there's no need.'

'None that I can see. Well, I'm glad. I'm selfish enough to be enjoying your company too much to relinquish it. But it's not like George to fall off a horse, is it?'

She managed a smile and agreed. But in her bedroom, as she gathered up shawl and bonnet, a heaviness lay on her. No word of apology or regret, no message to make her feel, even remotely, that he wanted the quarrel to be put right. No affectionate subscript — but she hardly expected that.

The fine weather was holding as they joined the line of carriages approaching the main entrance. A great many people were there and Sophie thought her father-in-law was right, that the crowds would be even larger when the price came down from five shillings to one.

Once inside Lord Randolph paused, leaning on his stick, quite amazed by the sheer beauty of the central court, with the sunlight patterning through the glass. 'Amazing,' he said, 'quite amazing. I'm glad to have seen it.'

They toured the stands he had chosen and he was fascinated by the display of clocks, always an interest of his, and one in particular — an ornate and curious skeleton clock without a case, its elaborate dial picked out in gold.

'It would collect the dust,' was Sophie's objection, and he laughed.

'You prosaic girl, or perhaps I should say there speaks the careful housewife. George must see the gunnery exhibits; he and Charlie Layton were always good shots. He ought to try his hand with a Colt revolver.'

On their tour he met a great many acquaintances, and could hardly be prised away from a new type of lantern for a lightship. 'How Maurice would like to see that. It might be a means of saving both ships and lives,' was his comment.

The two hours were soon gone and they had turned for

the door when a voice said, 'Mrs Randolph!'

She turned to see Major Bryce, apparently alone. Coolly she wished him good morning and would have moved on, but he had held out his hand and she could not ignore it.

'I hope you are enjoying this incredible affair,' he said. 'Is Mr Randolph not with you?'

'Not at the moment, but he expects to be in London shortly,' she said. 'As you see, my father-in-law is escorting me. Sir, may I present Major Bryce? I met him when he came to — '

In a voice of ice, Lord Randolph said, 'Thank you, but I know perfectly well who Major Bryce is. Shall we go?' And ignoring both the polite inclination of the head and the proffered hand, he turned away and Sophie had perforce to go with him.

Even in the face of this snub, the major laughed and said softly, 'Goodbye then, Mrs Randolph. I hope we shall meet at my balloon display,' and Sophie had cause to be thankful that her father-in-law had grown somewhat deaf, for the major's voice followed them. 'Has your husband been smashing any more china lately?'

Chapter Sixteen

A ball at the Granvilles was always a grand affair. 'Puss' was a man of considerable account, much involved in court circles, and one of the prime movers in the Crystal Palace project, and he was delighted with the success of the first few days. In his soft voice, with the manner to match that had earned him his nickname, he had a personal greeting for each guest as he and his wife stood at the top of their wide, sweeping staircase.

Going up on Nigel Storrington's arm behind Henry and Amabel, Sophie was determined to enjoy the evening. It seemed that all London Society was there as well as a great many of the foreign dignitaries who were crowding into the city. She was wearing a new gown of deep rose pink, low off the shoulders with little puffed sleeves dressed with silver lace, and there was a fringe of the same about the hem. Feeling confident in it, her hair nicely arranged by Phoebe, and adorned with two pink silk roses, she thought fleetingly how the last year had changed her. Without Great-Aunt Adela's legacy she would probably have lived quietly in Clapham, and married a local young man, never dreaming such a glittering world existed, and even with circumstances as they were, it was impossible not to relish the occasion. Knowing she danced well, she took the floor first with Nigel, and then with various acquaintances, after which she was glad to be captured by Jack Fleming, who was there with his sister and her husband.

He laughed uproariously at the thought of George falling off his horse. 'He's always called me the incompetent!'

adding that he hoped the dear old boy would soon be in town for all the festivities of this special season. Clearly Verity had kept her word and he knew nothing of the shattering tale confided to her, for which Sophie was very thankful.

'I mean to see the Exhibition tomorrow,' Jack said, 'and when Verity is confined and about again, I shall bring her. Did you think her looking well the other day?'

'Never better,' she answered, as they swept into a lively polka round the floor under the enormous chandeliers. 'I suppose you want a boy, Jack?'

His eyes sparkled. 'I do, of course, but as long as the baby's healthy I don't mind. I've captured my old nurse to care for them both and nothing could be more satisfactory.'

Sophie was going into supper with Nigel and they were following the crowd when she saw Major Bryce bearing down on her. How persistent he was! Only this time he had on his arm the most beautiful woman Sophie had ever seen. Gowned in green velvet with exquisite taste, her burnished hair in a perfect and elegant coiffure, there could be no mistaking who she was. Even Major Bryce's introduction, presenting Mrs Emily Horton as his betrothed, was unnecessary.

Instantly Sophie felt like an unsophisticated girl, her dress suburban, which it wasn't, her hair inadequately arranged, though Phoebe had learned to do it well. No wonder George had been intoxicated by this stunning creature!

Mrs Horton held out her hand. 'Well, so you are Sophie Randolph. I have heard a great deal about you, my dear.'

There was something so patronizing in her tone that it set up Sophie's hackles as well as sending a blush to her cheeks, which infuriated her. But she managed to say with admirable coolness, 'And I have heard a great deal about you, Mrs Horton,' though, to her annoyance, this only widened Emily's smile.

Hastily Sophie introduced Nigel, and the major said 'Are you interested in ballooning, Mr Storrington?' To which Nigel replied ingenuously, 'By Jove, I should say so.'

'Then,' — Edgar Bryce had the same mischievous look in his eyes that Sophie remembered from that day at Plummers — 'I am to make an ascent tomorrow, from the north-eastern end of the Park, about five o'clock. As Mr Randolph is away, perhaps you would care to come and bring Mrs Randolph?'

Nigel accepted this with great enthusiasm, having been far too young at the time to have known anything of the scandal, and glancing at Sophie, added, 'What do you think? Would you care for it? Do let me escort you.'

Before Sophie could answer Mrs Horton said, 'Perhaps such frivolous affairs are not to Mrs Randolph's taste?'

Stung, she retorted in what she hoped was a casual manner, 'We may stroll over to see it, if we are not too captivated in the Exhibition. Nigel, we had best take our places for supper.'

'We shall see you tomorrow then,' was the major's parting remark as they moved off.

Throughout the sumptuous meal Nigel talked about ballooning, explaining that he had once been up at Oxford and giving an account of it to their supper companions that lasted throughout several courses.

They were seated with, among others, her sister and Lord Bentley, and Sophie deliberately talked mostly to him, wanting to find out what sort of a man he was. He showed himself to be an intelligent man, a widower newly returned from a long spell in the West Indies and wanting to settle down and make a new start in England. He could hardly take his eyes from Alethea. His late wife, he told Sophie, had been older than himself, the daughter of his partner in a successful tobacco plantation, and from his tone she gathered it had not been a love match, but a convenient arrangement. Now, lonely and somewhat at sea in England, he explained that his elder brother had died, and he was taking up the threads of his old family life, of which he was now the head. Before they had talked for long she became aware that he had fallen headlong in love with Alethea. In a low voice for her only, he said, 'I would like to tell you, ma'am, that I want nothing more than to cherish your sister,' which she thought a rather precipitate remark considering what a short time they had been acquainted. But with the advent of a delectable concoction of ice cream, shredded chocolate and rum, the conversation returned to

232

ballooning and she was back to the prospect of tomorrow's ascent.

She wouldn't go, of course. George would be very angry if she did, but at the same time she was not going to be put down by Emily Horton. Yet, despite this determination to hold her own, deep down was the overwhelming feeling that she could not possibly compete with such elegance, charm and sophistication. What a striking couple she and Edgar Bryce made! No wonder George was so jealous, so unhappy, though he had no right to be. Having sacrificed Emily to Aunt Adela's money — she could hardly think it was to save her from the embarrassment of a cancelled wedding, albeit almost on the very day — she had to admit that he had exerted himself to shake off the past, to make Plummers his life. Only it seemed that the facade he had built up was all too fragile, as if they were living in one of Mr Paxton's glasshouses. If Major Bryce had not landed in their field, it might have worked well enough; indeed, there had been little indications of warmer feelings on George's part, especially after his father's illness but now that the whole truth had come out, it seemed quite hopeless.

They would go on, of course, keeping up some semblance of normality, entertaining, busy with their separate occupations, and now at last, she hoped and prayed fervently, with the advent of a child maybe they had a chance. Having made up her mind not to visit Clapham until she had seen George, and she knew where they stood with each other, she kept away. Her father would never be deceived, either into thinking all was well, or into ignorance of her condition, her talk with Verity having made her sure of it. Yet it had not brought the longed-for joy. Nor could it until matters were resolved between her and George.

Alethea, joining her sister in the upstairs room set aside for the ladies to refresh themselves, was full of her own doings. In the last year, despite her broken love affair with Maurice, Alethea did not seem to have matured very much, and now she chattered on about how good Lady Louisa was to her and the splendid time they were having. 'She says it is like taking another daughter about. There's all the season to come and Ascot and goodness knows what else.'

233

'But when are you going home?'

'Oh,' Alethea waved an airy hand, 'sometime. Lady Louisa wants me to stay at least until June, and Mama is so pleased for me. Lord Bentley' — her eyes were very bright — 'sent round to ask what colour I was wearing tonight, and brought me this pretty posy of primroses. He is so thoughtful.'

'Too old for you,' Sophie said absently and her sister gazed at her.

'He's not that old, and he's fabulously rich. He thinks I am wonderful and that's all that matters.'

Unable to keep back a smile, Sophie said, 'Dear Thea, you are so transparent.'

'What do you mean?'

'Only that you are still a butterfly.' The smile faded as she recalled it was George who had said that. So she was back to her own troubles and a long sigh escaped her.

'Sophie! What is the matter with you this evening? I noticed at supper that you were hardly listening to what Nigel was saying.'

'Nothing's the matter,' her sister said, 'nothing at all. Shall we go down? I expect Lord Bentley is waiting for you.'

'Oh, he can't have all my dances. So many others want a place on my card.' She glanced down where it dangled from her wrist. 'Yes, there's a very handsome officer next, though he's no use to anyone as he sails for India next week. After him Nigel, and then Lord Granville's nephew, but I've saved the last one for Lord Bentley. He was so insistent. You do like him, don't you?'

'I think,' Sophie said in some amusement, but with a serious thought behind it, 'that he might be the very man to keep you in order.'

Pleased, Alethea floated away on the arm of her officer. Really, Sophie thought, she had enough of her own problems without trying to sort out Alethea's affairs. Waltzing with a rather dull man who claimed acquaintance with George in Italy, she was quite glad when it was all over.

In the morning Lord Randolph declined to come down to breakfast and when Sophie went up to his room professed himself a little tired after yesterday's outing.

'I'm afraid it was rather too much for you,' she said in swift concern, but he answered at once, 'I would not have missed it for the world, especially in such charming company. A magnificent spectacle, but too many people.'

He sounded weary, so, to cheer him, she remarked that she was sure George would arrive later today or tomorrow.

He nodded, leaning against a mound of pillows. 'I'm afraid I will not be much entertainment for you today, my love.'

'Never mind,' she said cheerfully. 'Nigel and I are going to see the balloon ascent. Apparently it has been subscribed by a great many people so I expect there will be a crowd to see it.' She was thankful that the old man knew nothing of the ownership of the balloon. When he had asked her, after meeting the major yesterday, how she happened to be acquainted with him, she had said only that he had a house in Henley. Assuming from this the meeting had been accidental, he did not pursue the subject apart from calling the major a tiresome fellow for being where he was not wanted.

Sophie went away feeling slightly guilty, but thought no point to be served by recounting the landing in a Plummers field and the consequent scene in her drawing room. She and Nigel spent the whole afternoon at the Exhibition, discovering further fascinating objects and delightful vistas. At last, at about four-thirty they strolled to the ground reserved for the balloon flight and joined the assembling spectators, where Nigel insisted on elbowing their way to the front, proclaiming cheerfully, 'Friends of the owner, you know.'

The balloon was apparently a new one with red, white and blue chevrons patterning it and a pennon flying that bore the name, the *Royal Victoria*. Already it was being filled from the Edgware Road gas-main, bringing it slowly into the vertical position under the watchful eye of Stephen Fox and another young man who kept hold of the anchoring ropes.

'It's quite beautiful,' Sophie said, 'the colours and the name, so appropriate for the celebrations.'

At that moment Major Bryce, overseeing it all, spotted them and came over at once. Dressed in a red coat, blue waistcoat and white trousers, he looked distinctly theatrical.

235

'Doing it rather too brown,' was Nigel's comment, 'but striking, I suppose,' and Sophie remembered how George had called the major a mountebank. He was undoubtedly a good showman.

Raising his hat to her, he said, 'Mrs Randolph, I hoped you would come.'

Why, she wondered? Why should he seek her out, knowing how angry her husband would be? Perhaps that was the very reason. Pure mischief.

'I've saved two places for you and your escort, Mr Storrington, I think?'

'Oh no, no,' she said quickly. 'I never meant –' but Nigel broke in eagerly, 'I say, how splendid! Will you really take us up? What an adventure! Sophie, do come. I'll look after you.'

'Up there?' she laughingly indicated the sky. 'No, it's quite impossible.'

He looked so crestfallen that the major said, 'Here's my fiancée, Mrs Randolph. She's coming up too, so you will have a lady companion. Many ladies go up, I assure you.'

'I can't,' she said, though with less firmness. 'My husband is expected –'

'But he isn't here,' Mrs Horton broke in gaily. 'He's had so many exciting experiences in his life, I am sure, that he wouldn't grudge one to you. And if he knew I was going to accompany you . . .'

All the more reason for her not to go, Sophie thought, but almost at once the contrary thought came, that perhaps he wouldn't care. He didn't care for her at all, and the only objection would be his hatred of Edgar Bryce. With Mrs Horton on board too, what would be his reaction? She shuddered at the thought. Hesitating, looking round at the glittering Palace, the Park so green and fresh, the brightly coloured crowds moving about, she hardly knew what to say, standing there so perplexed that Nigel broke in.

'Do let's go up. Please, Sophie, please. Imagine floating over all this – oh do come. What a tale for the fellows at Oxford!'

In a last attempt to evade the issue she answered, 'You go then. I'll wait here.'

'I can't do that. Leave you alone? Not the thing at all while you are in my charge,' he exclaimed, for all as if he was a responsible man of years, rather than a student of eighteen. 'Do come. It will be such fun, something to tell the others.'

That was just the very objection, she thought. And then it seemed that it was quite pointless to concern herself with what George's reaction would be. Why should she? He would not be concerned about her. It needed only Mrs Horton to say, 'We shall have a perfect view of London from above,' adding a little slyly, 'but perhaps, Mrs Randolph, you think it too alarming, too daring . . .' for her to make up her mind.

Turning to Nigel with a bright smile, which did not in the least reflect her feelings, she said gaily, 'How gallant of you. Shall we be daring together?'

Nigel beamed and the major had a satisfied look on his face. 'Come along then,' he said, 'the balloon is about ready.'

The flight party consisted of the four of them and a Mr Asher and his son, friends of Emily's brother. Bryce helped the two ladies up the purpose-built steps and into the basket-like 'car'. Sophie gazed around at the intricate arrangement of ropes, bags of ballast tied to the side of the car, the coiled grapnel hanging ready for the landing, and she was waiting there when a voice exclaimed, 'Sophie! What are you doing? Where's George?'

She was dismayed to see Jack Fleming staring up at her. 'He's at Plummers,' she said in answer to his urgent question. 'He found he couldn't leave his horses just at the moment.'

There was such an edge to her voice that he was even more startled. 'Verity said he hadn't joined you yet, but was coming. I can't imagine what you are doing in this thing, but,' he lowered his voice, 'I'm very sure he wouldn't like it at all. Believe me — '

'Believe me,' she retorted, 'he wouldn't care greatly. Oh, we are off!'

Requested to stand back, Jack made one last effort. 'You can't mean that. Do come out of there, Sophie. Let me — '

But she made no response and the major requested him sternly to move away unless he wanted to be carried off by the now loose anchoring rope. More gas was released into the heart of the balloon and, with only the slightest jerk, it rose to the cheers of the watching crowd, much enhanced by encouraging yells from a party of schoolboys.

Sophie knew one moment of sheer terror. No captive balloon this, but a wilful monster with a mind of its own and all of them in its power. Hoping her stomach would settle down, almost at once she was conscious of a smooth, delightful sensation as the balloon rose slowly and gracefully. It was a perfect evening for a flight, only a light breeze stirring the air. The crowd receded, trees grew smaller, carriages, horses all diminishing. Greatly daring, she waved to those below, catching a last glimpse of Jack standing watching, his horse's bridle over his arm, the animal inclined to take fright. And then, to her utter amazement, and horror, she saw George striding up to Jack. What they were saying to each other she could neither hear nor conceivably imagine — well, at least George could never call her timid again!

The balloon was soaring over the Crystal Palace, a view revealing clearly its immense size and amazing beauty. Sophie's fears subsided and she listened as Major Bryce pointed out landmarks.

'We're above the Strand now, you can see St Clement's church — next is Fleet Street and there's the sun catching the golden dome of St Paul's. Quite a sight, eh?'

Nigel exclaimed to his companion, 'There, didn't I tell you it would be worth it?'

'I wish you wouldn't lean over,' she said, feeling as if she was in charge of him, but the panorama below was beyond anything she had ever seen.

Laughing, Mrs Horton said, 'Won't George be surprised, Mrs Randolph? An adventure he might envy, don't you think?'

'I don't in the least know what he will think,' Sophie said, resenting Mrs Horton's use of his Christian name in so familiar a way. Looking over at the silver ribbon of the Thames, she asked the major where they would land.

'With luck,' he answered, 'on Wanstead flats. There's a

good open landing space there and we can easily get transport back, which I have arranged. But I don't like the look of those clouds coming up. Very unexpected.'

A little uneasily Sophie looked and saw. There were ominous clouds scudding in, breaking up the evening peace, hiding the sun. It felt cooler and she wished she had brought a warm shawl. Thinking of George watching below, she began to feel a little sick. His sudden appearance at this particular moment could only make matters worse between them. A few spots of rain spattered into her face and she wished she was safely down.

Sophie's imagination of George's reaction fell far short of reality. Looking for his wife, he had walked over to the balloon site, remembering her pleasure in that Oxford visit, and suspecting that she might have gone there to watch. And then, as the thing rose gracefully higher and higher above the launching place, he encountered Jack Fleming.

'Well,' he said. 'So you've come to see the show. Bryce's balloon, I suppose?'

'Yes,' Jack said reluctantly. Without doubt this situation was going to turn awkward. 'He's taken a party up.'

'So I see. Well, one can only hope they all come safely down, not like that catastrophe I saw in Paris. However, I can't wait about here. I'm looking for Sophie. I gathered at Mount Street that she had come to the Park with young Storrington, and thought she might possibly be watching the ascent − though after our last encounter with that clown, I hope she didn't speak to him.'

'I'm afraid she did more than that.' Jack could see no way to avoid the truth. 'She's up there with Storrington, taking the flight.'

'My God! It isn't possible. Jack!' George almost shook his friend. 'She can't be! You must be mistaken.'

'I wish I was. Let me go, Randy.'

'Why in hell's name didn't you stop her? How could you let her − '

'Steady,' Jack said. 'I only got here at the last minute and I did try to persuade her out of the car, to say you wouldn't like it above half.' Jack looked at his friend, who

239

was still gripping his arm and staring upwards, something like anguish in his face. He added in a low voice, 'Mrs Horton is up there too, so Sophie's not the only lady – '

Hoarsely George said, 'Emily? *Emily* is up there too?'

'Yes. Ironic, isn't it?' He saw inexpressible emotions chasing across George's face, but went on, for it seemed to him time and more that George should wake up to certain truths. 'She told me you would not care. What *is* going on, Randy?'

'Great God!' George's voice was shaking, 'You don't know - how could you know?'

'Then what was Sophie meaning? What have you done to her?'

'Near wrecked everything! And she said I wouldn't care? Oh God! What haven't I done? But I know now I can't live without her! Jack, I've got to get her back.'

Stunned by this outburst, then light nevertheless began slowly to dawn on his friend. 'Of course you will, old fellow. They'll come down safely, though I've no idea where, and then be brought back by cart or carriage. That's the usual thing, isn't it? Try not to worry – '

'I'm not waiting for that. Lend me your nag. I'm going after the damned thing!'

'Willingly, but I don't see – '

What he did not see was lost on George as he vaulted into the saddle and was away into Oxford Street, galloping east, regardless of what or who was in his path, chasing the gaudy globe sailing peacefully, in contrast to the agony of the man below.

Chapter Seventeen

The unexpected swift summer storm broke when the balloon was floating above the winding Thames. Rain drove against it and into the faces of the passengers, a sudden contrary wind changing their direction and sending the balloon veering to the north-east.

'Too low,' the major shouted. 'Ballast – two, I think.'

Mr Fox leapt to his command, releasing one bag, the contents fanning out, while the younger Mr Asher, quite in the spirit of the adventure, emptied another on to anything that might be below. The balloon rose a little but still the wind had it and it was some while, skimming over houses and gardens, churches and streets, before open ground showed up ahead as they reached Islington. Major Bryce, valving gas rapidly, was aiming to take advantage of this first possible landing space, while Mr Fox pulled on the rope that released an envelope of silk in one panel to aid their descent. Telling the passengers to hold to the rim of the car, the major assured them they would get down safely, to which his fiancée replied without the slightest alarm that she was sure they were in good hands.

Sophie was not so sure. The rough ground became broken by trees and alder bushes, all shaken by the wind, and she saw a little stream meandering along. The balloon lifted a little and then sank, for it was too late to control it.

There were for the passengers a few moments of sheer terror as the earth seemed to come up to meet the falling car. It bumped along the ground, the grapnel swinging wildly without making contact with anything strong enough to hold it. For one moment the car turned on to its side. Sophie screamed and, being on the underside, tipped out before the balloon, like a monstrous wild animal, dragged the basket up and on another fifty yards until it hit the earth again. Turning and twisting, it entangled itself inextricably in a clump of trees, the cover ripped, releasing the last of the gas, the ropes a tangled mess in an oak tree.

Sophie had rolled down a slope almost into the stream, slipping and slithering in the mud before coming to a halt almost in the water. Stunned, for a moment she lay still, too shaken to think of anything but that she was safely back on earth, even if every part of her body seemed to hurt.

A sound like horses' hooves thudded suddenly in her ears — or was it perhaps the basket bouncing, or the flapping of the balloon? She had lost her bonnet, and her dress was draggled in the mud, but she was beginning to try to collect herself, to get up, when someone ran down the bank. She was gathered into firm arms and a familiar voice, low and desperate, was calling her.

'Sophie, my love, my darling, look at me. Speak to me, for pity's sake. How could you — how *could* you risk your precious life? Sophie!'

But this couldn't be from George. She must be dreaming, or in heaven, and rather foolishly she kept her eyes shut, not wanting to lose the illusion of sudden bliss. Then she became aware of being kissed, cheeks, forehead, eyes, his mouth too real for fantasy. The last moments of terror receded and with a little sigh she opened her eyes.

'George — it *is* you! I don't understand. How — how can you be here?'

'Never mind that now,' he said, almost overcome with relief. 'Are you hurt? Can you move?'

'I think I'm all right.' With his help she sat up, finding arms and legs seemingly undamaged, though she felt bruised from head to toe. And then saw an expression on his face that she never forgot for the rest of her life. She thought there were tears mingling with the rain. Letting her head rest against him, she murmured again, 'I don't understand.'

'No, perhaps not, but — my precious girl, you might have died in that thing! I was near frantic. But I must get you out

242

of this rain, and I'd better see if any of the others are hurt.'
He caught her hands to help her to her feet, and when she
gave a gasp he said instantly, 'Your hand is hurt? How —
was it when you fell?'

'No,' she murmured, 'the fire in the stables —'

Giving a smothered exclamation, he turned it palm
upwards, drawing in his breath sharply. 'Another harm
I've done you.'

'Oh no, no. That at least was my own fault.'

He caught her wet face between his hands and his mouth
sank on hers in a kiss such as she had never received from
him. Dizzy with happiness, she stood where she was, reluctant
to break the dream this must surely be, but he was getting
on with the practicalities, stripping off his coat to wrap it
round her, for she was shivering. Finding a convenient tree
stump, he told her with a swift caress of her cheek, to sit
there while he saw to the others, and then strode off to the
final resting place of the balloon.

None of the passengers seemed to be much hurt. Nigel
was slumped on the ground, his head in his hands, but when
George came up, he tried to pull himself together.

'Oh my God — Sophie?'

'She's all right, no thanks to you, you damned young
idiot. I'll have something to say to you later. Emily, are
you hurt?'

Mrs Horton was already on her feet, a little shaken but
perfectly cool. 'No, I don't think so. Good heavens, George,
how did you get here?'

'I followed you.'

'Well! I'm glad you did. Do go and help Stephen get poor
Edgar down.'

Then George saw, suspended in the branches of a tree,
entangled in ropes, the pilot of the unlucky craft. Stephen
Fox was already trying to disentangle the ropes while the
major dangled ignominiously.

'Get me down, damn you!' he was shouting. 'Randolph!
Good God! Come and be of use.'

Almost light-headed with the release from desperate
anxiety, George was shaken by a sudden desire to laugh.
'You look like the clown you are.'

243

'Don't,' Emily exclaimed, her voice shaking with rare anger, 'don't be so – so vindictive. Help him – '

'If I had my way, I'd leave him there to rot,' George retorted. 'Are you hurt, gentlemen?' this question directed at the others of the party.

'I think my father's arm is broken,' young Mr Asher said and George saw that the older man's face was grey with pain, 'but I'll help Stephen get the major down if you could find us some transport, sir.'

But help was already arriving. Two farm workers from a nearby field were running towards them, and a gentleman who had ridden over from the road was offering his services. In answer to George's query he said, 'The Black Swan, sir, is no more than half a mile away. Is that your horse? The road lies through that gap in the bushes.'

'I'll get my wife there then,' George said, 'and send back transport of some sort.'

'Quite the knight in shining armour!' Emily mocked. 'Once it would have been *me* you would have rescued.' She glanced up to where the farm hands were up the tree and cutting ropes, freeing her luckless future husband.

George was looking at her as if she bore no relation to the woman for whom he had thrown away so much. 'I'll never forgive you, either of you,' he said, 'for putting her life in such danger. I hope I never see you again.'

'Oh, so that's how the wind blows! Then go to your little suburban wife, George. I wish you joy.'

'Damn you, Emily,' he said quietly, and turning his back he walked away. He thought she laughed.

Returning to Sophie, looking forlorn on her log, he caught hold of Jack's horse, where it stood blowing and exhausted, drooping in the rain. 'Well, my darling, I'm afraid there's no helping it – this will have to be your first ride on a horse!' She gave a little gasp, but lifting her into his arms, with one movement he set her sideways on the saddle. 'It's not very comfortable, but the best I can do.' Then he set his foot in the stirrup and came up behind her, his arms on either side of her to gather up the reins.

Slowly in the gathering dusk they rode off. 'Are you all

244

right?' George asked in a low voice. 'You're quite safe, you know.'

She was leaning against his chest. 'Yes, quite safe,' she murmured into his drenched shirt. 'I don't think I'll ever be afraid of anything again. This dear old horse – '

He gave a low laugh. 'A nag. Jack's – he never did have any idea how to choose horseflesh.'

They didn't speak much, George concentrating on guiding the exhausted horse back to the road and along it to where the Black Swan stood in lonely isolation. There he lifted Sophie down and the landlord's wife made coffee for her, while George enquired about a carriage. Fortunately, as the inn was on a busy road, the innkeeper said there was one available. While it was being prepared he served George with a brandy which he thankfully drank off while Sophie finished her coffee.

'I want to get you home,' he said, 'and into a warm bed. My poor love, you look very pale.'

'My head aches,' she admitted, 'and I seem to be bruised all over, and cold because I'm so wet and muddy. But I don't care for any of that. Only that you said – you called me – oh George, did you really mean it?'

'Did I not?' he said in a low voice, glancing round. Two men in a far corner had left and there was no one else in the room. 'I know now how much I love you. Differently. What went before – with Emily – was nothing to what I feel now for you. When I saw you sailing away in that damned balloon – I can't tell you what I endured. I thought I'd lost you, that I'd never get you back. Foolish, I suppose, but I had to come after you, if only to ask you – can you ever forgive me for all the hurt, all the wicked things I have said and done? Oh my love, my love,' leaning across the table, he took one of her hands, careful that it was not the injured one, 'can you care for me at all after what has happened? Once I thought so, but now – I don't know.'

She covered his hand with her other one. 'I've loved you,' she said slowly and in great content, 'since that day at the windmill.'

Safely back at Mount Street, George delivered Sophie into

245

Phoebe's hands before going to tell his father what had happened. Jack had had the sense to call in and, without making it seem a very great matter, warned his lordship that Sophie might be delayed in coming home.

'After a balloon flight,' he explained, 'there's no knowing where it will land and there's always the business of getting the thing and its passengers back.' He tried to make it sound humorous but the old man had been badly shaken. Able to set his mind at rest now, George said nothing of the ownership of the balloon or its passengers, emphasising that Sophie's safe return was all that mattered. Lord Randolph could scarcely express his relief which, following on great anxiety, brought on a fit of trembling and George hurriedly poured a brandy.

'Drink this, father. And don't fret. There's nothing to fear now.'

After a few minutes the faintness passed and Lord Randolph murmured, 'Such a dangerous thing to have done. My poor little Sophie. What was that young man thinking of? Thank God you were there. If you had come sooner no doubt she wouldn't have gone at all.'

'I know it,' George agreed, his voice low. 'You can't reproach me more than I do myself. Such a thing will never happen again.' He put a hand on his father's shoulder and pressed it. At the door he paused. 'A few days ago you asked me if I knew what a treasure I had in my hand. I was in too wretched a state to realise it then, but I do now. Goodnight, father, I'll send Harper to you.'

Lord Randolph sat there in a state of euphoria until his valet came.

Upstairs Sophie was sitting up in bed drinking a cup of hot chocolate and demolishing bread and butter.

'I've sent a note to your father,' he said, looking down at her, 'though you do look better now. Poor darling, you must have been terrified when the flight went wrong.'

'I was,' she admitted. 'I don't know how I could have been so crazy as to go at all, only – well, never mind that now. I'm sure I'm only bruised and I'll be black and blue tomorrow, but I don't think you needed to call Papa.'

'I'm very sure he wouldn't forgive me if I didn't. And I

want to be reassured there's no real damage,' he said lightly, for Phoebe was still in the room.

'I expect you're right, and it will be so nice to see Papa. I hope Mama doesn't come fussing up. Yes, thank you, Phoebe, I've finished. You may go to bed now. And don't look so anxious. I've had an adventure, that's all.'

Phoebe disappeared, not entirely convinced, and George went away to his dressing room, reappearing ten minutes later in his night gear. Extinguishing the candles he slid into bed and took her gently in his arms. After a moment spent kissing her hair, her head on his chest, he murmured, 'Thank God I've got you safe back. When I saw you going further and further from me — '

Settling herself in the warmth and inexpressible comfort of his arms, for not one of their nights together had been like this, she gave a long deep sigh. They had talked only a little in the hired carriage; it had been musty and looked and smelled as though it had recently transported a crate of hens. Happy now to rest against George, she was still dazed at the revelations of the last few hours, inexplicable though it all was. Only once she said quietly, 'I met Mrs Horton at the Granvilles' ball last night. When I saw her — so beautiful — I knew I could never — '

He put his finger over her lips. 'I know what you are going to say, but don't. Even to think yourself less, never believe it, my darling. She has great beauty, yes, and it turned my head, among others, but that is nothing — an ephemeral thing. It is what *you* are that is real to me. Believe that, my Sophie.'

She did believe it, a spasm of joy running through her, though she could not help murmuring, 'Something must have happened . . .'

He gave a long, shuddering sigh, then recounted his distressing visit to London, his return to find her gone. 'And the place empty,' he added. 'I never knew it could seem so empty. I spent those few days thinking. My God, how I thought! I knew then that you mattered more than anything or anyone. Seeing Emily again last summer was a great shock, but I see now that I tried to live again the passion of a boy. It tormented me and in the end Emily threw me out. She called me a complication! I saw at last – what I should have seen long ago. You are all that matters to me now and for the rest of my life. That's what I learned those few days at Plummers without you. I left Jassy to Hedges and should have been with you sooner, soon enough to prevent your ballooning, you crazy girl. How could I have called you timid? It was a damned rabbit upsetting the new mare that stopped me.'

'I'd have come home, but your letter didn't seem to want me to. And I was so ashamed of the things I said to you that last day.'

'Which I richly deserved. But I didn't want to spoil your enjoyment of the Exhibition. Was the opening very grand?'

'Very. But oh, I did miss you so much.'

'I thought it best I should get over my confounded headache without being a nuisance to anyone. Sophie, can you, have you forgiven the way I behaved – oh, ever since our wedding day?'

'It's over, in the past,' she whispered. 'Now that I truly have your love – '

'That you have,' he said softly. 'We'll never lose each other again. But I think now, my precious darling, you should sleep. After such an adventure – '

'I do feel very tired,' she admitted, slipping an arm about him and settling herself comfortably. 'I don't think I can keep awake.' The secret of the baby, she thought, was a joy she would nurse until tomorrow, until Papa came to confirm it.

He lay wakeful, oddly glad that his first act of love was to deny himself the urgent desire to make love to her. Soon, very soon, he would come to her as he had never done before, teach her a depth of loving she had never had the chance to discover. Only not tonight. Tonight she needed rest and it was enough to hold her, experiencing a hitherto unknown desire to protect, to cherish, moments he wanted to savour. She might have been killed today and he could not suppress a shudder.

Drowsily she murmured, 'What's the matter?'

'Nothing,' he said, 'nothing. But I think balloons will be

in my nightmares for the rest of my life.'

She gave a little laugh and then asked drowsily, 'Did Jassy have her foal?'

'Yes, a beauty, and I wasn't even there! Hedges did splendidly.'

'I'm so glad.' She gave a long sigh and slept, warm and content in the circle of his arms, the place where she had longed to be.

George had hardly sat down for breakfast the next morning when, not surprisingly, Dr Sterling arrived, alone, to his son-in-law's relief.

'Well,' the doctor said, 'I came at once. You said an accident — what happened?'

'Let me give you some coffee, sir. Thank you, Beveridge, we can manage now.' And when the butler had gone, without mincing his words, he told the story of the flight.

Sophie's father was almost bereft of speech. 'Sophie! She went up in a balloon? I find that hard to believe. Your note only said an accident, and that you were sure she wasn't hurt.'

'Only bruised, I think,' George said hastily. 'She assures me this morning that she feels well, but I told her to stay in bed until you came.'

'Quite right. But *Sophie* in a balloon! Why? Do I gather you weren't there?'

'To my shame I was not,' George admitted in a low voice. 'Once I called her timid, and she has certainly routed that senseless remark. I know,' he went on with difficulty, 'I know, sir, that I have not so far been a good husband to her. I'm only too aware of my many failings and all I can do is to swear to you that from now on, Sophie will be my first care. I love her more than life itself, and I've only just discovered it.'

His father-in-law was touched. 'My dear boy, I'm glad, for I'm sure she loves you.'

George looked down at the half-eaten roll on his plate. 'She says so, little though I deserve it.'

'If we all got our deserts —' the doctor said and left the sentence unfinished. Having been anxious about his daughter for some time, yesterday's tumble suddenly seemed of less importance than today's happy revelation. He suggested he should go up.

George conducted him to Sophie's room and left them together. By the time he got downstairs again Lord Randolph had come down and was ensconced in his chair in the library.

'Well?' he asked. 'Harper says David is here. How is the darling girl this morning? What does he say?'

'Nothing yet,' George told him and listened patiently to his father's diatribe against ballooning, against Nigel Storrington for being such an irresponsible young fool, against Henry for having so senseless a brother. It was as if the enormity of what had happened had only just impinged on him, and when he had finished he was breathless.

'My dear father,' George said, 'I am aware the whole thing was a disaster and you had better blame me too for delaying at Plummers. If I'd been here none of this would have happened.'

'I'm glad you realise that.'

Leaning against the mantelshelf, George said, 'Oh yes, I realise it. But whatever has been amiss between us in the past is put right.' Looking down at the disturbed old man, he smiled and added, 'We are going to be very happy, you know.'

'Thank God for that.' His father gave a long sigh. 'I only want your happiness.'

Touched, George said only, 'Thank you, Father. We have it now.'

Dr Sterling came down then and as they turned expectantly to him, he said, 'Well, she is only bruised and so far as I can tell, there's no harm to the baby.'

He saw the astonishment in their faces and added, smiling, 'You didn't know? Yes, John, you and I are to be grandfathers. George, my dear boy — '

But the dear boy was gone, up the stairs three at a time to his wife's bedroom.

'There goes a happy man,' the doctor said in a satisfied voice. 'My Sophie too.'

Lord Randolph reached out a hand towards his cousin. 'David — so much joy — too much for — ' His hand fell;

there was a brief convulsive movement.

Dr Sterling was instantly on his knees by the chair, felt a pulse, listened, but there was no flutter of a breath.

They buried him in the churchyard at Plummers beside his wife, and when the mourners had gone, George and Sophie walked in the May twilight down to the lake.

'I wish,' she said in a troubled voice, 'that I didn't feel it was my fault. The shock of that flight, the accident — '

You mustn't blame yourself,' he said firmly. 'Your father said he was in a condition that could have ended his life at any moment, and that his last words were of joy about the baby.'

'I wish he could have lived to see it. Perhaps he would have if there hadn't been so much to distress him.'

He stopped and put a hand under her chin to lift her troubled face. 'You could trace it further back and say you wouldn't have done it if I hadn't made you so unhappy. The blame must lie, if anywhere, at my door.'

'Oh George, dearest, no — '

Kissing her lightly, he added, 'I think we should stop apportioning blame. His health was so precarious. What is important is that he was happy at the end.'

'Yes, oh yes, that's true.' She leaned against him. 'He must have been so glad for us, for Plummers.'

George glanced over her head at the much loved house. 'We shall make it what it was when Maurice and I were children.'

She gave a little sigh. 'He told me after Christmas that he didn't think he would see Maurice again. Poor Maurice will be so upset.'

'They were always close,' George said, and Sophie was silent, wondering if he was remembering the less than happy days of his youth. Well, the 'dark sullen boy' of those years had gone into the limbo of past unhappiness and at least of late George had known a new relationship with his father. At the edge of the lake they stopped and sat down on the wrought iron seat, placed for the best view.

For a while they sat in companionable silence, twilight falling around them. Thinking of her mother's barely concealed delight that she was now Lady Randolph, Sophie was thinking how much less that mattered than that she and George were sitting here together in their garden, so deeply in love. After a while she said, resolutely, 'I have been thinking. I'll never make a horsewoman, but do you think I could learn to drive a little pony and trap? Then I could go about the countryside, as Monica does, and oh, do so many things.'

He laughed, catching her hand in his. 'What a splendid idea. I'll find you the gentlest little mare and have a trap built for you, picked out in whatever colours you like. But not until after our child is born. No more risks, Sophie.'

'None,' she agreed with a contented smile, and leaned across to kiss him. A night bird swooped across the lake as they walked slowly back up the grassy slope, Plummers a dark shape against the translucent blue-green of the evening sky, lamps already lit in the lower rooms.

'Home,' Sophie murmured. 'Do you think the generations that have gone could have loved it any more than we do?'

George laughed and his arm tightened about her. 'I doubt it. Not one of them had the good fortune to be married to you!'